Disclaimer

This is a work of fiction rooted in truth. Though the characters and events are imagined, the mindset, struggles, and principles reflect the real power of vision, ownership, and community. It's storytelling with a purpose—to plant seeds of thought that grow into change

DEDICATION

Rih Son Devonta Ford
4/21/92 6/25/11
YOU FOREVER IN MY HEART AND THOUGHTS WILD MONEY

My Other Three Boys
Tierre Gresham
Chancellor Ford
Jackson Ford
DADDY LOVE Y'ALL. KEEP PUSHING FOR GREATNESS

My Wife
Emmaundia J Ford "Duchess"
THANKS FOR ALWAYS SUPPORTING AND HAVING OUR BACK AND
FRONT

My Mother
Brenda Barthell

My RIH
Joseph "Slow Joe" Ford

ABOUT THE AUTHOR

At just 12 years old, I started selling drugs in the 6th grade—following the blueprint I saw in my own home. My father was both a dealer and a user, and by the 7th grade, I had bought my first car, was paying my mama rent, and buying my own school clothes.

That same year, the school system labeled me as "slow." They placed me in a remedial reading class—embarrassed me, honestly. I was ashamed. But I still kept my swag, my gold chains, my Starter jackets, and my game face. I was one of the most popular kids in school, but truth be told, I had stopped learning. I was only there to show off.

Then one day, my reading teacher—who I'll never forget—looked me in my eyes and said, "You don't belong in this class. You're smart. Don't let them label you." Her words stuck with me, even though my CRT test scores said otherwise.

At age 12 years old I became my neighborhood's youngest drug supplier. I started with 10 dollars, and I flipped that all the way to over $500,000. Me and my Dad link up dealing together supplying the market. I dropped out of high school in the 10th grade. I bought my mother a house with a pool in the backyard, purchased luxury cars, before I was locked up at 19.

At that point in my life, I had never read a full book. Not one. But my father always told me, **"The mind is the most powerful tool in the universe. Street sense and book sense together? That's unstoppable."**

So I gave books a chance.

It started with street fiction. Then history. Then business. Then biographies about powerful and wealthy people. I started seeing myself in those pages— not always in their polish, but in their ambition, their boldness. Then I read **Think and Grow Rich and As a Man Thinketh.** Those two books changed my entire mindset.

That's when I met my friend Cool Harris. I saw some of his writing on a notepad, and it rocked my world. I realized I had something to say, too. From that moment on, I picked up the pencil—and I've never looked back.

I earned my GED, took business and college courses, and started studying resilience. I discovered that, back in the day, Black people were once forbidden to read. There's even a saying: **"If you want to hide something from a Black person, put it in a book."** That became my fuel.

2+2=8

TIERRE FORD

I

Now, I write both fiction and self-help books, covering everything from mindset and mental toughness to financial strategy and spiritual growth. I pour my soul into every page with one mission: to light a fire inside someone who's ready for change.

To everyone who's followed my journey—thank you. Let's set the world on fire with truth, with courage, with knowledge. Let's break every chain and every myth that says we don't read.

Peace—And Keep The Faith.

TIERRE FORD

SYNOPSIS

#2Plus2Equals8 – The Revolution of Legacy

In a city stitched with contradictions—Atlanta, Georgia—**Ezekiel Trueborn**, a struggling Uber driver and father of two, is pulled from survival into purpose. Buried beneath the weight of broken systems, generational cycles, and spiritual betrayal, Ezekiel's spark is lit when a ride-share conversation introduces him to the radical power of **financial literacy**.

Fueled by voices like **John Hope Bryant**, **Dr. Claud Anderson**, and the legacy of **Black visionaries past**, Ezekiel transforms his doubts into doctrine. What starts as a hashtag—**#2Plus2Equals8**—evolves into a movement that redefines the math of freedom. It means: **multiply your value. Break their system. Own your future.**

Alongside **Malik**, a former street general turned visionary strategist, and **Geneva**, a faith-rooted powerhouse with real estate grit and historical wisdom, they create **Legacy Land**—forty acres of revolution built by the community, for the community. But power has enemies.

As the movement grows—through podcast networks, school tours, real estate development, clothing lines, and financial education—the **IRS freezes their assets**. Homeland Security marks them as a threat. **Shanice**, once trusted, is flipped into a mole. **Jason**, a planted operative, aims to assassinate Ezekiel on live TV.

Yet through gunshots, betrayal, and spiritual warfare, **the mission never stops.** They:

- Build housing with ex-dealers and single mothers.
- Host career days and mentorship for Black youth.
- Teach passive income, compound interest, trust accounts, and entrepreneurship.
- Write books, produce films, and create content as currency.

From **Tasha's braid shop** to **Truth's transformation**, from boardrooms to barbershops, from Bible verses to stock portfolios—this is more than movement. It's a revolution.

The system threw everything at them: audits, moles, media slander, and violence. But the people?

The people chose Legacy.

Because this isn't a story about Black pain.

It's a story about **Black power**.

It's about rewriting the rules.

And when the smoke clears, they realize something deeper:

2 plus 2 equals 8...when you believe in more than just the math.

CHAPTER ONE

THE CHURCH OF SMOKE AND MIRRORS

Ezekiel sat in the last row of Kingdom Dominion Cathedral, slouched beneath the velvet arches and golden chandeliers. The sanctuary was a spectacle— forty-foot LED screens, fog machines hissing stage-side, praise dancers twirling in silk robes that cost more than his monthly rent. To the untrained eye, this was heaven on earth. But to Ezekiel, it was smoke and mirrors.

He was thirty. Still unsure of what he believed. He had grown up in the church, yes, but somewhere between the tithes and the manipulation, between the shouts of "Hallelujah!" and the empty echo that followed, he had grown suspicious of it all.

Bishop Armond Blackstone took the stage like a rock star. Tailored maroon suit. Diamond cufflinks. Microphone clipped to his cheek like a pop singer. The crowd roared as if God himself had walked in.

"God told me this morning," the Bishop began, pacing with flair, **"that if you want your miracle, you better sow a hundred-dollar seed right now!"**

Ezekiel's lips twisted into a slow, bitter smile. The screens flashed *Sow Now*. Ushers marched like soldiers, holding velvet baskets as they moved through the aisles. Some gave. Some hesitated. But no one dared walk out. The unspoken rule was simple: to doubt the man of God was to doubt God Himself.

Ezekiel stayed seated. Wallet untouched.

His friend Marcus leaned over. "You ain't gon' sow, Zeke?"

"I already gave," Ezekiel whispered. "My time. My rent. My sanity."

Marcus chuckled nervously and turned away.

But Ezekiel kept watching. Keep listening.

"Turn your Bibles to First Samuel," Bishop Blackstone shouted, opening his gold-plated Bible. **"Let's talk about David. Born of scandal. Forgotten in the field. And yet... called!"**

"Amen!" a thunderous chorus echoed.

"David's mother," Blackstone continued, **"was never even named in the scripture—but scholars believe her to be a woman of shame. And yet through her, God birthed a king!"**

The crowd was hooked. Shouts of "Preach!" and "Say that again!" rang out.

But Ezekiel listened between the lines. He watched the way Blackstone's hand gestures mirrored a salesman. He watched how certain scriptures were cherry-picked, how conviction was weaponized for currency.

"If David could rise from the pasture to the palace, so can you!" Blackstone thundered. **"But first, you must sow!"**

The organ flared. Feet stomped. A woman fainted in the third row. But Ezekiel remained still. Something about the entire performance—it no longer stirred reverence. It stirred reason.

That night, after service, Ezekiel wandered the back corridors of the sanctuary. He wasn't looking for anything. Just... searching. Hoping maybe his doubt was wrong. That this was just a moment of disillusionment.

But what he found confirmed what he feared.

Laughter spilled from the green room. He peeked through a half-cracked door and saw Bishop Blackstone with a woman half his age sitting on his lap, sipping champagne. Behind them, Deacon Harris and two choir members played cards, cursing like they were at a Friday night dice game.

Ezekiel stepped back, heart heavy. He wasn't angry. Not yet. Just... done.

That night, he walked the streets for hours. Past corner stores. Past liquor stores. Past broken people, some of whom he recognized from church—people who shouted on Sundays and suffered in silence Monday through Saturday.

For A few days, he didn't show up for midweek Bible study. The texts came: *Where are you at, bro? Are you good?* But he left them unread

Instead, he read Psalms. Proverbs. And the words of David struck him:

"Create in me a clean heart, O God; and renew a right spirit within me."

One night, he stood barefoot in a field under a low-hanging moon.

"God, if you are out there," he said into the wind, "show me You. Not them. Not their tricks. You."

No lightning. No booming voice. Just wind.

But in that silence, something stirred. Not an answer. Not yet. But a question:

What if I called you to build what they destroyed?

The words came from nowhere and everywhere. From within and without. It wasn't a voice. It was a conviction.

Ezekiel didn't sleep that night. He stayed up sketching ideas. Scribbling scripture. Writing visions. Not for a church. Not for a brand. For a movement.

He imagined a place with no fog machines. No theatrics. Just real people. Real prayer. Real power.

Where men cried without shame. Where women led without compromise. Where youth were taught ownership, not just obedience.

A place where the gospel wasn't just preached—but *practiced.*

Where legacy didn't start with a stage—it started with sacrifice.

Where Black boys could become kings without manipulation. Where mothers weren't shamed for broken homes but supported into healed ones.

Where the poor weren't shamed for being poor—but shown the path to wealth.

He was still in that field when the sun rose.

And with the morning light, Ezekiel stood.

Not just on the grass. But on purpose.

Because that night, the seed of something real was planted.

Not smoke. Not mirrors. But the truth.

And that seed would one day grow into fire.

Into Trueborn.

CHAPTER TWO

UBER, BABY MAMAS, AND THE BOOKS

Morning came with no mercy. Ezekiel's phone buzzed before dawn—Uber ride requests blinking on his cracked screen like digital lifelines. He slipped on his only decent jeans, grabbed a to-go cup of reheated coffee, and kissed his son Elijah on the forehead. Seven-year-old Elijah stirred beneath his Spiderman blanket, mumbling something about pancakes.

"I'll try to grab some when I get back," Ezekiel whispered.

He stepped carefully over a pile of laundry, sidestepping the creaky step outside the bedroom so he wouldn't wake Tasha's mother. Miss Ernestine ruled her basement like a warden. Her love came wrapped in shade and sharp reminders: "Three years. Three. Y'all still here. This ain't a hotel and you ain't no husband." She said it often, loud enough for the drywall to memorize it.

Tasha leaned against the bathroom door frame, arms folded, bonnet still on.

"Zeke... we can't live like this forever. I know you are trying. But I want more than Ernestine's basement and pity stares from folks at the hair salon."

Ezekiel nodded. Her voice wasn't angry—it was worn. Like dreams turned into dust.

"I'm working on something, Tash," he said. "I feel like... something coming together."

"Yeah? Well I hope it comes with a front door and a lease."

Outside, his dented Toyota Camry coughed like a man on his last prayer. He slapped the dash and whispered, "Come on, baby, not today."

By 8 a.m., he'd already picked up a college student still smelling like last night's tequila. Halfway down Moreland, the kid yelled, "Pull over, man! I'm gonna lose it!"

Ezekiel braked hard. The passenger leaned out the door and let it all go.

"My protocol, bro! My protocol!" the kid laughed between heaves, then, as if possessed by the spirit of chaos, began singing Bobby Brown at full volume: "Ain't nobody humping around!"

Ezekiel couldn't help but chuckle. Life had a weird way of slapping you and tickling you at the same time.

The next rider was a calm, middle-aged man in a hoodie who spoke like he read too many books. But his vibe was peaceful.

"Have you ever read John Hope Bryant?" the man asked.

"Nah, who's that?"

"Look him up. Talks about financial dignity. How poverty isn't just about money—it's about mindset. You want to win in this world? Information. That's the real gold. Hard work beats talent when talent doesn't know the rules."

The words hung in the air.

h nothing but a car and a Bible finds out faith is an investment.

He smiled. Crazy, maybe. But something in him buzzed.

At noon, he stopped by his daughter Naomi's school to eat lunch with her . Her mom, Candace, was a straight-laced elementary teacher with little patience for Ezekiel's "dream chasing."

"I hope you're working, Zeke," she said, arms crossed as Naomi grabbed her food.

"I am. Uber. Classes. Still writing."

"Writing ain't a career, it's a hobby."

He nodded, lips tight. He'd learned to pick his battles.

Back in the car, a new ping: Buckhead pickup. As he drove, he whispered, "God... I'm tired of being stuck between two women, two kids, and too many doubts."

Ezekiel parked near a Starbucks and pulled out his phone. He searched for John Hope Bryant on YouTube. The first video hit like prophecy:

"You can't fix what you don't understand."

Then another:

"The opposite of poverty isn't wealth—it's dignity."

And then:

"Nothing changes without mindset first."

Ezekiel repeated each line out loud as he wrote them in his notebook.

His hands trembled. A shiver passed through him.

He whispered, "2 plus 2 equals 8..."

His heart started racing. Not from anxiety. From alignment. Like he had just unlocked a door he didn't know he had the key to 2+2=8.

Not traditional math. Not book math.

Faith math. Seed math. Kingdom math.

He texted Tasha:

"We're not stuck. Just growing. I'm gonna show you. #2Plus2Equals8"

She didn't respond, but he saw the three dots appear. Then disappear. But that was enough. Maybe she was watching. Maybe she was waiting to believe.

His next passenger was a guy in a button-down and slacks. Clearly just promoted—he couldn't stop smiling.

"Just got the email this morning," the man said, buckling in. "Manager position. Been waiting three years. Almost gave up. But look... faith and discipline, man. Never lose hope. Everything unfolds when it's supposed to."

Ezekiel stared at him in the rearview.

"God talkin' to me through y'all today."

The man laughed. "Then you better be listening."

Ezekiel nodded.

He was.

Later that night, after putting Elijah to bed and tiptoeing past Ernestine's judgmental silence, he pulled out his notebook. The page was filled with scribbles. Half a sermon. Half a business plan. A few quotes. A budget. An app name.

He circled the center of it all:

2+2=8.

Below it, he wrote:

"If money is power, and faith is seed, then knowledge is the shovel. And we just started digging."

He didn't have it all figured out. He still had rent due. Still had no title to his name.

But he had fire.

And this time, it wasn't borrowed from a pulpit. It came from God's breath in an Uber car.

And it was just the beginning.

CHAPTER THREE

TASHA'S FIRE AND ERNESTINE'S SHADE

That evening, Ezekiel returned to the basement apartment. Elijah sat on the floor watching cartoons, a cereal bowl empty beside him. Tasha was still at work. She worked late nights as a cocktail waitress at a strip club—"just until we get right," she always said.

Miss Ernestine stood at the top of the stairs, arms folded like a statue of judgment. "He's been watchin' that TV all day. You said you'd be back hours ago."

Ezekiel sighed. "Rides kept coming'."

"Yeah, well, rides don't raise no boy."

He wanted to snap, but held it. Instead, he knelt beside Elijah and rubbed his head.

"You good, little man?"

"Can we do that voice thing again tonight? The Bible one."

Ezekiel smiled. It was their tradition. Before bed, he'd read Elijah a scripture and turn it into a superhero bedtime story.

"Bet. You pick the verse."

Miss Ernestine shook her head and disappeared back upstairs.

What Ezekiel didn't know was that she wasn't heading to bed. She was grabbing her keys.

GAS STATION – LATE NIGHT

The neon from the corner gas station flickered like a half-true promise. Inside, past the counter and racks of honey buns, was a glass door with a crooked sign that read: *WINNERS LOUNGE – NO LOITERING.*

The room stank of old cigarettes, cheap cologne, and desperation. Slot machines lined the walls, glowing like false prophets. You could hear coins clinking, tickets printing, and sighs deep enough to scrape souls.

Miss Ernestine slid into her usual machine—the one near the window with the faded Jungle Queen decal. She didn't greet anyone at first. Just lit a menthol, blew smoke to the ceiling, and started tapping the button.

Rose was already there two chairs down, hunched over her machine like it owed her an apology. A few other familiar faces sat near the back—church sisters on Friday, gamblers by Saturday.

LIT BIT (across the room): "Y'all watch this one! Come on, baby! Big money, big money!"

BEEP. SPIN. CHA-CHING.

LIT BIT (jumping up): "HA! Told y'all! Run me my blessings! We eatin' tonight!"

She danced around in her slippers, swinging her ticket like it was a winning lottery.

ROSE: "Don't get too hype, Lit Bit. You just gon' feed it back in by Tuesday."

ERNESTINE (dry): "Shoot, Tuesday? Try Sunday afternoon."

They all laughed, but there was no joy in it. Just a rhythm of routine. These machines had become their therapist, their confessional, their escape. Rent money. Light bills. Grocery cash. It all fed the beast one button at a time.

ROSE (softly): "Remember when we used to sit around praying for each other instead of praying for triple sevens?"

Ernestine didn't answer. Because the truth was… she didn't want to hear the answer.

BASEMENT – SAME TIME

Ezekiel sat with his laptop open, a half-eaten sandwich on the table. Elijah was finally asleep, Spiderman blanket tucked under his chin.

Ezekiel had just finished writing a few lines of a movie script:

Genesis. A Black man with nothing becomes the father of many. But first, he drives Uber. Struggles. Gets clowned. But then the equation changes.

He leaned back and grabbed the book sitting on the end table: *As A Man Thinketh.*

He flipped a few pages and read aloud:

"The vision that you glorify in your mind, the ideal that you enthrone in your heart—this you will build your life by. This you will become."

His chest tightened. Candace's voice echoed in his mind: *"Writing ain't a career, it's a hobby."*

He picked up a pen and started scribbling notes:

- Vision is currency.
- Thoughts shape struggle.
- Poverty ain't just broke—it's belief.

His phone buzzed.

MARCUS (text): *Where have you been, Zeke? Blackstone has been asking about you.*

Ezekiel stared at the message.

Bishop Blackstone.

The man with a golden tongue and a rotting core.

He hadn't been back to Kingdom Dominion in weeks. Not since that night. Not since he peeked through the green room and saw the hypocrisy dancing on the Bishop's lap.

He clicked his pen shut.

"I ain't ready to go back," he whispered. "But maybe I gotta face it to fix it."

Thunder cracked outside like a warning—or maybe a drumroll.

He looked at Elijah. Then at his notes. Then at the ceiling.

"God… if 2 plus 2 really can equal 8, I need a sign. Or maybe I just need to start moving like it already has."

And he wrote one more line:

The man they counted out will be the one who multiplies everything.

CHAPTER FOUR

CHAOS, COFFEE, AND CALLING

Ezekiel was halfway through brushing his teeth when Tasha burst in, tears streaking her makeup.

"I have to find something different, Zeke. That place gettin' more like a trick-off truck stop. They had me workin' VIP all night, and some old dude grabbed my ass—I poured a drink on him and security kicked me out."

Ezekiel dropped the toothbrush, wiped his mouth, and pulled her into a tight hug.

"Change is coming," he said into her hair. "We just gotta keep pushing. The storm always comes before the sun. The seed comes before the fruit."

She looked up at him. He wiped her tears, kissed her forehead.

She threw her purse on the bed and kicked off her heels like they were on fire. Elijah peeked from behind the hallway door.

"I need a break," she mumbled, voice cracking. "I need help. And your dreams ain't paying no bills yet."

He didn't argue. Not yet. He knew better.

Later that morning, Ezekiel dropped Elijah off at school, picked up three back-to-back Uber rides, and by 10 a.m., he was running on fumes. He pulled into a BP gas station and sat for a minute, head against the steering wheel.

His phone buzzed. Candace.

Candace: "Naomi said you promised to be at the Father-Daughter dance on Friday."

Ezekiel: "I did. I will."

Candace: "What's your title again? Uber prophet?"

He didn't reply.

Instead, he opened his laptop in the passenger seat and pressed play on a saved video from his online financial course.

"Money follows clarity. Faith follows vision. Vision follows truth."

He whispered, "Truth, Lord. That's all I want."

Then he started writing:

Episode 1: The Gospel According to Broke. A series about hope, hustle, and holy math.

His fingers flew. At that moment, he wasn't a struggling Uber driver. He was a messenger.

Even if the world didn't believe him yet. Even if his own house didn't.

Faith was compounding. And something was about to break.

Needing space to breathe, Ezekiel parked near Five Points Station and started walking.

The heart of Atlanta was pulsing with contradiction.

He passed a couple arguing in front of the MARTA escalator. The woman screamed about loyalty. The man kept yelling, "You always got a smart-ass mouth!"

A street preacher stood on a milk crate, shouting through a megaphone.

"The end is near! Babylon is falling! Repent and be saved!"

Next to him, a heated debate unfolded between two old heads sitting on a concrete ledge.

TRUMP SUPPORTER: "I don't care what y'all say, Trump helped my pockets. That PPP put food in my freezer. Obama? He just looked good on the podium."

OBAMA SUPPORTER: "Yeah? But at least Obama gave us dignity. Trump gave y'all clown suits. Now we are stuck with Biden, who can't remember what room he is in."

TRUMP GUY: "On that, we agree. Biden ain't it."

OBAMA GUY: "Ain't been it. Too old, too slow."

Ezekiel kept walking, absorbing it all.

A man with dreadlocks played guitar by the fountain, singing old Curtis Mayfield. Across from him, a kid in an oversized hoodie freestyle rapped into his cracked iPhone.

The city was a collage. Broken pieces, overlapping sounds. Beautiful. Chaotic. Honest.

His phone rang. New ping. Midtown pickup.

He got back in his Camry, adjusted his seat, and headed north.

The couple he picked up were two men in crisp button-downs and expensive sneakers. They got in mid-conversation.

MAN 1: "...and that's why I said, we take the second room and turn it into a podcast studio. Stream the passive income. Content *is* currency."

MAN 2: "And the vending machines? I got a guy. We place three in local schools—bam, residuals monthly."

Ezekiel listened, quietly impressed.

MAN 1 (to Ezekiel): "Have you ever thought about vending machines?"

Ezekiel: "No, but I've been thinking about legacy. Teaching kids the stuff we were never taught. Like that 2 plus 2 don't always equal 4... sometimes it multiplies."

They laughed. But they nodded.

"Ain't that the truth," one of them said.

By the time he dropped them off, Ezekiel had typed four new lines into his script. A scene about two men building something together in a city that never expected them to rise.

He wasn't just collecting rides anymore. He was collecting stories. Seeds. Signs.

The world was loud, messy, and uncertain.
But his vision was sharpening.
And the call on his life?
It was getting louder by the day.
 about to break.

CHAPTER FIVE

THE MOTHER, THE MARCUS, AND THE MATH

Before a man becomes who he was born to be, life often lets him simmer in the pot of contradictions. One foot in faith, the other in foolishness. One hand holding a dream, the other juggling baby mamas, overdue bills, and Uber fares. Ezekiel Trueborn didn't know it yet, but he was smack dab in the middle of his becoming. And before he could walk into purpose, he had to walk through people—some who loved him, some who used him, and some who would unknowingly push him closer to the man he was born to be.

Ezekiel sat in a folding chair off the BeltLine, waiting on his next ride request. The sun bounced off the concrete, heat rising from the pavement like steam off judgment. The smell of exhaust mixed with hot dog water from a nearby vendor made his stomach flip. Elijah had been coughing all night. Tasha blamed the basement mold. Miss Ernestine blamed Ezekiel's lack of income. Ezekiel blamed silence from heaven.

He thought of Moses—leading a stubborn, stiff-necked people. Even after God split seas and rained bread, they still doubted. He felt that. How easy it was for people to doubt rather than believe. To criticize the dream before ever understanding the weight of carrying one.

Another ride: a woman headed to Kingdom Dominion Cathedral.

He stared at the screen.

That church again?

He hesitated. But money was money.

The passenger was an older woman in a peach Sunday hat with rhinestones around the brim. Her Bible was covered in pink leather, bursting with bookmarks.

"Have you ever been to the Kingdom?" she asked as she buckled up.

Ezekiel grunted. "Used to be a member."

"Whew, child. That Bishop Blackstone is a man of revelation. Did you hear last Sunday's message? He said if we sow double, God gon' triple it! I gave my last hundred. I *know* my blessing is coming."

Ezekiel smiled tightly, knuckles tightening on the wheel. He respected faith. He just hated fraud.

He dropped her off, but instead of pulling off, circled the block. That's when he saw Marcus—outside the cathedral, dapping folks up like a neighborhood politician. Gucci sneakers, a silver chain, fresh cut and loud laughter.

Ezekiel parked, stepped out.

"Marcus."

Marcus turned, then broke into a wide grin. "Zeke! Boy, what's good? Still driving Uber?"

"Still dreaming. Are you still sowing hundred-dollar seeds?"

Marcus laughed and hugged him. "Don't knock it till it blesses you. I got a new girl, a new job, and the Bishop said my *bonus season* is coming."

"You're not Ruth."

"Nah," Marcus said, laughing, "but I might marry one."

For a moment, it felt like old times. Their teenage days. Before life got so complicated.

Then Marcus sobered up. "You really left, huh?"

"Had to. Couldn't keep pretending the smoke was the Spirit."

"So what now? You on that YouTube theology? TikTok prophets?"

"No. Just trying to find God outside the filters."

Marcus nodded, but there was a flicker of something behind his eyes. Ezekiel recognized it. Doubt. Not everyone who stayed believed. Some stayed because it was all they knew.

Then the crowd shifted. Bishop Blackstone approached, flanked by two deacons.

Blackstone: "So this how you turn your back on the church that pulled your mind out the gutter?"

Ezekiel stiffened. He felt 17 again. Back in juvenile. Lost and eager. The boy Blackstone once took under his wing.

Blackstone (low and heavy): "I remember that scared little boy in juvie, desperate for the Word. Now he's out here running."

Ezekiel stared him in the eye. For the first time, he didn't flinch. Just nodded and turned.

No more fear.

That evening, Ezekiel pulled up to his mother's house. The porch was cluttered with hanging plants and faded wind chimes. Gospel music played from inside, loud and off-beat.

She opened the door holding a tambourine in one hand, Bluetooth speaker in the other, blaring Bishop Blackstone's sermon.

"Baby! Are you hungry?"

"I could eat."

He stepped in. The house hadn't changed since he was fifteen. Same couch, same Jesus clock, same smell of fried catfish and menthol rub.

She turned the speaker down and handed him a plate.

"You ain't been back to church."

"I know, Ma."

"You think you are better than the saints now?"

"No. I just... I see too much."

She sat beside him, sighing deep. "Ezekiel, God uses flawed people to speak perfect truth. Moses was a murderer. David was messy. Peter denied Jesus with curse words."

"But they didn't sell blessings like concert tickets."

She smiled. "Maybe they did. Just with different currency. Baby, you are trying to build something perfect. But God builds with crooked sticks."

He wanted to argue. But she kissed his forehead, and just like that, the debate ended.

"Are you still writing them scripts?"

"Yeah."

"Then write. But don't lose your soul trying to save your story."

Later that night, Ezekiel put Elijah to bed and opened his laptop to study for his online finance course. But the moment his fingers hit the keyboard, Tasha came in hot.

"You know what my mama said today? That I need to get a man with a real job!"

"She says that every Thursday."

"It's Wednesday."

"Exactly."

They both laughed.

She slumped beside him. "Do you ever feel like we just stuck? Like no matter what we do, life keeps handing us the same test?"

Ezekiel leaned forward. "Yeah. But maybe we keep getting the same test 'cause we ain't learned the right math yet."

"Here you go with your weird logic."

"No, for real. What if 2 + 2 really does equal 8? What if we just been thinking too small?"

She studied him. "You sound like a preacher."

He shook his head. "Nah. Just a man tired of counting what's missing."

That night, Ezekiel sat in front of the mirror, looking at his reflection. He whispered questions into the silence. About purpose. Provision. Pain. He listened to John Hope Bryant again.

"It's not about how much money you make. It's about how you think about money."

"Wealth is not about dollars. It's about dignity."

The words pierced him. He wrote them down. Then made a note:

Buy John Hope Bryant's book. First chance you get.

By the end of that week, Ezekiel had no extra money, no guarantees, and no clarity—just a whisper. A whisper that said heaven's math ain't bound by calculators or clocks. That pain can be principal. That struggle compounds. And that when faith enters the equation...

2 + 2 doesn't have to equal 4.

It can equal 8.

And if you're crazy enough to believe it, maybe—just maybe—you're already halfway there.

CHAPTER SIX

DANCES, DANCERS, AND A DIAMOND BARBER CAPE

Faith isn't always fire from heaven. Sometimes it's a whisper in traffic. A quote that hits too hard. A daughter's dance. A twisted laugh in a barbershop. This was the day Ezekiel Trueborn started seeing the world not for what it was—but for what it could be. Because when life's math stops making sense, that's when divine multiplication starts kicking in. And today? Today was about to be funny, fragile, and full of flickers of something more.

Ezekiel rolled through morning traffic, dashboard dusty, the Camry's AC wheezing like a dying lung. His latest audiobook—*The Alchemist*—played through his Bluetooth speaker.

"When you want something, all the universe conspires in helping you to achieve it."

He slammed the steering wheel.

"Damn right."

He pulled up to Naomi's school just before 8 a.m wearing a The Vault outfit. He had one job this morning: show up for the daddy-daughter dance practice.

Naomi spotted him from the door, her face lighting up. She wore a sparkly gold tutu and a Black girl magic headband. Ezekiel's heart melted.

"You came!"

"Of course, girl. You think I'd miss this?

They entered the gym, surrounded by other dads—some in suits, others in construction boots, all awkwardly trying to follow the dance teacher's choreography.

Ezekiel spun Naomi, missed a step, and almost collided with a PTA dad doing too much.

Naomi giggled. "Daddy, you're stiff."

"It's the Camry seat. It locked my hips."

She laughed harder.

For the first time all week, Ezekiel wasn't thinking about bills or barbershop fades. Just this moment. This joy. This sacred foolishness.

Meanwhile, on the other side of Atlanta, Tasha leaned against the VIP bar in dim lighting while Destiny and Luscious, two dancers with more confidence than clothing, re-applied lip gloss.

"Girl, I don't care what nobody says," Destiny said, adjusting her lace top. "These men ain't nothing but cash with teeth."

Luscious laughed. "You are poetic today. Are you quoting Cardi?"

Tasha shook her head, wiping down glasses. "Y'all stupid."

"We are honest," Destiny said. "Are you still with that Uber dude?"

Tasha rolled her eyes. "He's Elijah's dad. He's... tryin'."

"Trying not to pay rent, baby," Luscious said, smacking her gum. "Unless he is trying to rob a bank."

Tasha grinned. "Nah. He has dreams. I just don't know if dreams come with health insurance."

Destiny pulled a few bills from her garter. "Keep the dreamers around long enough, and they either become legends or letdowns. There's no in-between."

Back at Miss Ernestine's house, the old woman was in her groove. Gospel music blared as she cleaned every inch of the house with militant precision. She wore a bonnet, rubber gloves, and a housecoat that doubled as armor.

She paused to watch her favorite court show, yelling at the screen.

"You let that man cheat and stole your mama's dog? Girl, you need Jesus and a stun gun!"

Then she went outside to water her lawn and curse at squirrels. "I see you diggin' in my tomatoes again, you fuzzy-tailed demon!"

Her day was structured, loud, and unshakably hers.

Meanwhile, across town, a white Rolls-Royce Phantom with gold rims pulled up to *Royal Cuts Barbershop*. Inside sat Bishop Armond Blackstone, wearing a linen Gucci robe and snakeskin slippers. His personal barber, Raheem, greeted him like royalty.

"Bishop in the building! Y'all hide your chains, he might ask for a seed."

Laughter broke out.

Blackstone grinned. "Y'all need to tithe just for these jokes."

He sat in the chair, and Raheem draped a custom diamond-stitched cape over him that said *BLESSED & BALDING*.

As Raheem lined him up, Bishop leaned toward him.

"Your hands are soft, Raheem. You've been moisturizing?"

"Every night, Bishop. Shea butter and child support."

More laughter.

"Mmm," Blackstone smirked. "That's biblical."

Then he locked eyes with Raheem's cousin Tierra, who was sweeping near the back.

"And who is that vision of Proverbs 31 in skinny jeans?"

Raheem rolled his eyes. "That's my cousin, Bishop. Don't even start."

"You sure she ain't a sermon? 'Cause I feel a message coming."

Even the old heads hollered. Barber shops in Atlanta weren't just places for fades—they were pulpits of gossip, gospel, and game.

Blackstone looked in the mirror, adjusting his collar. "Tell Tierra if she wants to join the usher board, I'll lay hands personally."

Raheem muttered, "This man is wild."

Back in the Camry, Ezekiel sat in traffic, playing back the dance video Naomi recorded.

He watched himself stumbling, spinning, laughing. And for once, he didn't feel ashamed of where he was.

His phone buzzed. A reminder from his online course: *Submit investment plan by midnight.*

He thought about the quote from this morning: *When you want something, all the universe conspires...*

But he paused.

"God... it ain't the universe. It's You, right? So if you're conspiring, say something. Show something. Drop me a clue."

A ping hit his phone: a scriptwriting contest. *Winner receives $25,000 and a development deal.*

He stared at it.

Deadline: three days.

He whispered, "Two plus two equals eight, right?"

Then he drove.

Every now and then, God moves in whispers and winks. A moment at a dance. A joke in a barbershop. A woman cursing squirrels. A writing contest that shows up when you ask for a sign. It doesn't always look like a miracle. Sometimes, it looks like the first domino wobbling. The first light in a dark hallway. But it's a movement.

And if you have the crazy courage to believe in math that doesn't add up... You just might see the impossible start to multiply.

And Ezekiel?

He was about to run straight into his turning point. One awkward dance step at a time.

CHAPTER SEVEN

DREAMS, DUETS, AND A WAFFLE HOUSE STICKUP

Some nights, life writes the chapter for you. You don't plan the plot twists. You just ride the wave and pray your faith doesn't drown in the foolishness. Ezekiel was learning that in real time. Between loud laughter through basement walls, tired Uber confessions, and a duet that ended in a robbery, Saturday had hands. But buried in chaos was a strange math—a spiritual formula whispering that even messes can multiply into miracles if you don't give up too soon.

All day, Ezekiel's mind replayed that contest flyer. $25,000. A shot at something real. He'd already scribbled a logline on a napkin: *Faith in a Toyota*. But writing was hard in a house filled with noise, and Miss Ernestine wasn't helping.

From the other side of the wall came cackling. Male voices. Ernestine and two of her old "church friends" were playing Spades and telling stories that didn't sound like they came from the Book of Psalms.

"Do you remember Deacon Lonnie back in '83? Lawd, that man could lay hands in all the wrong places!"

Laughter.

"Girl, I still got that oil stain on my sheet from the revival after-party."

More laughter.

Ezekiel turned up his audiobook to drown them out, but his earbuds were busted. He sighed, sat back in his chair, and stared at the laptop.

"God, I need this contest. Let me focus. Let me write this script... before I lose my mind to holy hoes and flashback freaks."

The next morning, Tasha brewed weak coffee and rubbed her temples. She hadn't slept well.

Ezekiel sat at the small kitchen table with his finance course pulled up on his phone.

"Babe," he said, "we gotta start thinking about compound interest. Even with just $100 a week."

Tasha squinted. "We don't even have $100 a week extra."

"I know. But we gotta start somewhere. The system ain't built for us to win—but the numbers don't lie. If we stack, invest, even in pieces, in a few years from now we could be out of this basement. Out of this cycle."

She stirred her coffee. "That some 2 plus 2 equals 8 talk again?"

He nodded. "Exactly. And I'm tired of living in 4."

Elsewhere in Atlanta, Naomi's mother, Candace, lay in bed with her new man, Darryl. He was a mortgage broker with smooth hands and too many colognes.

She scrolled through Ezekiel's latest Facebook post: a quote about believing in dreams even when broke.

Darryl kissed her shoulder. "That's your baby daddy again?"

She sighed. "Yeah. He is still talking about writing scripts and flipping Uber into something big."

Darryl smirked. "Ain't nothing wrong with dreaming... but it's hard to raise a daughter on vision boards."

Candace turned to him. "He's a good dad. Just... broke."

That afternoon, Ezekiel picked up two passengers in Buckhead.

The first was a man in a crisp suit, talking on the phone.

"Yeah, we just pushed six figures into crypto. Real estate's dead, bro. Digital is the new divine."

Ezekiel chuckled to himself. "Divine till it crashes."

The second was a college girl with green braids and a notebook filled with sketches.

"I'm gonna start a fashion line," she said. "But with scripture. Like, Proverbs 31 hoodies and Moses sandals but make it urban."

Ezekiel grinned. "You got vision."

She leaned forward. "You got that pastor's voice. You preach?"

He laughed. "Nah. I just Uber with style."

By the time he got home, the house was quiet. Tasha had done Elijah's hair and was watching *The Best Man* on mute.

Ezekiel took a long shower. Steam rolled off his back. His brain buzzed with ideas.

When he stepped out, Tasha was dressed in a red jumpsuit.

"You ready?" she asked.

"Where are we going?"

"You said you wanted Saturday night vibes. I found a karaoke spot."

He blinked. "Are you serious?"

She tossed him a clean shirt. "Let's go make fools of ourselves."

The karaoke bar was dim, smoky, and packed with 40-somethings reliving their 20s. Ezekiel and Tasha signed up for a duet. The DJ announced: "Give it up for... E&T!"

They stepped up and started singing *Ain't No Mountain High Enough*. Ezekiel missed the first beat. Tasha jumped in and carried him.

By the second verse, he was all in. Off-key. Off-beat. But his spirit? On fire.

The crowd clapped. Someone shouted, "Get them a record deal!"

Tasha bowed. Ezekiel winked.

They sat down, fingers laced.

"I needed this," she said.

"Me too."

Around midnight, they hit Waffle House. Greasy joy. Booth seat sticking to thighs. Everything smelled like hash browns and dreams.

Ezekiel ordered an All-Star combo. Tasha got smothered and covered.

Then... chaos.

Two guys in ski masks stormed in with pistols.

"EVERYBODY DOWN!"

Screams. The cook ducked behind the griddle.

One robber yelled, "You! Cook! Get back up and make us some eggs!"

The cook blinked. "Scrambled or over easy?"

Even the robber paused. "Scrambled. And don't burn my damn toast."

Someone giggled. Tasha whispered, "Is this real life?"

Ezekiel whispered back, "Only in the South."

The second robber, nervous and clearly high, pointed his gun toward Ezekiel. "Are you laughing?"

Ezekiel raised his hands. "Nah, man. Just... you gotta admit, this ain't exactly Ocean's Eleven."

More giggles. Even the first robber snorted.

They took a few wallets, got their food, and dipped.

The room sat in stunned silence.

The cook looked around. "Y'all still want your orders?"

Someone yelled, "Hell yeah, I'm hungry!"

Laughter erupted. Tension broke. People started clapping.

Ezekiel looked at Tasha.

"2 plus 2 equals eight, huh?" she said.

He nodded, still holding her hand.

"Or at least... dinner and a story."

Sometimes, the math of life includes stickups and scrambled eggs. But underneath the madness, God still multiplies joy, memory, and hope. Tonight wasn't perfect. But it was theirs. And Ezekiel, for the first time in a long time, felt like maybe—just maybe—the break wasn't just around the corner. It was already beginning.

Because in a world where dreams get robbed and eggs get flipped, faith still has the final say.

And faith always tips big.

CHAPTER EIGHT

THE SERMON, THE SCRIPT, AND THE SECOND PLACE FAITH

Every man chasing purpose comes to a fork in the road—grind or give up, faith or fear, church pew or computer screen. Ezekiel Trueborn wasn't just at a crossroads. He was mid-sprint on both paths. The contest deadline loomed like a sunrise he couldn't outrun. But the world around him still moved: sermons shouted, children laughed, and rent waited. And somewhere between the madness and the manuscript, Ezekiel realized that sometimes second place is still a divine setup. Because even when faith is tired, it's still working overtime.

Sunday morning.

Kingdom Dominion Cathedral was louder than usual. The choir wore gold robes that sparkled like royalty, and the sanctuary smelled of Chanel perfume and ego. Bishop Blackstone stood at the pulpit in a robe so embroidered it looked like it came with stock options.

Miss Ernestine swayed in the second row, eyes closed, purse clutched to her chest like it held a golden ticket. Beside her, Ezekiel's mother, Ms. Rosa, shouted "Glory!" every other sentence, though she missed the last two light bills.

Marcus was in the third row, fresh fade, custom suit, nodding like he was auditioning for deacon of the year.

"Turn to your neighbor and say, 'Your blessing is overdue!'" Blackstone bellowed.

The church erupted.

"This morning, God told me," Blackstone said, voice booming, "that somebody in this room is sitting on a dream... a script, a book, a billion-dollar business—and all it takes is one act of obedience!"

Ezekiel wasn't there to hear it. He was at home.

Laptop open. Hoodie on. Fingers flying.

He had turned the Waffle House robbery into a scene—funny, tense, brilliant. The robber demanded eggs while holding a Glock. The cook asked if he wanted cheese. A side character—a failed preacher turned Uber driver— used humor to defuse the situation and record it for his script.

It wasn't just good. It was **fire**.

He checked the word count: 4,972.

The contest required 5,000. He had twenty-eight words to go.

Outside, kids played. Tasha had taken Elijah and Naomi to the park. She told Ezekiel to meet them. But he couldn't. Not yet.

"God," he muttered, "let this win. Or at least let it change something."

He typed the final lines:

FADE OUT.

TITLE: 2 PLUS 2 = 8.

He hit submit.

The clock read: 11:59 a.m.

At the park, Elijah chased pigeons while Naomi did cartwheels in the grass. Tasha watched with a soft smile. For once, there was peace.

A few other moms watched her from the bench. One nudged the other.

"Is that the girl from Eden's? The club?"

"Yeah. But she cleaned up real nice."

Tasha heard them but didn't respond. She just pulled out her phone and texted Ezekiel: *Did you finish?*

A few seconds later: *Submitted.*

She smiled.

"Okay, Zeke. Okay."

Meanwhile, back at Kingdom Dominion, Blackstone was mid-sweat.

"Y'all waiting on a check. I'm waiting on a *call*!" he shouted.

The crowd roared.

"I don't need your applause—I need your obedience."

Marcus wiped a tear. Miss Ernestine screamed. Ms. Rosa danced in her orthopedic shoes.

But as the church spun, the real miracle was happening miles away—in a small, dusty basement, in a browser tab marked **Submitted**.

Later that afternoon, Ezekiel finally met the family at the park. Naomi ran up first.

"Daddy, I did a whole cartwheel and didn't fall!"

Elijah shouted, "We fed ducks!"

Tasha handed him a water bottle. "You look like you wrestled with a cloud."

"I did," he said. "And I think I pinned it."

They sat under a tree. For a moment, everything was still.

"You think you'll win?" she asked.

He shrugged. "I don't know. But they said second place gets ten grand."

"You'd take a second?"

He nodded. "Faith without works is dead. But works without patience is stupid. I'll take a second. I'll take momentum."

Tasha smiled. "You sound like a preacher."

"Nah. Just a man who finally turned his pain into paragraphs."

Winning isn't always a miracle. Sometimes, just submitting your dream into the world is the win. Sometimes, second place is God's way of making sure you're humble enough to handle first when it finally comes. And sometimes, while the world is screaming for blessings, the real blessing is peace. Ezekiel was broke, behind on rent, and praying into silence. But he had submitted something divine.

And now, the math was in motion.

2 plus 2 equals 8.

And heaven was watching the formula unfold.

CHAPTER NINE

SLOT MACHINES, LIVE STREAMS, AND THE MINDSET SHIFT

The world doesn't change with a bang. It shifts in whispers—in barrooms, gas station corners, and late-night Waffle Houses. While some chase jackpots with quarters and faded dreams, others fight for peace with broken hearts and borrowed Wi-Fi. The equation doesn't always make sense. But when 2 plus 2 starts to look like 8, you learn to trust the rhythm before the reward. This was the week the odds looked rigged—but Ezekiel? He started betting on something bigger.

After Sunday service, Miss Ernestine and Ms. Rosa hit the corner Shell station like clockwork. They weren't alone.

Three more seasoned women joined them, each with a beer in hand, wigs slightly tilted, cigarettes lit like incense offerings to the luck gods. The gas station had a little back room—a row of dusty slot machines humming like temptation.

Ms. Rosa wiped sweat from her upper lip. "I'm feelin' this one today."

Ernestine snorted. "You say that every Sunday and leave broke as last week."

"Faith, fool. Faith."

Two older men sat nearby, laughing loud about the Falcons and ex-wives, while two younger dudes watched the ladies, fascinated.

"Yo, these grannies are serious. I swear one of 'em just cussed out a penny slot."

From the back came an eruption: "DAMN! I almost hit the triple crown!"

"That machine rigged!" another voice yelled.

Beer bottles clinked. A woman in a neon top lit another cigarette with the last one.

Across town, Ezekiel sat in the basement with his phone propped up on a cereal box. His ring light was crooked, and Elijah's drawings hung behind him like a bootleg backdrop.

But his spirit? Sharp.

He tapped *Go Live.*

"Yo, what's up family? Ezekiel here. I wanted to drop a few money gems I've been learning by reading these finance books. Real talk: the system ain't built for us, but we can still learn how to work it..."

He broke down compound interest with an example, shared how he started a no-fee investment account, and explained how even $50 a week could turn into $20K over time.

A few comments popped up:

"Bro talkin facts."
"A Uber driver teaching finance? Lol ok."
"Nah this deep. I'm taking notes."

Then his phone vibrated. A text.

Congratulations. You're in the Top 5 finalists. Winner will be announced one week from today. Live on YouTube. Stay tuned.

Ezekiel stared at it. Heart pounding.

He breathed deep. "Let's go..."

That evening, Tasha was getting ready for her shift at Eden's Lounge.

Ezekiel stood in the doorway, watching her fix her hair in the cracked mirror.

"You ever think about five years from now?" he asked.

Tasha paused. "Like what?"

"Where we'll be. What we'll have. What are we building."

She didn't answer. Just sprayed perfume and reached for her earrings.

"Tasha?"

Her voice was flat. "I don't know, Zeke. I just know I gotta be at work by eight."

She grabbed her purse and walked past him.

"I see us owning property," Ezekiel said loudly as she headed up the stairs. "I see a business. Elijah going to private school. You not clocking in for tips. You makin' moves."

She didn't look back.

But she heard him.

Eden's Lounge pulsed with neon lights and bass drops. Tasha wiped down the bar while dancers prepped backstage.

Then he walked in.

Rowe "Kilo" Dunn. A local legend. Big time dealer turned Instagram celeb. Loud. Flashy. Dangerous. He wore a gold chain thick enough to anchor a yacht. His entourage flooded in behind him.

"Look at my old flame lookin all sexy and fine?" he said.

His boy smirked. "That's Zeke baby mama now ."

Kilo strutted over. "Tasha, you still fine as hell. You need to stop servin' drinks and let me buy you a business."

She rolled her eyes. "Kilo, the best thing I did was leave you drugged me through the mud?"

He laughed and tossed a stack in the air. It rained twenties.

Someone pulled out a phone. Live started.

Kilo grinned. "Tell Zeke I said go back to his Camry. Broke Uber baby daddy. I got his upgrade right here."

The comments exploded.

"Damn! He said that on live?"
"Not the Camry shade!"
"Tasha better not fall for it."

Tasha picked up a drink.

Without warning, she threw it dead in Kilo's face.

Gasps. Phones raised.

She turned and walked away. Didn't look back as Kilo whipped his face.

Back at the gas station slots, Ms. Rosa and Ernestine sat slumped.

"I spent my grocery money and bills money," Rosa mumbled.

"I'm way past that I'm in deep waters, don't even like to talk about it" Ernestine replied.

They looked at each other.

"Are you hungry?"

Rosa nodded. "Got four dollars left ."

" I have three, Waffle House?"

They limped out, purses lighter, dreams delayed.

Inside Waffle House, the two women shared an All-Star special.

Ernestine sipped water slowly. "I ain't always been like this."

"I know," Rosa said. "Me neither."

"I used to teach Sunday school."

"I used to run a soul food kitchen."

They sat in silence, chewing toast, mourning something unnamed.

Then Ernestine whispered, "Maybe it ain't too late. Maybe we just need... better math."

"Maybe we can start selling plates, " Rosa smiled.

"get our kids make us a tik toc page."

Tasha got home late. The house was still. The TV was off. Elijah snored in the next room.

Ezekiel was on the couch, passed out. A book on investing rested on his chest. A notebook with scribbled ideas lay on the floor.

Tasha walked into the bathroom and stared at herself in the mirror.

Smudged makeup. Tired eyes.

She whispered, "I want more."

Not just more money. More peace. More joy. More meaning.

She wiped her face, then picked up Ezekiel's notebook. Read a few lines.

Mindset is the gateway to miracles.

She smiled.

In the mirror, she traced the phrase on the foggy glass:

2 + 2 = 8

The shift doesn't always start with applause. Sometimes it starts in silence, in reflection, in Waffle House confessions and quiet courage. Tasha didn't know it, but her turning point had already begun. Ezekiel didn't know it, but his words were seeds taking root in the woman he thought had stopped listening. And Ms. Ernestine? Even she felt it—that the next spin might be a new kind of chance.

Because when you change the math in your mind, you change the equation of your life.

And that's when 2 plus 2 stops being four...

...and starts becoming destiny.

CHAPTER TEN

GRAVY, GROWTH, AND THE FIRST INVESTMENT

Progress doesn't always come in paychecks and praise. Sometimes it shows up in strangers, scriptures, or a fifty-dollar risk made on faith. The people of Ezekiel's world were reaching, stretching, stumbling toward change. Some toward the light. Others toward anything that felt like stability. But underneath the chatter, gossip, sermons, and setbacks, something new was beginning to break ground. Because when a seed hits good soil—even in concrete—it's only a matter of time.

The sun hadn't fully risen when Ezekiel started his Uber shift. The Camry's radio was low, gospel humming beneath the hum of tired tires. He picked up a man in his fifties, clean beard, kufi hat, and fire in his eyes.

"Have you ever studied Marcus Garvey?" the man asked as they pulled onto Peachtree.

Ezekiel shook his head. "Only what I heard growing up."

"Garvey was a prophet. Misunderstood. Misused. But never moved off purpose."

He held up three fingers.

"One—**economic independence.** Own your lane. Buy Black. Circulate the dollar."

Ezekiel nodded.

"Two—**mental liberation.** If you don't own your mind, your body follows orders from fools."

"Facts," Ezekiel muttered.

"Three—**pan-African unity.** We are stronger when we ain't fighting each other for scraps from the same table."

They rode in silence for a second.

Then Ezekiel smiled. "Appreciate the download, brother."

The man tapped the seat. "Just make sure you upload it somewhere it counts."

His next ride was a woman dressed plainly, with gentle eyes and a tote bag full of flyers.

"You drive full-time?" she asked.

"Yeah. For now."

"We have a little church on the east side. Maybe twenty-five people. But we are heavy on growth. Not just spiritual—financial, emotional, all that. You should visit."

Ezekiel raised an eyebrow. "Where is it?"

"Old Payless store in the shopping plaza near Glenwood. We rent the back. Ain't fancy, but it's real."

He took the flyer. *Renewed Grace Assembly. We don't play church. We become it.*

He tucked it in his sun visor.

Elsewhere, Tasha sat in a buzzing hair salon, head tilted as her friend Trina twisted faux locs into a client's scalp.

"Are you really thinking about coming back?" Trina asked.

"I miss it," Tasha said. "My hands miss it. The money. The sisterhood."

Trina popped her gum. "Girl, we got room. Everybody wants locs now. And these girls don't clean their parts like they used to. You'd kill it."

In the corner, someone laughed loud. "That's 'cause they are too busy taking' selfies to wash their hair!"

Another stylist chimed in. "Are you still with that Uber prophet?"

Trina rolled her eyes. "She ain't never really *left* him. They just on pause-play like one of them mixtapes with no label."

Tasha laughed, but deep down, she wasn't laughing.

She was thinking.

Meanwhile, Miss Ernestine stood on her porch holding a letter.

FINAL NOTICE. MORTGAGE DEFAULT.

Her hands trembled.

She called a car and went straight to Kingdom Dominion.

Inside, Bishop Blackstone lounged in his velvet chair, scrolling his phone.

Ernestine walked in with tears already forming. "Pastor... I need help. They are talking about foreclosure. I have done tithes for twenty years. I cleaned toilets, served food, and sold pies. I just need a little help. A loan. A prayer."

Blackstone barely looked up. "Ernestine, you know I love you. But we are not in the business of handouts. We gotta keep the ministry afloat. Maybe try the county. Or a GoFundMe."

Ernestine's lips quivered. "You told us God would provide."

He smiled without warmth. "Sometimes He provides through struggle."

She walked out without a word.

Outside, she sat in her car, eyes red.

"Twenty years," she whispered. "Twenty damn years."

That evening, Ezekiel sat on the floor, Elijah doing math homework beside him. Naomi on FaceTime, telling him about her new sneakers.

He flipped open his Bible and read aloud from Proverbs:

"The plans of the diligent lead surely to abundance, but everyone who is hasty comes only to poverty."

Tasha walked in, dropped her purse, and slumped onto the couch.

"Long day?" he asked.

"Loud day. But yeah."

He handed her the phone. "I downloaded that investment app. We talked about it. Are you still down?"

She nodded.

They each deposited $50.

The screen blinked: **First Investment Complete.**

"2 plus 2," Ezekiel whispered.

"Equals 8," she finished.

They smiled.

Later that night, Ernestine sat in her kitchen with her friend Maybelline. Two cups of instant coffee steamed between them.

"I gave that man everything," Ernestine said. "And now I might lose my house."

Maybelline patted her hand. "Baby, that ain't God. That's greed in a robe."

"I believed him. Believed in him."

"Do you still believe in God?"

Ernestine nodded slowly.

"Then don't you stop. Just change who you're listening to."

It wasn't a firework moment. It was slow-burning. Silent. But something had shifted in everyone. Ezekiel planted his first financial seed. Tasha remembered who she was behind the bar. Ernestine saw through the glitter to the greed. And somewhere, between broken trust and new beginnings, the equation started adding up.

Because faith ain't always loud.

Sometimes it's just a $50 step.

Sometimes it's what you do when nobody claps.

And that's where 2 + 2 stops being survival.

And starts looking like an increase.

CHAPTER ELEVEN

LAUGHTER, LOSS, AND THE WEIGHT OF TRUTH

Sometimes, progress comes with a smile. Other times, it shows up as fire in the streets, truth too loud to ignore. In a world that keeps trying to sell silence, Ezekiel found himself caught between comedy and chaos. But even in the madness, he kept collecting pieces of the puzzle—because when your eyes are open, even pain can feed the script. Even laughter can teach. And when the world starts shaking, some folks preach, some protest, and some... finally wake up.

Ezekiel opened his email, expecting spam or a payment reminder.

Instead:

Congratulations, Ezekiel Trueborn. You passed your Financial Foundations Exam.

He jumped from the chair like he'd won the lottery.

"Let's go!"

He danced a little jig in his socks, then pulled out his notebook and wrote:

Pass the test. Build wealth. Share the truth.

He whispered, "2 plus 2..."

"...equals 8," Elijah said from the couch, half-asleep.

His next Uber ride was a comedian named J. Milly. Gold chain, mismatched socks, and energy like four Red Bulls.

"Yo, my man, this car feels like if it hits 80, the engine is gonna file for unemployment!"

Ezekiel laughed. "You're right. She got arthritis in the steering wheel."

"Your seats ain't got no cushion. I feel like I'm ridin' a bus stop bench with dreams."

Ezekiel wheezed laughing. "Do you want a bottle of water or a back brace?"

J. Milly held up his phone. "I'm goin' live. Y'all meet the homie Zeke, prophet of the pavement. He is drivin', studying finance, and probably about to cast out demons from his brakes."

Ezekiel smiled big. "As long as they pay surge pricing."

They laughed the whole ride.

Later, Ezekiel got stuck near downtown.

Traffic was blocked. People were marching. Signs waving. Chants echoing:

"Say Her Name!"
"Justice for Nia Brooks!"

He parked, grabbed his notebook, and got out.

The crowd was electric. People of all shades standing up for a Black woman gunned down in her own home. Police claimed she was selling drugs. But the neighborhood knew better. Nia Brooks was a preschool teacher.

Ezekiel stood still.

A man on a bullhorn shouted, "They murdered a mother and tried to bury her story under lies!"

Cheers erupted.

"Where are our safe spaces? Our parks? Our playgrounds?" another speaker yelled. "You shut down every positive outlet for our kids and wonder why the streets got 'em!" Malik shouted

Ezekiel filmed on his phone. Jotted notes. His script was evolving. Truth was becoming flesh.

At the same time, inside a luxury office lined with gold plaques and mahogany cabinets, Bishop Armond Blackstone sat across from Congressman Gerald Wright.

They watched the protest on a muted TV.

Wright sipped his scotch. "Can you calm your people?"

Blackstone adjusted his cufflinks. "They're passionate. But they trust me. I can steer the conversation."

"We've got the Super Bowl bid. Olympics scouts watching. This city can't afford chaos."

Blackstone leaned forward. "I'll give them purpose. A reason to look away."

That evening, the bishop appeared on a televised roundtable alongside city officials.

"We hear the community's pain," he said with trained sorrow. "But instead of protests, let's propose solutions. Our parks have closed due to funding—but what if the churches opened their doors?"

Ezekiel watched from his phone, disgusted.

"Man's trying to spin the truth into applause," he muttered.

He rewound the video. Took more notes.

This wasn't just a script anymore.

This was testimony.

At the hair shop, the TV played the protest in the background. Tasha sat under a dryer while Trina, ever loud, shouted from across the room.

"That's Nia Brooks' cousin! I've known her since middle school! And they tryin' to say she was movin' weight? That girl couldn't lift a gallon of milk!"

Someone else chimed in. "My cousin said the cop who shot her already got complaints. But they keep transferring him like mold in a rental kitchen."

Tasha leaned back, eyes closed. Her head wasn't just under a dryer.

It was full.

Of doubt.

Of anger.

Of a quiet fire.

That night, Ezekiel returned home. The house was dark. Quiet.

Miss Ernestine lay on the couch asleep, glasses tilted, her mail open on the floor.

Ezekiel picked it up.

FINAL NOTICE: Foreclosure proceedings will begin within 15 days.

He stared at it.

"God..." he whispered. "She gave her life to a church that won't give her a dime."

He set the paper down gently.

Downstairs, Tasha was in the basement watching YouTube. A man's voice filled the room—steady, deep, full of conviction.

It was Bob Proctor.

"You must begin by seeing abundance in your mind. Not your bank. Your results don't come from your hustle—they come from your beliefs."

Ezekiel sat beside her.

"Are you watching mindset videos now?"

She nodded. "Your books. Your talks. They are rubbing off."

He smiled. "It's compound faith. Grows slowly. Hits big."

They sat quietly, listening.

Proctor's voice rolled on:

"When you shift your perception, you shift your outcome."

Tasha whispered, "I'm tired of reacting to life. I want to design it."

Ezekiel reached for her hand.

"Then let's build the blueprint."

Laughter won't fix injustice. Protests won't replace policy. But when people wake up—really wake up—systems start to crack. Tonight, Ezekiel learned that growth isn't always loud. Sometimes, it's in the way a woman sits under a dryer and hears a new voice. In the way a son writes truth while others shout. In the way faith, finally fed, begins to move.

And as the city stirred, as lies unraveled, and dreams rewrote themselves...

2 plus 2 was still four on paper.

But on purpose?

It was looking more like destiny.

Every story has a chapter that humbles the dreamer. Where the world doesn't hand you nothing but a flat tire and a silent sky. But it's in these dark spaces where seeds start to stir. Not because the sun is shining, but because something in the soil refuses to stay buried. Today, Ezekiel learned that before fruit comes pressure, before revelation comes resistance. And some truths only grow when you're forced to stand still and ask the right questions.

Ezekiel went live on Instagram, standing under a cloudy Atlanta sky.

"Peace, y'all. Real quick—I wanna talk about passive income. I don't care if it's dividend stocks, royalties from your art, or flipping vending machines. It's time we stop trading every hour for a check. Speak what you want. Design the life you see. Because faith without works is dead—but so is faith without a vision."

He tapped the screen. "Type '2 + 2 = 8' if you know you're planting something bigger than your struggle."

He ended the live, smiled, and walked toward his car.

Then—*ssssshhhhh.*

He looked down.

Flat tire.

He shook his head, then looked up.

"Romans 5:3," he muttered. "Suffering produces perseverance. Perseverance, character. And character, hope."

He grabbed the jack.

"Lord, let this struggle be a setup."

Meanwhile, on the west end, Bishop Blackstone stood near the front of a crowd gathered outside a closed park. His robe was shorter than usual. His voice, smoother.

"We must protest with purpose," he told them. "But not with rage. The city will listen if we approach with strategy. Let me help guide the message."
A young organizer named Malik stepped forward, fist raised.
"Respectfully, Bishop, we don't need handlers. We need solutions. Kids dying in the street. Cops lying'. Y'all churches are full of money, but the parks are still boarded up."
Murmurs of agreement spread.

Blackstone adjusted his collar. "I understand your pain—"

"No, you understand cameras," Malik snapped. "Where was Kingdom Dominion when Nia Brooks got shot? When Jaheim got locked up on a trumped-up charge? We are grieving. You're politicking."

Blackstone opened his mouth but nothing came out.

The crowd turned their backs.

Ezekiel finished tightening the spare and wiped his hands with a shirt from the trunk. As he got in, another Uber request came through—three girls headed to Southlake Mall.

When he pulled up, the energy hit before they even opened the door.

The one in the front seat, nails like stilettos, smacked her gum. "Uh-uh. This ride got a donut. I'm not gettin' in no car with a *fake* tire."

The second girl stepped back, inspecting. "I'm good."

The third girl paused. Hood, quiet, eyes tired.

"I ain't tryna walk nowhere," she mumbled, getting in.

Her name was Tammy. She didn't talk much, but something about her felt different. She stared out the window.

"Are you always the one that commits?" Ezekiel asked.

She shrugged. "Somebody gotta stick to the plan."

He drove in silence, respect growing for the girl who didn't flinch.

Ms. Rosa stood on her porch with her phone to her ear.

"Yes, ma'am, I got the notice. I'm askin' for an extension. I just need two more weeks before they shut my gas off."

The voice on the line gave her another script.

"I have been paying on time for years. Just behind this once."

She sighed, sat on the porch swing, and stared out at the sky.

"Lord, I don't need a miracle. Just a lil' mercy."

At the salon, chaos was peaking.

Tasha was halfway through braiding a new client's hair when Sexy Red's voice exploded through the Bluetooth speaker.

"Pound townnnn... just left pound town!"

Half the shop started hollering. Stylists dropped combs to twerk. Clients pulled out phones.

Trina shouted, "This is the anthem, y'all!"

One lady in the back muttered, "Lawd, take the wheel."

An older woman near the front looked offended. "This what y'all call music now?"

Tasha laughed while still parting hair. "Everybody got a different soundtrack, ma'am. Some of us just braid to beats."

The whole place cracked up.

But somewhere inside, Tasha wondered what her own soundtrack used to sound like.

And what it could sound like again.

Later that night, Ezekiel sat alone on the porch, sipping lukewarm tea. The streetlights buzzed. In the distance, kids laughed on a corner.

He looked up.

"Am I doing enough? Am I wasting time chasing dreams while rent inches higher? While gas gets cut off?"

He opened his notebook.

Patience is a seed.
Every fruit starts in darkness before it hits the light.

He looked toward the stars.

"God... I'm still watering. Just let it grow."

It wasn't a day for glory. It was a day for grit. A day when tires flattened and voices rose. When laughter clashed with politics and doubts danced with dreams. But Ezekiel didn't quit. Tasha didn't crumble. Even Rose, the quiet one, showed what commitment looked like.

Because sometimes the real fight isn't loud—it's loyal. It's what you keep showing up for.

And even on spare tires and soft prayers, 2 plus 2 still equals 8.

CHAPTER TWELVE

THE TIPPING POINT

Every movement needs a moment. And sometimes that moment doesn't come with permission—it comes with pressure. Pressure from the people. From the pain. From the truth that's been suffocated too long under robes, titles, and a hush-money gospel. Today, the city wasn't just stirred. It was waking up. And Ezekiel? He was standing at the center of a narrative nobody could control—not even the man who once owned every amen in town.

Ezekiel woke up to his phone vibrating like it was fighting for its life.

Comments. Shares. Reposts.

A protest clip had gone viral overnight—the one with Malik calling out Bishop Blackstone in front of a fired-up crowd.

Ezekiel watched it three times.

Then an idea hit.

He opened his notes app and recorded a voice-over to the footage.

"When truth stands up, power sits down. This ain't about religion—it's about redemption. For every grandma who gave her rent to the pulpit and got silence in return. For every kid told to pray while systems failed them. We done praying to buildings. We are praying through action now."

He overlaid it with a beat.

Posted it.

#2Plus2Equals8

Within an hour, the views passed 15,000.

At Kingdom Dominion, Blackstone scrolled the clip with tight lips. The comments were brutal:

"This bishop ain't been real in years."
"Ezekiel preached better from his Camry than Blackstone from his throne."

His assistant entered. "City Council's on line one. They want to know if you've lost control of your flock."

He waved her off. "They still need me. Just gotta remind them who owns the mic."

But even he knew—the crowd was listening to a new voice.

Tasha braided a client's hair when Trina came flying into the shop with her phone up.

"Y'all seen this clip? Zeke broke the internet!"

The video blasted from the speaker. Clients nodded, stylists cheered.

Tasha stood still.

Pride. Fear. Hope. All wrapped in one emotion.

Her client smiled. "That's your man?"

Tasha blinked. "That's my family."

At Rosa's house, she sat in her living room, gas off, lights dim, tears falling.

She watched Ezekiel's clip with her neighbor's Wi-Fi.

Her hand trembled, but she whispered to the screen:

"Keep going, baby. Keep going."

In a local high school, a teacher played the video for his history class.

"This," he said, "is what real leadership looks like. Don't wait for a platform—build your own."

A student raised their hand. "He is like a new Fred Hampton."

Another said, "Nah, he's just Zeke. And that's enough."

Malik called Ezekiel directly.

"You got fire on your hands, bro. Are you ready to do more than post? We got youth. We got elders. We got *energy*. Let's organize something real."

Ezekiel leaned back, overwhelmed but focused.

"I'm down. But we do it our way. Not with politics. With purpose."

"Say less. You just became the voice of something bigger."

That night, Ernestine sat with Rosa in a dark kitchen.

Rosa lit two candles.

"I watched him today. Your boy. He ain't preaching, but he is ministering."

Ernestine sniffled. "He made me feel seen. After all these years of feeling used."

"Maybe that's why God saved him for now. To say what needed to be said."

At home, Ezekiel stood at the sink washing dishes when Tasha walked in.

She slid her phone on the counter.

"You're trending."

He laughed. "I don't care about trends. I care about the truth."

She wrapped her arms around him.

"You're doing something they can't ignore."

He exhaled. "Then we better be ready. Because once they see you for real… they start trying to shut you down."

It started with a video. A verse. A voice. And now it was bigger than a platform—it was a movement. The city was tipping. The masks were slipping. And Ezekiel? He was no longer just a man in a Camry. He was a mirror. A message. A new kind of preacher in a world starving for something real. The seeds were growing.

And 2 plus 2?

Was starting to equal revolution.

CHAPTER THIRTEEN

PEOPLE VS. POWER

When truth walks into a room, comfort runs out. And when that truth echoes through the streets, shaking pulpits and city halls alike, people start choosing sides. This wasn't just about a viral clip anymore. It was about vision. About whose voice would shape the future—and who would finally be held accountable for selling salvation while the streets bled. Lines were being drawn. And Ezekiel? He wasn't running from the tension. He was stepping into it.

Ezekiel sat on the porch, notebook in hand, the city still humming from yesterday's digital earthquake. Tasha brought him a plate of eggs and toast, but his mind wasn't on breakfast.

"Malik wants to set up a town hall," he said. "Real talk. No filters. He asked if I'd come."

Tasha sipped her tea. "Are you going?"

Ezekiel nodded. "I have to."

At Rosa's house, a truck pulled away after disconnecting her gas line.

She didn't cry. Just watched it leave like it had taken the last bit of her pride with it.

"I'm still standing," she whispered.

She packed her bag and called Tasha.

" tell your mom I'm coming over with food and my overnight bag for the weekend"

In a packed barbershop, Ezekiel's name sparked heavy debate.

"Zeke out here tryna be Malcolm with a camera," one man said.

"Nah," another replied. "He just saying what everybody was scared to say."

Raheem the barber laughed. "When the truth comes with a clean fade, folks listen differently."

An old head near the door added, "Preachers got rich while we got evicted. Bout time somebody flipped the script."

Tasha visited her old client Keisha, who now ran a boutique downtown.

" You left the club and never looked back," Tasha said. "I'm ready to bet on myself."

Keisha nodded. "Then do it. Open your braid shop. You got skill. You got the story and skill. That's branding with backbone."

Tasha breathed deep. "I want to teach girls how to hustle legit. Build something that doesn't need a pole or pity."

Keisha smiled. "Then start planting. The streets are already watching."

The town hall buzzed. Folding chairs. Hot lights. Journalists. Elders. Kids. Everyone came. The energy was thick, not with tension—but with a shared sense that something meaningful was about to go down.

Blackstone showed up in a fitted suit, smile tight and eyes scanning the room like a general entering enemy territory. His entourage flanked him, but none of them dared touch the mic first.

Ezekiel walked in last. Hoodie. Calm. Focused. No crew. Just conviction.

Malik grabbed the mic. "Tonight, we ain't throwing shade—we throwing light. Bishop Blackstone, Ezekiel Trueborn, the mic is open."

Blackstone stepped forward, adjusting his lapel, nodding at a few familiar faces.

"I've served this city for decades," he began. "Mistakes? Sure. But I've prayed, paid, and poured into this soil. I buried our dead, baptized your babies, and fought politicians so we could have food banks and school drives."

A few claps. Some respectful nods. But mostly silence.

"I gave y'all faith when the government gave up on you. And now y'all let a hoodie and a hashtag make you forget who fed you?"

Ezekiel rose slowly. Walked to the mic.

"I ain't here to replace no pulpit," he said, voice steady. "I'm here 'cause I'm tired of watching y'all survive when we could be building. Faith without accountability is just noise. And we made enough noise."

A ripple moved through the crowd.

"I ain't perfect. I Uber. I struggle. But I believe in legacy. And if I gotta be the first seed to break ground so y'all can rise? So be it."

Roars. Applause. Some tears.

Blackstone raised a hand to respond, but a woman stood up in the crowd.

"Question for both of y'all—where was the church when my son OD'd last year? Y'all had balloons, but where was the plan?"

Murmurs. Heads nodding.

A man in a work uniform spoke up. "All due respect, Bishop—but I have been tithing fifteen years and I still can't get a call back when I need help. Is it about faith or favoritism?"

Another voice. "Ezekiel, we love what you sayin'. But how do you make sure it doesn't become just another hustle? We've seen movements. We've buried too many dreams."

Ezekiel stepped back to the mic.

"I don't need y'all to follow me. I want you to lead with me. This ain't about my name. It's about shifting mindsets. Ownership. Literacy. We are not waiting for saviors—we are planting seeds."

More applause.

Blackstone stepped forward again, his voice sharper.

"Talk is cheap. And the streets are ruthless. Are you prepared to carry what comes with the weight of being a shepherd, Ezekiel?"

Ezekiel locked eyes with him.

"I already carry weight. The question is, are you ready to release yours?"

Silence.

Malik walked back to the mic and lifted it with authority.

"We ain't here to tear down no man. But we are not gonna keep building on shaky ground either. #2Plus2Equals8 ain't just math—it's motion. It's the mindset. It's multiplication by faith and by function. If you plant the truth, you grow the people. And right now, we are choosing to grow."

The room erupted.

Real dialogue. Real debate. And something bigger than egos started to rise in that room: clarity.

The shift wasn't coming.

It had already begun.

Later that night, back at home, Ezekiel held Elijah while he slept.

He whispered, "One day you gon' ask what your daddy did when the city shook."

He looked at Tasha, scrolling through commercial lease options on her phone.

"And I'm gonna say—I showed up."

Real power doesn't come from robes or microphones. It comes from the people who never stopped believing—even when no one believed in them. Tonight, the people chose. Not a celebrity. Not ceremony. But the truth. And that truth wore worn-out sneakers, carried notebooks, and told the system: your time is up.

Because when people stand together?

Even the biggest throne can shake.

And 2 + 2?

Still equals more than they ever expected.

Title: The Making of Trueborn

CHAPTER FOURTEEN

A NEW KIND OF CHURCH

When old walls crack, it ain't always the end. Sometimes, it's just space being made for something better. A church without steeples. A community without gatekeepers. A movement without permission. Ezekiel wasn't trying to preach—he was trying to plant. And Tasha wasn't just braiding hair—she was weaving power back into her own story. What they were building couldn't be boxed in pews or barber shops. This was a new kind of sanctuary. One born in struggle, shaped by truth, and rooted in something deeper.

Ezekiel pulled into the Glenwood strip plaza, parking outside a former Payless. The windows were still dusty. The sign out front read: *Renewed Grace Assembly* in hand-painted letters.

Inside, folding chairs, a Bluetooth speaker, and about 25 people greeted him with smiles and sincerity. No robes. No collection plates. Just presence.

Pastor Geneva, a woman with silver locs and fire in her words, stepped forward.

"You Ezekiel?"

"Yes, ma'am."

"We watched your clip. Some of us twice. We don't have much, but we have a purpose. You're down to lead a financial class?"

Ezekiel smiled. "I'm more comfortable with a whiteboard than a pulpit."

She laughed. "Good. We're more about doing than preaching."

He looked around. Real people. Real hunger.

"Let's build something that outlives us," he said.

Geneva stepped closer, voice low but full of urgency. "Ezekiel, the people don't just need checks—they need clarity. They don't just need hope—they need help. You know what Hosea said? *'My people are destroyed for lack of knowledge.'* We've been shouting and shouting and still losing ground because nobody taught us how to plant seed in the soil we got."

Ezekiel nodded slowly, taking it in.

"I've seen what happens when folks get fed just spirit with no strategy," she continued. "They fall. Over and over. And in Jeremiah, the Lord said, *'I know the plans I have for you... plans to prosper you and not to harm you... to give you a future and a hope.'* But plans mean work. Plans mean infrastructure. Faith without a foundation collapses every time the wind blows."

Ezekiel's gaze swept the room—mothers, teenagers, elders, all with the same look: open palms. Not begging. Ready to build.

"We don't just need inspiration," Geneva said. "We need instruction. We need blueprints, budgets, group chats, workshops, gardens, co-ops. We need to know how the system works so we can stop bleeding at every turn."

Ezekiel exhaled. "Then let's teach 'em. Let's give 'em what they never got in school. Let's talk about credit, compound interest, passive income, trust funds. Let's teach the mindset."

Geneva smiled, eyes watering just a little. "Then let's get to work."

Tasha met with Trina and two stylists at a small café. They flipped through lease options for a community braid bar.

Trina pointed. "This one has two stations already. And a break room."

Tasha hesitated. "It's a big leap."

Trina leaned forward. "We've been building other people's dreams for years. I say we start charging rent instead of paying it."

The third stylist added, "And make it a teaching salon too—braids, branding, business. Bring up the next girls the right way."

At Ernestine's place, a new letter arrived. Final foreclosure notice. 7 days.She didn't cry this time. Just folded it neatly.

Then she whispered, "Maybe this is the chapter where I rise."

That evening, Ezekiel launched *Faith Hustle Fridays*, live on social media. His backdrop? A handwritten sign that read: **Plant. Water. Harvest.**

He spoke on budgeting. On mindset. On miracles and management.

Within an hour, 10,000 views.

Tasha watched from the braid shop. Rosa watched from her neighbor's tablet. Malik reposted it with the caption: **This the church now.**

Later that night, Ezekiel and Tasha sat on the porch.

"Feels different now," she said.

"It is," he replied. "We are not just surviving anymore. We are designing."

She looked up at the stars.

"You ever think maybe all this—our pain, our past—was never punishment? Just pressure building something solid."

Ezekiel nodded.

"Pressure makes diamonds. Or cracks. We just chose to shine."

The new sanctuary ain't made of stained glass. It's built on sweat, truth, and a seed called faith. No robes required. No offering needed. Just vision and a vow to do better. Ezekiel and Tasha weren't just changing their lives—they were changing the math.

And from the cracks in old systems, something holy was growing.

2 + 2...

Still equals 8.

And the blueprint was just getting started.

CHAPTER FIFTEEN

FULL CIRCLE

Before purpose, there's pain. Before triumph, trauma. Every man who rises carries a version of himself that nearly didn't make it. Some get buried in the system. Some are buried by silence. But the ones who survive? They don't just live—they testify. This chapter ain't about winning a prize. It's about remembering the price. Because before Ezekiel taught the word, he had to survive the wound. And some wounds cut so deep, even time has to tread softly around them.

The summer heat clung to Atlanta like guilt on a preacher. Fifteen-year-old Ezekiel stood on a street corner, dopestories sweatshirt, eyes sharp. The weed tucked into his sock was barely enough to get noticed—but enough to get caught.

Him and his two boys, Dre and Kemo, ran the block like it owed them something. They weren't gangbangers. Just kids who'd seen too much and decided fast money made more sense than food stamps and empty refrigerators.

They argued that day over something dumb—who owed five dollars for a blunt. Dre shoved Kemo. Kemo swung back. It was petty. Loud. Stupid. But being loud was dangerous. And danger had eyes.

Blue lights flared before they even noticed.

"DOWN ON THE GROUND!"

The boys scattered—but Ezekiel didn't make it far.

Handcuffs. Concrete. Cold silence.

The juvenile intake smelled like Pine-Sol and despair. Ezekiel's shoes were taken. His sweatshirt was replaced by an orange top two sizes too big.

That night, the screams started.

First, a fight. Two boys went at it over a honey bun. Blood on the wall. No one stepped in for ten minutes.

Then came the silence. Too quiet.

A counselor opened a cell door and screamed. A boy named Ronnell had tied his t-shirt around the bars and his neck. His legs kicked. Eyes rolled.

Two guards rushed in, cut him down.

He lived.

Barely.

They stripped him to nothing. Suicide watch.

Ezekiel sat on his cot, fists clenched, chest heavy. He couldn't sleep—not with the sound of Ronnell's bare feet dragging on the floor all night, the sound of soft whimpering from a kid two cells down, or the loudest sound of all:

The door kicking.

All night long, another boy named Rico kicked the metal door. Over and over.

"I WANNA GO HOME!"

BANG. BANG. BANG.

"I AIN'T EVEN DO NOTHING!"

BANG. BANG.

"I WANNA SEE MY MOM!"

No one came.

They let him kick.

And cry.

Until his voice broke.

Ezekiel watched the ceiling. His stomach growled. His eyes refused to close.

"If this is where you end up when you slip," he whispered, "the streets ain't life. They just the path to a slow death."

The next afternoon, a visitor came in.

A preacher in a sharp suit. Clean shoes. Bible in hand. Bishop Blackstone.

He spoke with smooth thunder.

"You are not your charges. You are not your past. You are not forgotten."

Some boys laughed. Others ignored him.

But Ezekiel listened.

Blackstone walked past his cell.

"Have you ever read Psalms 23?" he asked.

Ezekiel shook his head.

"Read that. And Psalms 51. And Proverbs. Let it feed you until the world doesn't scare you anymore."

He slid a Bible through the bars.

Ezekiel took it.

He didn't know why.

But he took it.

That night, Ezekiel stared at the ceiling, the screams still echoing, the door still getting kicked.

And he opened the book.

The Lord is my shepherd, I shall not want...

He got out two weeks later.

The city didn't look different.

But he did.

He came home to Rosa's house. She was washing dishes, humming low.

That night, after dinner, he finally asked her.

"Ma... who's my dad?"

She stopped. Her back stiffened. The dish in her hand slipped into the water.

She turned slowly.

"It's... a long story, Zeke."

"Why haven't I ever met him?"

She looked away. Eyes full.

"Because... some things ain't easy to explain. Some things hurt too much to say out loud."

He nodded, but inside, something cracked.

He went to his room.

Opened that same Bible.

And cried into the pages.

Present Day.

Ezekiel stood on the lawn, tossing a football with Elijah.

Naomi jumped rope, counting loud.

Tasha sat on the porch, her smile small but present.

Ezekiel's phone buzzed.

LIVE: 2 Plus 2 Equals 8 – Contest Results Premiering Now

He clicked.

Everyone gathered.

The announcer's voice cut through the speaker:

"After a national vote, Ezekiel Trueborn has been selected... as the **first place winner** of the $25,000 prize."

Gasps. Shouts. Naomi screamed. Elijah dropped the football.

Tasha covered her mouth.

Rosa stepped onto the porch with wide eyes.

Ernestine just wept.

Ezekiel stood up. Calm.

"Ms. Ernestine. I read the letter. Don't worry. Your house is safe."

She broke down. "Thank you, baby. Thank you, God."

"Ma," he said to Rosa. "Your lights and gas? Will be back on."

She nodded, wiping tears.

He turned to Tasha.

"And baby... let's get that building. I believe in your vision."

Tasha hugged him.

Naomi grinned. "2 plus 2!"

They all answered in unison.

"Equals 8!"

Before the win, there was a wound. Before the light, there was a long night full of kicking doors and silent screams. But Ezekiel didn't fold. He planted faith in pain—and watered it with purpose.

Now? That seed was rising.

And what they were building would outlive all the lies that tried to bury it.

2 plus 2?

Still equals 8.

Because God doesn't do regular math.

He does resurrection.

CHAPTER SIXTEEN

THE POWER IN NUMBERS

Victory doesn't always wear crowns. Sometimes it stands on a cracked porch, holding a phone with cracked glass, speaking truth into Wi-Fi signals while the world finally listens. This wasn't about money. It was about momentum. About math that didn't make sense on paper, but made perfect sense in purpose. And when Ezekiel stood up to speak, he didn't just claim a win. He claimed a generation.

Live on YouTube

The comments flew in faster than Ezekiel could read them. Over 32,000 tuned in. He stood in front of a white backdrop hand-painted with the words: **"Plant. Water. Harvest."**

Tasha held the phone steady.

Ezekiel adjusted his collar, exhaled slowly, and began.

"I want to thank everybody who believed. Who voted. Who saw more than just an Uber driver with a notebook. This win ain't just mine—it's yours. It's ours. Because when they told us 2 plus 2 equals 4, we smiled, nodded… and built something that proved otherwise."

He paused. Steady.

"You know what I learned from growing up without much? That the power isn't just in income—it's in outcome. In what you *do* with what you have. In what you plant while everyone else is sleeping. That's compound interest. That's a spiritual return."

Tears welled in Rosa's eyes.

Ezekiel looked directly into the lens.

"We are not begging no more. We are building. We are not waiting any more. We walking. And if this voice can reach y'all from the basement, imagine what we can do with a platform built on truth, not titles."

He closed strong:

"Thank you for showing me that faith, when backed by patience, still wins. We are not done. We are just starting. 2 plus 2 equals…"

The live chat exploded: **"8!"**

In a private lounge, Bishop Blackstone watched the stream on a flatscreen with two deacons.

He smirked.

"Boy got passion," he muttered.

One deacon said, "He got power, Bishop."

Blackstone sipped his drink. "So did Lucifer."

At a trap house up in Buckhead, Kilo sat on a couch rolling a blunt while the YouTube live replayed.

"That boy thinks he is better than me now?" he said, jaws tightening.

Across the room, a woman in a headwrap smiled from her corner.

"That boy walking in the light. And it's burning your demons."

Kilo glared.

She smiled wider.

"I told you God was gon' raise someone from the block. Now look at Him."

Across town, Malik and the protest organizers gathered around a laptop.

When Ezekiel finished, the room erupted in claps and cheers.

"That's our next speaker," Malik said. "We done following noise. We are following the builders now."

Later That Night – Dinner

The family sat at a round booth in a soulful diner off Ponce. Chicken and waffles. Sweet tea. Laughter.

Elijah colored on the menu while Naomi taught him how to spell "victory."

Ernestine leaned in.

"Baby," she said, voice low. "I wanna tell y'all something."

Rosa looked at her. "Go on."

"I was behind on bills 'cause… I went to the slot room. Feeding machines more than my fridge."

Rosa sighed. "Me too."

Ezekiel didn't flinch.

"You're human. But it stops now. You gave too much to luck. Time to give to legacy."

He reached into his coat. Pulled out two envelopes. Each thick.

"One for your mortgage, Ms. Ernestine. One for your utilities, Ma."

They both stared.

"Are you serious?"

He nodded. "We are no more. We are building. We are multiplying."

Naomi whispered, "Compound interest."

Tasha beamed.

Next Day – Southside Commercial Plaza

Ezekiel and Tasha toured a small but clean unit with a wide front window and two back rooms.

Tasha's fingers grazed the wall.

"I can already see it. Six chairs. A sign that says 'Crowned by Design.'"

Ezekiel smiled. "Let's start the lease paperwork."

She turned. "Are you sure?"

"I'm sure about you. And I'm sure about faith. That's enough."

Later That Afternoon

A used but clean 2017 Tahoe pulled into Rosa's driveway.

Naomi screamed. "It's ours?!"

Ezekiel tossed the keys in the air. "Ain't brand new. But it runs like hope."

Rosa hugged him. Ernestine kissed him on the cheek.

Tasha got behind the wheel. "Room for growth," she said.

Elijah climbed in the back. "We rich now?"

Ezekiel laughed.

"No. We *right* now."

They didn't win because they had the most. They won because they did the most with what they had. Ms. Ernestine let go of the slots. Rosa faced the truth. Tasha stepped into her calling. And Ezekiel? He didn't just lead. He lifted. He gave. He built.

Because that's what the blessed do.

2 plus 2?

Still equals 8.

Because faith, when multiplied by vision… always pays dividends.

CHAPTER SEVENTEEN

POWER, PAIN, AND THE PUSH FORWARD

Some chapters don't start with fanfare. They begin in silence—thick, sacred, and searching. And when that silence speaks, it ain't always loud. But it's holy. On this day, healing walked into the room without knocking. It didn't ask permission. It just whispered to the wounds, "It's time." This was that day. For Rosa, for Ezekiel, for all of them. Because when the soul says "I'm ready," the rest of you have no choice but to rise.

Rosa – Bathtub, Morning Light

Steam curled around her face, softening years of lines drawn by struggle. Rosa sat still, letting the warm water soak into her joints, her scars, her silence.

The lights were on.

The gas was back.

But peace? That was still making its way home.

Her eyes grew heavy. The hum of the heater became a lullaby.

And the past slipped in like smoke under a closed door.

Flashback – Motel 6

Rosa sat at the edge of a stained bed, her hands shaking like she had just held lightning. The man across the room buttoned his shirt slowly. No affection. No acknowledgment.

"I'm pregnant," she said. Quiet. Terrified.

The man didn't flinch. Didn't look at her.

"You knew the rules," he muttered.

He grabbed his keys from the dresser.

"That wasn't one of them."

She sat up straighter. "So that's it?"

He turned to her with a shrug that felt colder than the night air outside.

"Good luck."

He closed the door like she was a memory he didn't want.

Back to Present – Bathtub

A song played softly from a Bluetooth speaker.

"He loves me... even when I fall beneath His will..."
 Kirk Franklin.

Rosa's eyes opened, fog meeting tears.

She pressed her hand to her chest.

Her voice cracked, not from weakness—but from release.

"I was never the mistake."

She looked at the ceiling, then into her reflection in the faucet.

"And neither was my baby."

The water rippled as she sat forward.

"I survived men walking out, nights I didn't eat so my son could. I survived shame. I survived silence."

Her fingers tightened into fists.

"But I ain't just surviving no more. I'm done sitting in the ashes. I'm standing in the story."

Ezekiel – In the Tahoe, Late Morning

The sun glared off the dashboard as Ezekiel rolled down Moreland. The truck hummed beneath him like it understood its assignment.

Ping. Pickup request: Buckhead.

He pulled up to a modern office building. A sharp-dressed man in his 40s stepped in.

"Afternoon," the man said. "Nice Tahoe."

Ezekiel nodded. "Thanks. Just got it. Humble upgrade."

"You drive full-time?"

"I do more than drive. Writing, speaking... building something."

The man smiled. "That '2 Plus 2' video was you, right?"

Ezekiel chuckled. "Yes sir."

"I'm Dante. Financial advisor. Wealth management. I've seen a lot of speeches. Yours? That one was truth with teeth."

He pulled out a card.

"I mentor a few young professionals. If you're serious about changing lives— let's talk. You already got the voice."

Ezekiel took it like it was a divine appointment.

"God bless you," he said.

Dante smiled. "Looks like He already is."

Southside – Trina's Braid Shop

Tasha leaned over a young girl's scalp, parting with precision.

Behind her, the stylists laughed over a viral video.

But Tasha? She was in another mode.

"You know why I love braiding?" she said aloud.

The shop went quiet.

"It's not just hair. It's the mindset. You build while you speak. You lay edges, but also truth. That's power."

Trina nodded. "Go ahead, preacher."

Tasha grinned. "I'm about to open my own space. I'm scared. But being scared doesn't mean stop. It means trust louder."

The younger stylists listened closely.

"And if y'all don't hear nothing else—hear this: The tongue carries life. Speak what you need. Speak it until it shows up."

One girl whispered, "I needed that."

Kingdom Dominion – Private Office

Blackstone stirred shrimp and grits on a hot plate.

"Bishop," a deacon said, walking in, "he was on the news again. Ezekiel. Folks listening."

Blackstone stirred slower.

"He's got momentum."

"He's got *people*," the deacon added.

Blackstone set the spoon down. "Time to bring him back into the fold."

His phone buzzed.

Text: Congressman Wright – "You're losing your grip."

Blackstone stared at the screen.

Then whispered, "Not yet. Not while I still breathe."

Ezekiel – Live on Instagram

He pulled into a quiet park. The sun dipped low.

He tapped *Go Live*.

"Peace y'all," he said. "Real quick—I just wanted to remind somebody today… don't let your yesterday speak louder than your tomorrow."

He looked into the camera.

"You are not what left you. You are what stayed."

Tears blurred his vision for half a second.

"You're not broken. You're just under construction. So build. Even if you're scared. Even if nobody claps. Even if it's quiet."

He smiled.

"Keep going. God ain't done yet."

He ended his live.

And sat still.

Letting the Spirit breathe through him.

They were still climbing. But now? They knew what they were climbing toward. Rosa reclaimed her voice. Tasha spoke with power. And Ezekiel? He didn't just inspire—he aligned.

Because purpose is like breath.

You don't realize how much you need it… until it fills your lungs.

2 + 2 still equals 8.

And the air had never felt clearer.

CHAPTER EIGHTEEN

THE GHOSTS THAT STILL SPEAK

There's a power in history that refuses to stay buried. It doesn't ask permission to rise—it just does. And when it speaks, it echoes through cafés, courthouses, and communities like a drumbeat demanding to be heard. On this day, Ezekiel didn't just sip coffee—he drank in the legacy of men who died with fire in their throat and revolution in their bones. Men who didn't live long, but lived loud. And now? Their ghosts weren't haunting. They were guiding.

The café smelled like cinnamon, ink, and truth.

Ezekiel sat across from Malik at a corner table, dim light dancing off the chipped wood.

Malik slid his phone across the table.

"Watch this."

The YouTube video played.

Fred Hampton, young, fierce, unstoppable.

Fred Hampton (clip): "You can jail a revolutionary, but you can't jail the revolution. You might murder a freedom fighter like Bobby Hutton, but you can't murder freedom fighting. And if you do, you'll come up with answers that don't answer, explanations that don't explain, and conclusions that don't conclude."

Hampton's voice hit like a thunderclap.

Next clip. A grainy video of Malcolm X.

Malcolm X: "We declare our right on this earth... to be a human being. To be respected as a human being. To be given the rights of a human being in this society, on this earth, in this day—right now."

Then another.

Medgar Evers: "You can kill a man, but you can't kill an idea. You can silence a voice, but not the cause. Not the cry of mothers. Not the prayers of our people. If I die, let it be in service of truth."

Then Dr. King.

Dr. King: *"We don't have to argue with anybody. We don't have to curse and go around acting bad with our words. We don't need any bricks and bottles. We don't need any Molotov cocktails. We just need to go around to these stores and to these massive industries in our country and say,*

'God sent us here to say to you that you're not treating His children right. And we've come by here to ask you to make the first item on your agenda fair treatment, where God's children are concerned.'

But not only that. We've got to strengthen Black institutions. I call upon you to take your money out of the banks downtown and deposit your money in Tri-State Bank—we want a bank-in movement in Memphis. Go by the savings and loan association. I'm not asking you to do something that we don't do ourselves at SCLC."

Then Malcolm again.

Malcolm X: "I believe in action on all fronts, by whatever means necessary. I'm for truth, no matter who tells it. I'm for justice, no matter who it's for or against. I'm a human being first and foremost, and as such I'm for whoever and whatever benefits humanity as a whole."

And just before he was shot at the Audubon Ballroom, his last known words were:

"Brothers! Brothers, please! This is a house of peace!"

Malik paused the screen. Folded his hands.

"Can you imagine if they all lived to be sixty-something?" he said. "Just sixty. Think about that. Where would we be?"

Ezekiel stared at the still frame of Medgar's face. Quiet. Weighted.

Malik continued, voice low.

"I'm showing you this... because I need you to understand what we're up against. What happens when we really start uplifting our people. It's bigger than speeches. Bigger than protests. They come for you when you stop being noisy and start being powerful."

They both sipped their drinks. Steam rose.

Ezekiel looked up.

"Remind me," he said, voice steady, "when Pharaoh heard a boy child was born in Egypt, didn't he order all male babies under two to be killed?"

Malik nodded. "He did. Trying to kill Moses before Moses could rise."

Ezekiel leaned forward.

"That's why we gotta be bold. Not afraid. Because they'll send threats. Lies. Spies. All of it. Every race gets to uplift their own except us. Look at his-story."

He tapped his chest.

"But now? We telling ours. The real story. And this time—it doesn't end with a casket."

Malik smiled, eyes burning.

"Let's write it, then."

Ezekiel nodded slowly. "We can't just be echoes of the past. We gotta amplify the future. Structure, education, economics. We bring those together, we are not just protesting—we are building empires."

Malik leaned back. "What we saw on that screen? That's legacy. That's the blueprint. They left the notes, we just gotta follow the rhythm. It's time we turn our ideas into systems. Into schools. Ownership. That's what they fear."

Ezekiel's voice dropped. "And that's what we'll give 'em. Not another hashtag. A headquarters. Not just unity. Infrastructure."

Malik chuckled. "The next generation gon' speak in dividends and declarations."

Ezekiel grinned, tapping his knuckles on the table. "Let's make sure they never have to guess who started the shift."

They clinked their mugs together.

No more ghosts.

Only blueprints.

Only purpose.

And the pages were still turning.

Sometimes, you don't need permission to begin—you just need a chair, a coffee, and the courage to carry the fire of the ones who came before. Ezekiel didn't just listen to history. He understood the cost. And he accepted the calling.

2 plus 2 still equals 8.

And this time, the revolution had a notebook.

On the Block – Kilo's Corner

Kilo leaned against a parked car, gold chain swinging, giving orders like a drill sergeant in the middle of a hush war.

"When that red light drops, Truth, I want heads movin'. Move like the law's watching, 'cause they *are.*"

His right-hand man, Truth, leaned against the door with arms crossed.

"Boss," he said, low, "I've been thinking."

Kilo lit a blunt. "That's dangerous."

Truth continued anyway. "We've been beefin' with Ezekiel. But everything that man says? It makes sense. We are the only ones still fighting each other like that's gonna fix anything. Always been divided and conquered. And guess who wins every time?"

Kilo took a long drag. Blew the smoke slowly.

Then turned.

"You been smoking' *my* dope or you just went damn crazy?"

Truth didn't flinch. "Nah. Just tired of seeing us eat each other while they collect our crumbs."

Kilo chuckled. "You sound like a politician."

Truth stared off. "Maybe it's time we build something' instead of burying it."

Revolution doesn't just whisper through books—it moves in real time, through back alleys, church gardens, coffee shops and the concrete blocks where dreams get strangled daily. What Ezekiel and Malik were building wasn't just a movement. It was a resurrection. And not everyone was ready. Some were still playing God. Others were still chasing ghosts. But the shift had already begun. And nothing shakes a system like a people waking up together.

Ernestine's Yard – Afternoon Sun

She stood barefoot, watering the last line of her marigolds, humming softly.

A black car pulled up slowly.

Bishop Blackstone stepped out. Fine suit. Too clean.

"Miss Ernestine," he called.

She didn't stop watering.

"I was wrong," he said. "You were right. Here…"

He handed her an envelope.

"This should take care of your mortgage."

She looked at it. Then looked him up and down.

"You're late," she said calmly. "Ezekiel already paid for it."

Blackstone cleared his throat. "Still. Take it. You never know. Might need it on a bad day… at the slots."

She raised an eyebrow. "You're right. 'Cause I don't know who's had more of my money—the machines… or your church."

She took the envelope.

Then she set down the watering can.

"Let me tell you a parable, Bishop. Flowers? They don't bloom because you visit 'em once. They bloom because they tend to bloom daily. Your church stopped tending."

He nodded slowly.

"Well… maybe y'all can come back. Don't let one mishap erase what we built over decades."

She stepped closer.

"You already lost Ezekiel."

Blackstone smiled tight.

"You must not know the power of a man of God."

And with that, he turned, coat flaring behind him, and walked off.

Back in the Coffee Shop – Early Evening

Ezekiel leaned over the table, eyes burning with vision.

"We got a chance here, Malik. But we can't come in begging. We have to teach,our people to build. To create. To own. Ownership is the new revolution."

Malik nodded. "Financial literacy… that's the real power. That's what they fear. 'Cause when we start understanding money—we start understanding freedom."

Ezekiel tapped the table. "No more marching without building. No more noise without structure. We create curriculum. Launch workshops. From barbershops to block corners. Teach 'em what they never taught us."

Malik leaned in.

"You already got the people online. I got the streets. Let's build something special."

He grinned.

"Something unbreakable."

Ezekiel smiled.

"Something that finally teaches our kids that 2 plus 2?"

Malik raised his cup.

"Equals 8."

Ezekiel sat back, quoting John Hope Bryant: "Being poor is not just a lack of money; it's a lack of hope."

Malik nodded slowly, then added from Dr. Claud Anderson: "To make it in this world, we must become producers, not just consumers. Otherwise, we're only surviving, never thriving."

Their words hung in the air like prophecy. Like strategy.

Because this wasn't just a moment.

It was the blueprint.

The revolution wasn't televised this time. It was organized. It was calculated. It was divine. And while some were still busy protecting pulpits and corners, others had begun blueprinting a world no longer built on scraps.

The ancestors whispered. The people listened. The movement breathed.

And 2 plus 2?

Still equals 8.

Because this time, they weren't marching into traps.

They were building exits.

CHAPTER NINETEEN

THE SOIL AND THE STORM

Weeks later

Jesus once told a parable about a sower. Some seeds fell by the wayside and got eaten by birds. Some landed on rocky ground, sprouted fast but withered in the heat. Others fell among thorns, choked out by the cares of the world. But some? Some landed on good ground. And those? They produced thirty, sixty, even a hundredfold. The test was never about the seed. It was always about the soil.

And this—this was the soil season.

Ezekiel stood before a packed room in the back of a rec center. Fold-out chairs. Whiteboard. Smell of old basketballs and cheap carpet.

But what was he building? It Wasn't cheap.

Malik stood by the door, counting heads. A mix of barbers, teachers, single moms, hustlers, and high school kids who wanted better.

"Before we start," Ezekiel said, "let me say this: what we're building here, it's dangerous. Not 'guns and gangs' dangerous. But *clarity is dangerous*. Power is dangerous. The kind they sabotage before it blooms."

A silence settled over the room.

Then he began the workshop.

Budgeting. Credit. Ownership. Passive income. Group economics.

And then the test came.

That night, a man in a gray suit pulled Ezekiel to the side.

"I work with a nonprofit downtown," he said. "We love what you're doing. Got access to some serious grant money. Half a million. All you gotta do is let us *advise* your programming. Shape the language. Keep it 'light.' No talk of race. No ownership. Keep it surface-level. Safe."

He slid a folder across the table.

Ezekiel opened it.

$500,000.

No more Uber. No more folding chairs. Instant elevation.

He looked up.

"Have you ever read that parable?" Ezekiel asked. "The one about seeds and soil?"

The man blinked.

"I'm not in the ministry."

"Exactly," Ezekiel said. "That's why you don't get it."

He pushed the folder back.

"I ain't a seed looking for shade. I'm good soil. And good soil doesn't sell its roots."

Meanwhile, a government email pinged inside a Homeland Security office.

Subject: Monitor activity of grassroots org—'2 Plus 2 Equals 8'

A line at the bottom read:

Organizing urban youth, teaching sovereignty, increasing influence. Watchlist recommended.

Back at the rec center, someone vandalized the door overnight. Spray paint:

"Stay in your lane."

Ezekiel showed up early. Malik stood beside him.

"You scared?" Malik asked.

Ezekiel shook his head.

"I'm *ready.* You can't have rain without thunder. Wouldn't know what the sun means if it never stormed."

Malik nodded. "We ain't just leaders. We are soil-tested."

They opened the doors again.

And the people came.

More than before.

The storm doesn't break the ones planted deep. It breaks the shallow. The hollow. The sellouts.

But Ezekiel? Malik? They were rainproof. Rooted. And while the system plotted behind curtains and envy whispered in corners… something sacred was growing.

2 plus 2 still equals 8.

And this time, it wasn't up for negotiation.

The Soil and the Storm

The seed ain't the story. The soil is. That's where roots form, where storms hit, where decisions get made. It's the test ground. And when the rain falls—because it always does—only the planted rise. This wasn't just about empowerment. It was a war. But not with bullets. With blueprints. With buildings. With boldness. Ezekiel and his people weren't just gathering. They were growing. And in that growth? Eyes were watching. Some with hope. Some with hunger. Some with hate.

Few days later

The community room buzzed with energy. Folding chairs filled fast. No stage, just a whiteboard and a mic on a stand. Ezekiel stood in the center, hoodie sleeves pushed up, eyes scanning the crowd.

"Tonight," he began, "we ain't just talkin' money. We talkin' movement. Ownership. Power."

He clicked the remote. A slide lit up behind him: 'Passive Income vs. Time Slavery.'

"Most of us were raised thinking if you ain't grinding, you ain't eating. But they never told us we could make money *while* we sleep."

He pointed to the list on the board.

"Digital products. Royalties. Real estate. Dividend stocks. Vending machines. T-shirts. Apps. If you can sell your time, you can sell a product. If you can hustle on the block, you can flip a business. It's the *same muscle*. Just a different mindset."

A young man raised his hand. "My name's Marcellus. I did it for three years. I got a record. Who's gonna let me in the bank?"

Ezekiel stepped forward. "The same folks that *won't* are why we build our *own*. CDFIs. Credit unions. Cooperative economics. You don't need their seat when we build our own table."

Another woman, mid-40s, hand calloused from years of cleaning houses, spoke up. "But what if you don't even know where to start?"

"Start here," said a woman from the back.

It was Geneva—from the Renewed Grace Assembly.

She stood tall, silver locs wrapped in cloth.

"Black Wall Street started with less. And it grew. Businesses. Schools. Banks. But you know what destroyed it?"

The room fell silent.

"Fear. Envy. And a system that couldn't stand to see us independent. They dropped bombs on Tulsa because they couldn't drop chains anymore."

A few gasps. A few nodded hard.

"You know how long the Black dollar stays in our community?" she asked. "Less than three days. The Jewish dollar? Seventeen. Asian dollar? Thirty. That's not poverty. That's policy. But we can change that—if we *circulate*. If we trust."

At the snack table, Rosa and Ernestine handed out bottles of water and fruit trays like they were serving communion.

"You ever think we'd be here?" Rosa whispered.

Ernestine grinned. "I thought I'd be playing slots tonight."

They laughed.

Truth stood in the back, arms folded, watching.

Malik took the mic.

"I know some of y'all used to seeing me in marches. But we are about to start taking it to the traps. Not to shame. Not to police. But to reach. 'Cause them drug dealers? They ain't the enemy. They just ain't seen the light yet."

Truth stepped forward.

"Let me say somethin'."

The crowd turned.

"I ran with Kilo. I know what that life feels like. You either numb or you run. But Zeke? He made me *feel* again. Reminds me that I got value that doesn't gotta come in rubber bands."

Applause broke out.

Tasha took the mic next.

Her voice was calm. Warm.

"We just secured the building for our braid shop. But it ain't just a salon. It's a program. We gon' teach young Black girls not just how to do hair—but how to do life. Contracts. Branding. Self-worth."

A few young girls cheered. Mothers wiped tears.

"My son asked me if we were rich," Ezekiel added from the side. "I told him we're right. Right in heart. Right in spirit. And that's where it starts."

But in the corner, near the coat rack, sat a man no one knew. Eyes too quiet. Clothes are too plain. His phone never left his hand.

One of Blackstone's spies.

He watched. Took notes. And texted three words:

"It's taking root."

This was no ordinary night. It was a night of alignment. Of callings. Of confessions. But even among the builders, a Judas lingered. The system wasn't sleeping. And neither were its servants.

But Ezekiel? Malik? Tasha? Rosa? They had something deeper.

Soil. Soul. And strategy.

2 plus 2 still equals 8.

And what they were building couldn't be bombed this time.

It would bloom.

CHAPTER TWENTY

THE DREAM SEED

Some nights don't end with sleep—they end with revelation. And when love and legacy meet on a pillow soaked in dreams, that's when the real seeds are planted. You don't need a stadium to shift a generation. Sometimes, all you need is a voice, a mic, and a vision that won't shut up. Tonight, the storm had calmed. The fire still burned. And in the quiet? Purpose whispered.

Social media was on fire.

Clips from the community session flooded TikTok, IG, YouTube Shorts. Tweets, memes, duets—everywhere you looked, someone was quoting Ezekiel or tagging #2Plus2Equals8.

The world was watching.

The basement, in a dim bedroom, Ezekiel and Tasha lay in bed, tangled in sheets and breath.

2:03 a.m.

Tasha rolled over and laid her head on his chest.

"You know you can't keep driving Uber, right?" she said softly.

Ezekiel chuckled. "I know."

"I'm serious."

"I've been thinking about that story. When Jesus told Peter to step out the boat. To walk on water."

Tasha lifted her head. "You feelin' like Peter?"

"I feel like I've been paddling too long," Ezekiel said. "It's time I walk. More time at the center. Less time grinding for gas money. Between YouTube, the workshop donations, and now the attention… if we focus, we can build a flood from these streams."

Tasha smiled. "Then start a podcast. From the center."

He looked at her, eyes wide.

"You, Malik, and Pastor Geneva. Three different lenses. One mic. Call it…"

Ezekiel sat up.

"You are a genius."

Tasha kissed his shoulder. "I know."

"We print up shirts. Hoodies. #2Plus2Equals8.' Run it through Shopify. The message is the movement now."

"I was just about to say that," she laughed. "Plus, baby… we are about to shoot our own movies."

Ezekiel raised an eyebrow.

"You're submitting scripts," she said. "Hen has the cameras. I got girls ready to do hair and makeup. Why are we waiting for studios to approve our stories?"

He kissed her deep.

When they broke, he whispered, "about planting my last $5,000 and making it grow."

She held his face. "We gon' multiply it. You watch."

They curled up again, skin on skin, purpose on top of passion.

The city buzzed outside.

Inside? It rested.

Morning – Sunlight Through Curtains

Ezekiel blinked awake, heart still racing from a dream he couldn't shake.

He grabbed his notebook off the dresser. Scribbled fast.

Podcast name: Seeds & Smoke

He stared at the words.

Because that's what it was.

Truth planted deep.

And real talk they'd have to fight through fire to deliver.

Some names come from logos. Others from legacy. And this one? This one came from the belly of a vision wrapped in truth.

They were no longer waiting.

They were walking. On water. In faith. On fire.

2 plus 2 still equals 8.

And the podcast?

Seeds & Smoke

Was just the beginning.

It's one thing to speak of vision. It's another to *start* it. With no blueprint. No funding. Just a favor. Faith. And a fire that won't go out. That's where Ezekiel was now. Not waiting. Not dreaming. *Building.* And when God breathes on something, even chipped tables and tight budgets become sacred ground.

Back at the House – Late Morning

Ezekiel sat hunched at the computer desk in the living room, eyes dancing between tabs. On one screen, a rough sketch of a t-shirt. Bold print:

#2Plus2Equals8

On the other, a YouTube video titled "Best Podcast Setup on a Budget."

He clicked through microphone reviews, mixers, and design apps. Shopify pricing plans. Canva templates. Shipping costs. Every number he typed stabbed at his balance.

He sighed.

"Mic… $109. Adapter… $29. Monthly hosting… $15. Shirts… whoa."

Ernestine, sweeping in the hallway, paused.

She peeked in, broom still in hand.

"You alright, baby?"

Ezekiel rubbed his temples. "Just trying not to start a movement in the red."

She walked over, quiet. Listened to the numbers again.

Then without a word, she went to her nightstand. Pull open the drawer. Came back with an envelope.

"I was stashin' for emergencies. I think a new world counts as one."

She dropped it in his lap.

Ezekiel blinked. "Ms. Ernestine—"

"Shhh," she said, hand up. "Don't insult me. Take it. God moves mysteriously. Sometimes through old women with shaky hands."

He laughed, eyes misty.

"Thank you."

She patted his shoulder. "Print the shirts, baby. Speak the word. Let the world wear it."

College Park – Tasha's New Shop

The walls were freshly painted—lavender and cream. Mirrors leaned against the wall, waiting to be mounted. Boxes of hair products stacked near the back.

Tasha and her girls laughed as they danced to the radio.

"Actin' bad like a boss in my lace front..."

They shouted lyrics, moved furniture, unpacked, braided each other's hair just to test angles at the chairs.

One stylist twirled. "We got a shop, y'all!"

Tasha stood at the center, hands on hips, smiling like a proud momma.

"We are not just styling crowns," she said. "We saving queens."

Somewhere Else in Atlanta – Blackstone's Office

The room was dark, blinds closed. Only the glow of a screen.

A man sat beside Blackstone. The same one who'd offered Ezekiel the $500K grant with hidden strings. Name: Richard Wynn, political liaison with hidden ties to the city council.

"He turned it down," Wynn muttered. "Didn't even flinch."

Blackstone exhaled slowly.

"What's the boy building?"

"Momentum. Influence. Currency."

Blackstone narrowed his eyes. "Then we cut it before it blooms."

He nodded to one of his men.

"Send in the second wave. The ones who don't ask questions. Let's learn everything. I want names, funds, locations. He's got the people. I need the pressure."

The Bluff – Westside Atlanta

Malik stood on a crate, megaphone in hand, as kids in dusty sneakers and hoodies gathered.

"We will march next week!" he shouted. "Through the Bluff! We are not running' from our pain anymore—we walkin' through it."

Cheers. Applause.

Truth stood beside him, passing out flyers.

Kilo, a few blocks over, counted money at a folding table. Wads of it. Rubber bands. Silence.

He looked up. "Truth still runnin' with them tik tok prophets?"

"Yep."

"He is chasing' pipe dreams."

Truth walked past at that moment. Paused.

"Dreams are free," he said. "But so is hell. I'd rather walk toward the light."

He kept going.

Two other hustlers followed.

Midtown – Geneva Showing a House

Geneva opened the door to a modern townhome. A young woman in a red power suit walked through, looking around.

"I've seen you somewhere…" she said.

Geneva laughed. "Probably on TikTok. I teach workshops with Ezekiel Trueborn."

The woman's eyes lit up. "*That's* where! He's brilliant."

Geneva nodded. "He's bold. Different."

The woman stopped walking. "I'm executive operations for Coca-Cola's cultural initiative division. Bring me the right pitch. I can open some doors. Sponsorship. Real support. But it needs structure. Bring me the *paperwork.*"

Geneva smiled. "I'll bring the *plan.*"

A fire was lit. Across living rooms, salons, neighborhoods, and corporate suites, the ripple was now a wave. Ezekiel and his people weren't chasing approval. They were building a legacy.

And even while Judas wrote memos in the shadows…

The kingdom kept rising.

2 plus 2?

Still equals 8.

And the blueprint just found its ink.

CHAPTER TWENTY-ONE

MIC CHECK, GATEKEEPERS & CODES

Every movement needs a mouthpiece. But when the voice is real—when it speaks with soil still on its hands—the people don't just listen… they *lean in*. And while some build, others break. Some offer water, others set fires. This wasn't about what's already been said. It was about what still needed to be spoken.

Community Center – Late Morning

The sun poured through the front windows of the 2+2=8 Center, lighting up dust particles and blueprints.

Ezekiel, Malik, and Geneva sat around a folding table near the back, a chalkboard behind them already smeared with brainstorming from days before. A few volunteers moved quietly in the background—organizing, sorting flyers, checking emails. Energy buzzed low but steady, like an engine warming up.

Ezekiel tapped the chalkboard with his knuckles.

"So… *Seeds & Smoke*," he said with a grin. "Still love that name."

Malik nodded. "Feels gritty. Feels grounded."

Geneva smiled. "Feels *true*."

Ezekiel uncapped a marker. "Let's build the show outline. If we got an hour and a half, what's our first arc?"

Malik leaned in. "Start with *roots*. Our stories. What woke us up."

Ezekiel wrote: **EP 1: Where We Come From—The Awakening**

Geneva added, "Then tie that into history. How our personal soil lines up with our cultural soil. Black Wall Street, Tulsa, all of it."

EP 2: The Soil They Burned

"Then switch gears," Malik said. "Let's talk about the economy. Ownership. Hustle vs. wealth."

EP 3: Ownership is Oxygen

They kept going:

- **EP 4: Church Hurt & Healing**
- **EP 5: Raising Kings & Queens (Parenthood Talk)**
- **EP 6: The Currency of Trust**

Ezekiel leaned back, marker between his fingers.

"People gon' feel this," he said. "They gon' see themselves in it."

Geneva's phone buzzed.

She looked down, then back up.

"Oh—and speaking of doors opening…" she smiled wide. "The woman I showed that house to? Exec at Coca-Cola. She recognized me from the TikToks. Told me to bring her a solid pitch. She's talkin' corporate sponsorship."

Malik blinked. "Coke?"

"Coke," Geneva repeated.

Ezekiel sat still for a second.

Then smiled slowly. "God don't miss."

Uptown – Private Conference Room

Bishop Blackstone stood in a tall, glass-walled room surrounded by power: a congressman, a city councilwoman, two real estate developers, and Wynn, the political liaison.

The congressman stood.

"We brought you into this to *control*, Bishop. Not get outshined by some kid with a mic."

"I have influence—"

"You *had* influence," the woman interrupted. "Gatekeeper pass? Revoked."

Wynn added, "We're shifting the narrative. You're no longer the channel. You're the cautionary tale."

Blackstone's jaw clenched. His hands trembled.

But he said nothing.

Truth's Apartment – Westside

Cash poured from an old Jordan shoebox onto the bed.

Truth counted it out loud.

His baby mama stood in the doorway with arms crossed.

"You really done with the streets?" She asked.

"Yeah."

She laughed. "So what? Gonna rap now? Go viral? You've been in the trenches since sixteen."

"I've been surviving since I was sixteen," he snapped. "Now I'm ready to *live*."

"You really following' lame ass' Ezekiel and them?"

"Yep. They talkin' wealth. Ownership. *Freedom*."

She shook her head. "You're crazy."

He stared back.

"Maybe. But I'd rather be crazy and clean than comfortable in chains."

He folded the money.

"You coming' or not?"

She stayed silent as he walked out.

Tasha's Braid Shop – Afternoon

The door swung open and two city officials stepped in, clipboards in hand.

Tasha looked up from organizing edge control.

"Afternoon. Can I help y'all?"

One frowned. "We did an inspection. Your electrical code is off. Ventilation too. Fire clearance missing."

"What?"

"Until it's corrected, you can't open it."

Tasha stood frozen.

Her girls watched from the mirrors.

The city man handed her a red-tagged notice.

She looked down at it.

Then looked up. Fire in her eyes.

"Then we fix it. Every wire. Every screw. This place is opening whether y'all like it or not."

The movement wasn't just gaining momentum—it was gaining enemies. But the foundation was too rooted now. The vision was too clear. And even as systems threw up roadblocks, the mission just kept building.

2 plus 2?

Still equals 8.

Because when the gates fall, the voices rise.

And now?

The mic was on.

CHAPTER TWENTY-TWO

SEEDS & SMOKE – THE FIRST EPISODE

When the people won't go to church… the word finds a mic. The streets don't need another sermon—they need soil and fire. Seeds and smoke. And that's exactly what this was. Not entertainment. Not politics. But a pulpit powered by pain, love, and vision. The first episode didn't just launch a podcast. It launched a whole new way of testifying.

The 2+2=8 Center – Podcast Studio Room

Ezekiel sat in front of the mic, headphones on, voice steady but eyes burning. Malik leaned back in his seat, hoodie pulled tight over his head, arms folded like a soldier. Geneva had her journal open and pen in hand, ready to quote history, scripture, or the ancestors at any moment.

A hand-painted sign hung behind them: **SEEDS & SMOKE – TRUTH THAT GROWS & BURNS.**

"Welcome," Ezekiel said, "to the very first episode of *Seeds & Smoke.*"

Malik clapped once, slow and loud.

"This ain't just a show," Geneva said. "This is reckoning."

Ezekiel nodded. "Today we talk about where we came from. Not just individually. *Culturally*. Because if you don't know your soil, you can't grow fruit. First topic—'The Awakening.' Malik?"

Malik cleared his throat. "I grew up in Vine City. Caught my first case at thirteen. Not because I wanted to wild out… but because I didn't think I had another option. I didn't wake up until I saw a funeral where the casket looked like it should've had a report card in it."

Geneva wiped her eyes.

"And that's the lie we've been sold," she said. "That survival is the same as living. It's not. Next up—we talk about the economy. How do we build when we have never been taught?"

Ezekiel tapped the whiteboard.

"Passive income. Real estate. Group economics. It's time we stop chasing checks and start building *streams.*"

Malik leaned in. "Ownership is oxygen. If they control your water, your housing, your food—you ain't free. You're managed."

Geneva snapped her fingers. "And that's why we teach. That's why we reclaim what was stolen. Black Wall Street didn't die from poverty. It was *burned* because it worked."

Ezekiel raised a finger. "And now, we are planting again."

Guest of the Week: Raynisha Ford – Former Hustler Turned Nonprofit Leader

Raynisha sat in the fourth seat, mic close, a silver necklace of Africa around her neck.

"Ten years ago, I was in the trap every day," she said. "Now? I run a program for girls with incarcerated mothers. You know what changed me?"

"What?" Geneva asked.

"Someone told me I was *worth saving.* That's what this podcast is. A voice saying 'you still got value.' Even if the world doesn't see it yet."

Westside – On the Block

Truth sat on a crate next to a busted Crown Vic, phone turned up to max volume. Three younger dudes leaned over, listening to the podcast stream.

One laughed. "Man, y'all really listening to this?"

Truth didn't blink.

"They talkin' about building. About legacy. You ain't tired of selling death?"

The tallest one stood up. "I'm my own god."

He pulled out a wad of cash and threw it in the air. The bills rained down like dirty snowflakes. The group hollered. Cars honked. Somebody lit a blunt. The street echoed with chaos.

Truth stood up, brushing off.

He looked dead in the tall one's eyes.

"You gods? Then act like it. Build something. Protect something. Speak life. Or shut up."

Silence.

Then Truth walked off.

Alone.

Back at the Center – Podcast Still Rolling

Ezekiel looked into the camera.

"To the ones in the trap. In the shop. In the cell. In the silence. This is for you. You're not alone. You're not lost. You're still good soil. And with the right words, you can grow fruit that lasts."

He paused.

"Remember, you can't plant freedom in borrowed dirt. Reclaim your land. Reclaim your mind."

"Because 2 plus 2," Malik said, grinning.

"Still equals 8," Geneva whispered.

Geneva leaned toward the mic, her voice calm but filled with fire. "And if you don't believe the truth can shake an empire, remember David Walker. A man who didn't just speak freedom—he dared to write it."

She continued, her tone rising. "His *Appeal to the Coloured Citizens of the World* was so dangerous they banned it across the South. Put bounties on his head. Why? Because strong, independent Black truth terrifies a system built on silence."

She quoted him:

"America is more our country than it is the whites—we have enriched it with our blood and tears."

"If liberty is not given to us, we must take it."

"I will not shrink from asserting the rights of my brethren."

"They tried to bury him," Geneva said, looking around the room, "but his words grew roots. We carry his fire."

The silence that followed wasn't empty.

It was sacred.

It was history.

And it was just getting started.

The mic was hot. The truth was louder. The fire had found its fuel. And even though the streets mocked, and the system watched, the seeds had already been planted.

Now?

It was time to grow.

A word can raise the dead, break a curse, or build a future. That's what was happening now—not just talk, but transformation. And as the voices echoed out from the center into living rooms, cars, barbershops, and back blocks, the question wasn't who was listening. It was who was being changed. Because some seeds don't sprout in gardens—they rise from concrete.

Inside a Small Apartment on the East Side

A little girl named **Aniyah** sat cross-legged on the carpet, cradling a tablet in her lap. On screen, Ezekiel's voice came through, calm but powerful.

"...you're not broken, you're planted. And planted things? They grow."

Aniyah turned to her mom, eyes wide.

"Mama, he's talking like Jesus."

Her mother smiled, braiding her hair slowly. "That's a man speaking his destiny into existence, baby."

The front door opened. Her boyfriend, Dre, walked in with a grocery bag and side-eye.

" Zeke lame fake ass have got y'all hypnotized?"

"He is not a preacher," London said. "your old childhood friend, saying something real."

Dre scoffed. "Real don't pay the rent."

Aniyah looked at him, then back at the screen.

"He is talking about building. Maybe you should listen too."

Dre rolled his eyes but said nothing.

Back at the Center – Later That Day

Ezekiel sat in the front office checking analytics on the podcast when his phone buzzed.

Message from: Dante (Uber Client)
"Been following you since that ride. I got something to run by you. Let's do lunch?"

Ezekiel stared at it for a beat, then typed:

"Name the time. I'm there."

At Rosa's Apartment

Rose sat at the dining table with two friends, all holding plates of cornbread and baked chicken.

"You hear that boy talking about freedom?" one said, mouth half-full. "He makes sense."

Rose nodded slowly.

"He makes faith sound like something you can hold in your hand."

They listened in silence as *Seeds & Smoke* poured through the speaker.

North Atlanta – In a Mansion Kitchen

Chardonnay swirled in a glass. **Elena Matthews**, the Coca-Cola executive, sat barefoot in a designer kitchen, podcast streaming from her Bluetooth speaker.

Her husband, Bradley, walked in, raising a brow.

"Are you still listening to that inner-city activist?"

She didn't respond right away.

He leaned against the counter. "You've worked hard, Elena. Just be careful what hills you die on."

She stood up.

"I'm not dying. I'm investing. I just want to help my people."

Bradley raised an eyebrow. "Without disrupting your *position*?"

She nodded slowly.

"That's the tension, isn't it?"

She walked to the window.

Then she whispered to herself:

"*If you can control a man's thinking, you don't have to worry about his actions.*"

A pause.

"Carter G. Woodson said that. The *real* curriculum."

She turned toward the speaker.

"Maybe it's time I stop being comfortable."

From hood apartments to mansions, from tablets to trap houses, the first episode of *Seeds & Smoke* didn't just broadcast—it *breathed*. And somewhere in all those rooms, a new question was rising:

What if we believed in us… the way they fear we might?

2 plus 2 still equals 8.

And the fire was just catching.

CHAPTER TWENTY-THREE

LICKS, LESSONS, AND LUNCH WITH LEGACY

Some roots don't show until the pressure hits. And when your past and future show up at the same time? You either fold, or you figure out which one you're standing on. For Ezekiel, the choice had always been growing beneath it all— trying to do right while the wrong circled like wolves. But sometimes the test doesn't come in silence. Sometimes, it comes loud. In your face. With weight on it.

Flashback – High School Gym

Ezekiel bounced the ball slowly, each dribble echoing across the quiet gym floor. Sweat glistened on his neck, his #BattleTested tee clinging to his chest. He took another jumper. Swish.

"You ain't goin' nowhere but broke and tired," he whispered to himself. "But maybe… maybe tired got a different ending if you keep shooting."

He lined up another shot.

Then I heard the gym door slam.

Two figures walked in—Dre and Kemo. Both dressed loud: The Vault jackets, jeans crisp, eyes sharp. Dre's grill flashed when he smirked.

"Look who's still hoopin' like it's gonna save him," Dre said.

Kemo laughed. "Thought you were snitchin' last week. Word said you gave names."

Ezekiel let the ball bounce away.

"I ain't said nothing'. Y'all just paranoid 'cause you know what you're doing ain't built to last."

Dre stepped in close.

"We got a lick lined up. Pounds. Clean flip. You in?"

Ezekiel shook his head. "I'm not chasing crumbs any more."

Dre spat on the floor. "You actin' like some prophet now. Soft."

Kemo added, "You gon' be broke with a bible. We gon' be rich with options."

Ezekiel bent down, picked up the ball.

"Be careful. Some bags come with body counts."

They walked off, laughing.

Present – Aniyah's Bedroom

Aniyah sat cross-legged, scrolling YouTube. Ezekiel's voice poured from the screen.

"Being bold doesn't mean being reckless. It means choosing truth when fear shows up wearing power."

Kamilah stood behind her, washing and detangling her hair gently.

"This who you been watching?" she asked.

"Every week," Aniyah said proudly.

Just then, Dre walked in. Shirt loud, chain heavier. He eyed the screen.

"This dude again?" he muttered.

He stepped over and snatched the laptop.

"What are you doin'?!" Aniyah yelled.

Kamilah stood straight, towel in hand. "You outta line."

"He poisoning' her head with that revolutionary talk. Got her thinking we all need to be saints."

"She is thinking for herself. That scares you?"

Dre clenched his jaw.

"You've been scared of real change your whole life," Kamilah added. "Now your girl is thinking differently, and you're breaking screens like it's gon' stop growth."

He dropped the laptop on the bed. Walked out.

Aniyah looked at her mom.

"He's scared, huh?"

Kamilah nodded. "Of you becoming something he never will."

Downtown Café – Ezekiel & Dante

They sat outside beneath a striped umbrella. Dante wore a Watch God Work blazer, calm but crisp. Ezekiel sipped iced tea, eyes focused.

"You know what our biggest downfall is?" Dante asked.

"What?"

"We don't pool resources. Every other race moves as a *unit*. Arabs, Jews, Koreans, Latinx. They don't need approval. Have structure."

Ezekiel nodded. "Dr. Claud Anderson talked about that. Powernomics."

"Exactly," Dante said. "The collective dollar. Not individual wealth. That's what the system fears."

He slid his tablet over.

"Look at this chart. These companies—Pfizer, Microsoft, Amazon—don't just grow by luck. They grow by *information*. The rich don't get rich by working harder. They get rich by knowing first, moving fast."

Ezekiel leaned closer.

"You gon' teach me?"

Dante grinned. "You're showing' people how to wake up. I'll show you how to *own the alarm clock.*"

Ezekiel laughed. "You gotta come on the podcast."

"Name the day. I'm bringing charts and chains—we gon' break both."

They shook hands across the table.

Two builders.

One blueprint.

Destiny doesn't avoid danger. It walks through it. Truth doesn't hide from the hood—it *confronts* it. And power? Real power? Comes when knowledge, strategy, and faith sit at the same table.

2 plus 2 still equals 8.

And the lesson just went live

When pressure hits, real power doesn't shout—it chooses where to stand. The city was shifting, the people were waking up, and as the old guards watched the light move from their pulpits to the pavement, decisions had to be made. Will they change with the times—or try to choke out the sunrise? This chapter wasn't just about survival. It was about the battle between legacy and illusion.

Blackstone's House – Private Bedroom

The Bishop sat in a silk robe on the edge of the bed, hands steepled, jaw tight.

"They are trying to strip me of everything," he muttered. "That boy Ezekiel… he is growing too fast. Making noise that echoes."

His wife, Camille, stood by the window, curling lotion into her palms. She turned, calm but firm.

"Lil Zeke? Rose's boy? The one we helped with school clothes and summer lunches?"

He looked up. "Yes. That one."

Camille walked over.

"You can't beat him with envy. You gon' have to stand with authority."

Blackstone raised a brow.

"You are still a man of God, but don't forget—you *Black Atlanta*. You want the people back? You better show it."

He nodded slowly.

"I'll host a community event. Make it big. Let them know this city still runs through me."

Camille kissed his forehead. "Then walk with purpose. Because that boy? He's moving with destiny."

The Bluff – Daylight Rally

Malik stood on top of a crate, #2Plus2Equals8 jacket on, bullhorn in one hand, passion in his chest. Around him, twenty people gathered—young mothers, teenagers, ex-hustlers, elders in folding chairs.

Truth stood beside him, arms crossed, silent but solid. Respect walked in his shadow.

"We've been dying over blocks we don't own," Malik shouted. "Shooting each other over corners that pay *them*—not us."

Murmurs. Nods.

"It's time we take it back. Not with guns. With deeds. With equity. With mindset. unity black power"

He looked over at the crowd.

"I'm talking about raising kings and queens who don't fear change. Like Frederick Douglass said: *'It is easier to build strong children than to repair broken men.'"*

Applause.

Suddenly, Tires Screech

A black car pulled up fast. Kilo jumped out, flanked by J-Rock and two others.

Kilo's Dopestories shirt clung to his chest. He looked around like a wolf denied a meal.

"Y'all messing with my money!" he barked.

He pulled a pistol. Fired three times in the air.

People screamed. Ducking.

J-Rock stepped out next. Let three more off.

"Back up!" he yelled.

Truth stepped forward, two boys behind him, cool but unshaken.

"Don't do this," Truth said, stepping closer.

J-Rock pointed the gun directly at him.

Kilo grinned.

"One more step, I tell him to shoot to kill. You started this, Truth. But I *will* finish it."

Truth looked at the gun, then at Kilo.

"We were brothers," he said. "But ever since I changed my mindset, I realized—*they* don't even gotta divide us. We do it ourselves. Just what the white man likes."

He turned. Walked off slowly.

J-Rock's hand trembled on the trigger.

But he didn't fire.

The revolution wasn't just outside. It was *inside*. Inside the trap. Inside the church. Inside the soul of a city wrestling with who it was and who it could be.

And as guns smoked and voices rose, the difference between enemies and brothers became clearer.

2 plus 2 still equals 8.

And the truth just walked away from a bullet to prove it.

CHAPTER TWENTY-FOUR

THE SILENCE BUSINESS

Every system has a strategy. And silence? That's not a side effect. It's a product. Bought, sold, manufactured. For decades, power didn't fear riots—it feared a rhythm. A voice. A vision. And when a movement starts speaking with both? The silence industry starts preparing its next campaign. This time, the threat wasn't loud—it was *smart*. And now, they were in trouble.

Washington, D.C. – Undisclosed Homeland Security Briefing Room

Ten men sat around a long steel table, papers stacked, screens glowing. Mostly white. Mostly grey-haired. Suits crisp. Tone colder than the air-conditioning.

A large screen at the front played old black-and-white footage—Malcolm. Martin. Panthers. Protests. Followed by images of crack-era destruction, gang arrests, private prison blueprints.

Agent Wallace stood.

"Gentlemen, our systems worked. For a long time."

Click.

A slide flashed: *'Containment Strategy – 1975–2020.'*

"We flooded Black communities with drugs, redirected their movements into fractured, performative energy, and amplified voices that preached consumption, not creation."

He clicked again.

"Sports and entertainment. That's where we focused the spotlight. Let them dance, run, dunk, but never *build*. Give a few the illusion of inclusion. Billionaire athletes. Rap stars. But no systemic economic control."

One man with glasses added, "We replaced Malcolm with rap beef. Coretta with Instagram models. Revolution with reality TV. And the scary thing?"

He turned to the board.

"It worked."

Another agent stood up, holding a tablet. She spoke with clipped precision.

"But something is shifting."

Click.

A hashtag filled the screen: **#2Plus2Equals8**

"They're not just talking revolution—they're talking *economics*. Passive income. Ownership. Currency control. And worse—unity. We've identified a cluster network. It's gaining traction in the South, primarily Atlanta."

Names appeared on the board.

Targets of Interest:

- Ezekiel Trueborn (Community Leader / Speaker / Activist)
- Malik (Street Organizer / Mobilizer)
- Geneva (Faith-Based Connector / Real Estate)
- Truth (Former Hustler / Symbolic Shift in Hood Allegiance)

"The danger here," the lead agent said, "isn't what they're saying. It's *how many are listening.* And how fast."

He tapped a map showing heat clusters of engagement.

"They're not preaching violence. They're preaching ownership. That makes them ten times more dangerous."

Another man stood, older, sharp jaw, military pins.

"Who do we still have in our pockets?"

He flipped a folder open.

Assets / Leverage Points:

- Bishop Blackstone – Compromised. Heavy real estate debt. Controlled via city grants.
- Richard Wynn – Liaison with council. Monitoring, feeding data.

- Local Codes Enforcement – Used against their new business fronts.

- Social Influence Algorithms – Active shadow suppression across major platforms.

A pause.

One man leaned in.

"What's the play?"

Agent Wallace didn't blink.

"We target the network. Disrupt cohesion. Trigger ego splits. Weaponize whisper campaigns. Pressure funders. Collapse credibility through overexposure and fabricated scandal. Start with influencers—shame, doubt, divide."

Another added, "And whatever you do—*never* let them get syndicated media or corporate backing."

"Already working on it," someone muttered.

Power doesn't panic when you protest. It panics when you *plan*. And in this room, the truth was clear: they didn't just want to silence Black voices. They wanted to keep Black minds rented out—never owned. But something was shifting now. A sound too sharp to ignore. A truth too big to shadow.

2 plus 2 still equals 8.

And this time, they heard it coming.

While the system was whispering war in dark boardrooms, the builders were still building. Still speaking. Still shaping futures out of ashes. There was no pause in their purpose. The fire had already caught, and now it was spreading—through podcasts, platforms, and power moves rooted in unity. The silence business had officially met its disruption.

2+2=8 Center – Strategy Room

Ezekiel stood at the head of the table with a projector behind him, **Watch God Work** sweatshirt on, eyes alert. Malik leaned over the table, reviewing a printed layout. Geneva sat beside him with a notepad, calculator, and iced coffee that hadn't been touched.

The screen behind Ezekiel flashed: **Seeds & Smoke – Episode 2: The Fire That Didn't Burn Us.**

"We gotta move quick," Ezekiel said. "The numbers from the first show are wild. Comments. Shares. Sponsors even peeking in the door."

Malik tapped the laptop.

"Truth's moment in the Bluff?" he said. "We open with that. Raw. Ain't no editing truth."

He pulled up a slide.

"The whole neighborhood watched him stand up to Kilo and J-Rock with no fear. Now the block calls him 'Pastor of Peace.' He ain't just respected—he *trusted.* That's currency."

Geneva nodded. "We have to bring him in as a guest. Let the streets hear it from someone who *was* them. That transition is proof."

Ezekiel added to the board: **Guest: Truth – From Trap to Trust.**

Then he pulled up another slide: **Merch Report.**

"'2 Plus 2 Equals 8' gear just passed 1,200 units. That's 8k in net profit in two weeks. Monetization from YouTube and stream sites kicked in. That's another $2,700."

Malik grinned. "And we are just getting started."

Geneva finally sipped her coffee.

"Let me take it a step further."

They turned.

"I say we put the money in a pot. Start a collective land trust. Buy five lots. Build affordable housing. Another ten for community farming."

Ezekiel blinked.

"Urban ownership. Food security. Generational independence."

Geneva smiled. "Exactly. We start growing from the root. No more renting legacy."

Malik leaned back in his chair.

"We planting Black future into the same soil they said would never feed us."

Ezekiel wrote on the whiteboard in all caps:

LAND. LEGACY. LIFELINES.

While the system studied how to dismantle movements, Ezekiel and his crew were designing a blueprint they couldn't steal. A model they couldn't mimic. A movement built not just on survival—but succession.

2 plus 2 still equals 8.

And they were about to buy the land their enemies prayed they'd never see.

The Silence Business

Just because the blueprint is blessed doesn't mean the road will be smooth. In fact, the rougher it gets, the more proof you have that you're shaking the foundation. And on this day, while plans were being drawn on whiteboards and land was being spoken into existence, real life still kept swinging. Testing faith. Testing loyalty. And revealing who was truly built for the mission.

Tasha's Braid Shop – Morning

The smell of paint and fresh wood still hung in the air. Tasha stood with two contractors, one flipping through inspection papers, the other double-checking outlets and ventilation.

"Minor stuff," one said. "Seen a lot worse and opened with no issue."

"Still fixing it though," Tasha said, arms folded, her **#2Plus2Equals8** crop top tight over her stomach. "I want it right."

One contractor nodded. "Respect."

As they walked out, her friend Keisha walked in, holding iced coffee.

"You good?" she asked.

Tasha exhaled. "Yeah. Devil stays busy. Soon as you close in on purpose, he starts throwing shade, codes, people."

Keisha chuckled. "Girl. Say that. You know I went from shaking it on stage to running my boutique in two years flat. They laughed. Now I hire folks with degrees."

Tasha smiled. "That's what I'm talkin' about."

In the back, Elijah sat on the floor drawing superheroes with Keisha's son, Josiah.

East Side – Candice's Apartment

Candice sat on the couch in a long tee, laptop open, YouTube full screen.

Ezekiel's voice played through the room.

"You don't change the hood by preaching—*you build it a new language.* Ownership. Clarity. Protection."

She nodded slowly.

"He talkin' different now."

Darryl, her boyfriend, sat at the kitchen table, scrolling.

"Oh now you Ezekiel fan club too?" he muttered.

Candice didn't respond.

Their daughter walked in, eyes bright.

"That's Daddy!" she pointed. "He's famous now, huh Mommy?"

Candice looked at her. Smiled.

"Yeah, baby. He is."

Darryl made a long, annoying sound, grabbed his keys, and walked out.

Candice rolled her eyes and whispered to herself.

"Don't gotta like him. But truth is truth."

London's House – Afternoon

Trash bags sat by the door. Stuffed with clothes. Sneakers. Hat bent in one.

London sat on the couch, lip split, eyes swollen, fingers shaking.

Her mother stood beside her, silent at first. Then finally spoke.

"I told you, baby. I saw it in him the first time he smirked when you spoke about your dreams."

London wiped her nose. "Why was wanting more so threatening to him?"

Her mother sat down. Pulled her close.

"Because when you level up, people either rise with you… or try to break your wings so you'll stay grounded with 'em."

London cried harder.

And her mama held her tighter.

The movement wasn't just on the mics or in the marches. It was in the salons, the living rooms, the bedrooms, and broken places where people finally said *enough*. Not just to the world. But to themselves.

2 plus 2 still equals 8.

And the power was shifting in real time.

CHAPTER TWENTY-FIVE

SEEDS, SMOKE, AND STAGE PLAYS

While power tried to distract the people with polished speeches and cookouts, the real freedom was being cooked on a different grill—the slow burn of wisdom, finance, and unfiltered truth. Some tried to win the people with gifts. Others were planting roots. But on both sides of the city, voices were rising, and the crowd was starting to decide what kind of future they wanted to follow.

Podcast Studio – Seeds & Smoke: Episode 2

Ezekiel leaned toward the mic, calm and full of fire.

"People keep asking how to break the cycle. Truth is, it ain't always loud. Sometimes it's $50 a check into the S&P. I knew a brother who worked as a valet. Nothing fancy. But he stayed consistent. Every pay—$50. Rain, shine, broke or tired."

He paused, looking at Malik and Geneva.

"Twenty years later, man had over half a million. Off what? Compound interest. Small moves. Right sacrifices. It ain't about big leaps—it's about daily steps. Now he is pulling in five grand a month without even touching his principal."

Malik nodded. "That's what they don't want us to know. Freedom's a math problem with discipline as the answer."

Geneva added, "And time is the tool. Not talent. Not luck. Just time and truth."

Ezekiel leaned back, eyes locking on the camera.

"You know who figured that out? Byron Allen. Black billionaire. Built a media empire when the doors were locked. Didn't knock. He kicked 'em in. From owning The Weather Channel to twenty-plus TV stations—brother's worth over a billion dollars now."

He looked straight ahead and let the words drop:

"We have to achieve economic inclusion so we can achieve social inclusion."

"The way we're going to make America better is by making it fair and balanced for everyone—especially African Americans who helped build this country for free."

"Black people don't control anything. We don't control our image. And when you don't control your image, people can put out any image they want about you."

"That's why we do what we do," Ezekiel said, voice grounded. "Control the narrative. Own our platforms. Teach the math behind the miracle."

Malik clapped once, leaned forward.

"'Cause 2 plus 2?"

Geneva smiled. "Still equals 8

South Atlanta Park – Blackstone's Event

Grills sizzled. Kids bounced on inflatables. Teenagers shot jumpers for prizes. Music bumped soft through speakers. Blackstone stood in a **Watch God Work** blazer, holding the mic like a seasoned actor.

"Look around," he said. "This is love. This is *legacy.* But beware of false prophets. People good with words but not with *works.*"

The crowd murmured. Some nodded.

"Plenty of layers out here. Not enough doers," he continued, quoting from the pulpit.

"Even the serpent spoke scripture to Eve."

Some in the crowd glanced at each other.

"Is he talkin' about Zeke?" one man whispered.

Behind Blackstone stood Camille, regal and poised. And beside her, passing out flyers for his next church seminar, was Tierra—Raheem's cousin from the barbershop who once called him out. She smiled fake. Posed real.

Raheem stood off to the side, arms folded, shaking his head.

"Hypocrite," he muttered.

Back at the Studio – Podcast Rolling

Malik leaned into his segment.

"Let's talk about the Bluff," he said. "We held a rally. Trying to bring light. And shots rang out. Real ones."

He looked at the camera.

"We ain't leave. We stood up. And *Truth* stood taller."

He turned to Truth.

Truth adjusted the mic.

"I ain't no saint," he said. "I sold poison for years. Lied, ran, fought. But I'm here now. Tryna fix what I helped break. I'm about ownership now. Teaching my son stocks. Protection' instead of plotting'. That's team #2Plus2Equals8."

Somewhere on the West Side

Kilo leaned against a car, watching the podcast from his phone, surrounded by four other men.

They passed bottles. Laughed at parts.

Then Kilo froze.

"They're naming names now. Bringing me up without saying it."

One dude asked, "So what we on?"

Kilo lit his blunt slow.

"Next time we aim."

A pause.

"And we don't miss."

Two stages. Two missions. One truth. While one group fed the crowd with hot dogs and parables, the other fed minds with principles and plans. The crowd was watching. Listening. Choosing.

2 plus 2 still equals 8.

And now... so does the cost of legacy.

CHAPTER TWENTY-SIX

THE COST OF INTEGRITY

Every movement reaches a crossroads—the moment when the devil doesn't show up with horns, but with paperwork and promises. Not every enemy kicks in doors. Some slide across blank checks with stipulations dressed in opportunity. And the scariest part? Most people say yes.

But not Geneva.

New Beginnings Baptist Church – Saturday Afternoon

Geneva stood inside the sanctuary with three church members, stringing lights around the altar, prepping for Sunday service. Fold-out chairs aligned. Bibles stacked. The aroma of lemon-scented polish filled the air.

The door opened.

"May I help you?" Geneva asked, turning.

Richard Wynn walked in, smiling, too smooth.

"Geneva. It's good to see you."

She put down the lights, straightened up. "What brings you here?"

He pulled a folder from his briefcase. "I offered Ezekiel a $500,000 grant. Turned it down."

She folded her arms.

"He knows who he is. That doesn't surprise me."

Wynn stepped closer. "But *you*... You could build a new sanctuary. Community housing. Outreach. I could fast-track it all. Just one condition."

Geneva's eyes narrowed. "What condition?"

"Stay away from the 2Plus2Equals8 movement. Publicly and privately. No more podcasts. No more affiliations."

He placed a blank check on the pulpit.

"God opens doors," he said, "but sometimes you need help getting the keys."

He walked out.

One of her members squealed. "Pastor, that's God answering prayers! We've been struggling!"

Another whispered, "Maybe this is God making room for our growth."

Geneva looked at the blank check like it was poison.

"No," she said slowly. "That's not God. God doesn't come with stipulations to abandon truth. That's the *enemy's* check—disguised as a blessing."

She held it up. "Why would God need conditions? We did this with faith, not favors. And if we stand in truth, we stay in truth."

She tore the check down the middle.

Online – Social Media Eruption

Twitter. Instagram. TikTok. Threads. All lit up like fireworks.

#2Plus2Equals8 trending… but not for the right reasons.

"Pastor Geneva jumps ship to build her own church." "Ezekiel baby mama, a former stripper?! False prophet!" "Sources say Ezekiel's stealing money from the community fund." "Malik is just a gangster with new PR. Still extorting hoods."

Screenshots, false receipts, even fake DMs flooded timelines.

Ezekiel – Sitting in the Center

His phone buzzed nonstop.

He scrolled, disbelief washing over his face. Then he created a new group text:

The Big Three: Me, Malik, Geneva.

"We are under fire. Truth gotta talk louder now."

Café Downtown – Rose and Ernestine

Waitress at the counter whispered to another.

"Have you seen the drama with that Zeke movement?"

Rose turned around. "It's false."

They blinked. "You know him?"

"Know him? Helped raise him. And I know a lie when I hear one. That boy's heart is clean."

Salon – Tasha and Keisha

Keisha showed her the phone. "Girl, they are dragging your man."

Tasha's hands shook.

She whispered, "Now I feel it. Malcolm. King. All of 'em. When the truth starts rising, the system throws everything but a bullet."

Blackstone's Office – Evening

He leaned back in his chair, arms crossed, watching the chaos unfold online.

Camille stood behind him. "What's happening?"

He smirked. "He wanted light. Let's see if he can handle the heat."

D.C. – Homeland Operations Command

Agent Wallace sipped coffee, watching trending topics.

A young tech turned to him. "They're imploding."

Wallace smiled wider.

"Perfect. Let them burn their own heroes."

It wasn't the bullets that hurt most. It was the lies. The betrayal. The silence of those who knew better but said nothing. But the fire wasn't consuming the movement—it was purifying it.

2 plus 2 still equals 8.

Even when they try to divide it.

Every lie they tell becomes a confirmation that you're doing something they fear. The pressure doesn't break you—it reveals you. And in rooms filled with power and whispers, decisions are being made. Not all in favor of truth. But the truth? It doesn't beg. It builds.

Coca-Cola Regional HQ – Executive Floor

Elena walked briskly down the long glass hallway. Inside the VP's office, **Ellis** waited with a stern expression and a thick printout in his hands.

"You've seen this?" he asked, sliding the papers across the desk.

Headlines. Tweets. Fake articles.

"Coca-Cola considering endorsement of movement linked to strippers, former drug dealers." "False hope campaign #2Plus2Equals8 exposed."

Elena scanned the lines, her heart sinking—but not in shame. In frustration.

She looked up.

"These are lies, Ellis. Who's the source? Why not put a name on it if it's truth?"

Ellis folded his arms.

"That's the point. We don't know yet. All I know is that PR flagged it. And the board's asking questions."

Elena didn't blink. "They're not begging for help. They're creating help. I thought it made sense—linking with them before the world sees what they're building."

Ellis sighed. "I get it. But for now… let's pause the endorsement. See how this plays out."

Elena stood, eyes firm but heavy.

"Of course."

She walked out with her chin up, but her spirit was wounded.

In the elevator, she typed a message to Geneva:

"Tried to push forward. They're scared. Said it's too hot to touch right now. I know it's a lie. But I couldn't hold it. Don't give up. - E"

Her phone buzzed again.

Text from: Husband

"Told you to stay away from *them people.*"

She stared at the words.

Them people.

Then looked up, catching her reflection in the elevator mirror.

"And who am I?" she whispered.

Meanwhile – Phone Screens Light Up

Tasha →Ezekiel

"We must be winning. Now they are telling lies on us. Keep pushing, baby."

Ezekiel →Tasha + Big Three

"They just lit a fire that can't be put out. Let's pour gasoline."

Malik →Big Three

"We finally have their attention. Now let's show up and show OUT."

Geneva →Big Three

"Someone once told me—if they are not telling lies on you, you are not doing anything worthwhile. Meet at the center in an hour."

Phone notifications blinked:

"LIKE" "LIKE" "LIKE"

They threw dirt and expected the seed to die. But this seed knew what it was. What it came from. And now? The ground was shaking. Because the real ones weren't folding.

They were meeting.

Planning.

And about to multiply.

2 plus 2 still equals 8.

And this storm just turned prophetic.

CHAPTER TWENTY-SEVEN

THE ANSWER KEY

Sometimes the most dangerous thing you can do is tell the truth without raising your voice. Not defensive. Not rattled. Just steady. Measured. Unshakable. And when the lie is loud, the response must be louder in wisdom, not volume. Ezekiel didn't react. He *responded*. And the world? It listened.

2+2=8 Center – Strategy Table

The energy was electric but still focused. Ezekiel stood in front of the whiteboard, typing on his laptop with intensity, while Malik and Geneva hovered close, occasionally throwing out lines, facts, scriptures.

"No name-calling," Geneva said. "Just the truth. Fully clothed and undeniable."

Ezekiel nodded. "We ain't replying to lies. We are writing the chapter that will outlive them."

He cleared his throat and began to read aloud what they were about to post:

"To all who've asked if we're shaken—no. We're planted. They called Marcus Garvey a fraud. Dr. King an agitator. Malcolm a threat. They bombed churches filled with children. Burned down towns like Tulsa and Rosewood—not because of crime, but because of ownership.

Under this American sun, they've lynched Black boys for whistling. Lied on men and women for daring to speak clearly. And now? A hashtag that's helping people think financially is suddenly under fire.

We see the pattern. When truth rises, lies panic. When we talk about community wealth and land ownership, fear whispers through the halls of power—because control is slipping.

But remember: the devil sometimes looks like us. Dressed like us. Talks like us but not like us. Sold out truth for a seat at a table built to feed only them.

This movement isn't perfect. But it's ours. And it's open. The books are open. The numbers are public. And lies? They always travel fast. But the truth? Truth walks in after—slow, clean, and forever."

He looked up. The room was silent.

"Let's post it," Malik said.

Geneva nodded. "And let it breathe."

Ezekiel hit 'Post.'

Then Geneva added softly, "Like Nikki Giovanni said: *'If now isn't a good time for the truth, I don't see when we'll get to it.'*"

Malik chimed in: "*'Mistakes are a fact of life. It is the response to error that counts.'*"

Ezekiel leaned back, quoting her final words with conviction: "*'There's always something to do. There are hungry people to feed, naked people to clothe, sick people to comfort, and make well. And while I don't expect us to save the world, I do think it's not asking too much to love those with whom we share it.'*"

The room didn't need applause. It just needed action.

And they were already in motion.

Seconds Later – Online Response

Comments poured in.

"This was poetry. Facts." "I knew they were lying. This just confirmed it." "Protect this movement at all costs." "2+2=8. Period."

Engagement skyrocketed.

The post trended globally.

Merchandise Orders

Shirt orders exploded. Within an hour, over 10,000 units were sold.

People posted photos in **#2Plus2Equals8** gear. Schools. Barbershops. Hospitals. Bookstores. Streets.

It was no longer a movement.

It was a declaration.

Washington, D.C. – Homeland Command Center

A young agent ran into the room.

"Sir… the response backfired."

Agent Wallace stared at the screen, watching the numbers rise.

"You didn't kill it," he muttered. "You amplified it."

His skin turned pale.

Blackstone's Office

Blackstone sat at his dinner table, untouched ribs in front of him. The sound of Ezekiel's post being read aloud played from Camille's phone.

He pushed his plate away.

"No appetite?" Camille asked.

He said nothing.

Just watched.

Just listened.

The shift wasn't coming. It had arrived. Not by force—but by clarity. Not with riots—but with reason. The lie had a spotlight.

But the truth?

It had the people.

And now… it had the floor.

2 plus 2 still equals 8.

And this movement was now undeniable.

When truth takes hold, not everyone claps. Some plot. Some fold. Others float toward the noise, hoping to grab attention, distraction, or revenge. But this chapter? This was where the unseen started moving in the shadows. Quiet. Calculated. And yet, the light kept getting stronger.

West End – Late Evening

Truth's baby mother, **Shanice**, walked down the sidewalk with her earbuds in, purse slung low. Her energy was calm, but her mind raced—child support, school clothes, trying to keep balance.

Kilo pulled up slowly in a matte-black Challenger.

He leaned out the window.

"Shanice,?"

She paused.

He smiled. Flashy, all gold.

"You look like you're tired of carrying somebody else's dream. Roll with me… you'd be pushing a Benz in two weeks."

She blushed a little. Then scoffed. "Your boy is tripping. Following this… false hope movement."

Kilo saw an opening. He reached out, handed her a folded stack of money.

" Put my number in your phone. Call me. When you are ready to win."

She hesitated… look at his number lock it in

Kilo grinned. "Tell Truth I said bless up."

Liquor House – East Side

Dre leaned back in his seat, sipping from a solo cup. Marcus and Kemo sat with him, all half-lit.

"Man, Zeke thinks he is better than us," Dre said. "We from the same blocks. Same pain. He doesn't even know who his daddy is."

Marcus shook his head.

"Nah. Zeke is cool in my books. I saw him become who he is. Solid. I even have been thinking' about leaving the Kingdom Dominion Cathedral. Might pull up on that #2Plus2Equals8."

Kemo nodded. "You might be right. Sometimes you gotta swallow your pride. That boy shining bright. Teaching people how to win."

Dre waved them off. "Y'all sound soft. I need another shot."

Salon – Next Afternoon

Tasha sat in the back room, scrolling through the #2Plus2Equals8 thread, comments flying. Kim and another stylist stood nearby.

"Girl," Kim said, "you got Malcolm and Marcus Garvey on your hands. When are y'all getting married."

Tasha smirked. "We talkin' about it. But truthfully? No ring or paper gon' make me feel more secure. We are tighter than a tire on a rim."

The other friend laughed. "Well when is the grand opening?"

"Next week," Tasha said. "Just waitin' on the code lady to sign off."

2+2=8 Center – Meeting Room

The Big Three stood side by side.

Ezekiel looked around the nearly complete space.

"Wow," he said. "They are behind us now. For real."

Geneva placed a hand over her heart.

"Then it's time to pour. We've been planted long enough. Now? We bloom."

Malik stepped forward.

"In the words of Huey P. Newton—'The revolution has always been in the hands of the young. The young always inherit the revolution.'"

Ezekiel nodded.

"Then let's give them something worth inheriting."

He turned, then added with a grin, "And like Dick Gregory said—'Because I know who I am, I'm not going to let anybody else run my life.'"

Geneva smiled wide, finishing the moment: "And let's not forget—'If they took you out of history, it would take them years to rewrite it.'"

The room fell quiet.

Not out of silence.

But reverence.

They weren't just building a center. They were building a future wrapped in roots, resistance, and resilience.

Every side was moving. Some with hope. Others with heat. But the people? They had chosen. And now, what was once just a ripple… was becoming a flood.

2 plus 2 still equals 8.

And this movement wasn't just about rising.

It was about reigning.

CHAPTER TWENTY- EIGHT

THE PIVOT

Months Later

When a movement grows too big for silence, it invites war. But not the kind with bullets—yet. The kind fought in headlines, whispers, boardrooms, and between people you once trusted. Pivoting means pressure. And under pressure, only the truth expands. On this day, #2Plus2Equals8 didn't just pivot.

It planted a flag.

The Center buzzed with activity. Cameras mounted, chairs aligned. Tasha and Kim finished setting up merchandise tables near the front. New designs, bold lettering:

"WE DON'T RENT REVOLUTION. WE OWN IT."

"PASSIVE INCOME IS ACTIVE POWER."

Outside, a line stretched around the block.

People weren't just showing up—they were *arriving.*

Inside, Ezekiel stood at the center podium, flipping through notes, calm but charged.

His phone vibrated. A message from Geneva:

"Confirmed. Press will be watching. Speak what can't be misquoted."

Malik walked in behind him, wearing a fresh **Battle Tested** tee. "You ready?"

Ezekiel nodded. "It's time we pivot the conversation. No more defense. We teach. We lead."

Opening Remarks – Live Broadcast Begins

Ezekiel looked directly into the lens.

"Some of you heard the rumors. Others read the lies. And many watched us be mocked for choosing clarity over chaos."

He took a breath.

"But what they didn't expect… was that we *knew* this would come."

He clicked a remote, revealing a slide:

THE ECONOMICS OF OPPRESSION.

Behind him: photos of Black Wall Street, redlined neighborhoods, timelines of policy-based disenfranchisement.

"We've never just been hated for who we are. We've been *targeted* for what we're capable of building."

Geneva stepped forward.

"In 1921, they dropped bombs on Black-owned banks, barbershops, and schools. In 1955, they murdered Emmett Till for a lie. In 1969, they gunned down Fred Hampton as he slept."

Malik added, "Today, they shoot with algorithms. With shadow bans. With disinformation. But the goal's the same—stop us before we unify our money and message."

The Teaching Segment

Ezekiel shifted into financial literacy.

"Let me give you a number: 7%. That's the average return of the S&P 500. If you invested $100 a month for 30 years, you'd have nearly $120,000. Passive income is the quiet rebellion—they can't stop time, and they can't reverse knowledge."

He walked to the front row. Held up a mock debit card.

"This is what they expect us to chase. Spend. Swipe. Survive. But what if this became a tool… not a chain?"

He paused, then looked at the crowd.

"Let me tell y'all about Robert L. Johnson—the founder of BET, Black Entertainment Television. He became the first Black billionaire in America by building a platform for our voice, our culture. He once said:

'We must not let the illusion of inclusion fool us. Ownership is the beginning of real power.'

And another one for your spirit:

'You can't play in the economic game if you don't own a seat at the table.'"

Ezekiel moved along the row, hands now gripping a whiteboard marker.

"And for y'all that love legacy, let me introduce you to Fawn Weaver. She's the powerhouse behind Uncle Nearest Premium Whiskey—the first major spirit brand led and owned by a Black woman. She uncovered the true story of the Black man who taught Jack Daniel how to distill. And she turned that truth into a brand that now outsells many of the industry's giants."

He paused, voice rising.

"We don't need a seat at their table when we can build our own." — Fawn Weaver

"The legacy we build today becomes the standard they study tomorrow." — Fawn Weaver

Ezekiel stepped back.

"You see, the numbers don't lie. And neither does ownership."

The Breakthrough Moment

Tasha stepped up, holding her phone.

"Y'all need to see this."

She turned the screen to Ezekiel.

Viral Tweet: "I came for the drama. Stayed for the data. This movement is different. #2Plus2Equals8."

Over 1 million retweets.

Geneva smiled. "Now they know we teach. Now we're unignorable."

Somewhere in D.C.

Agent Wallace stared at the screen.

"They weren't supposed to survive that smear. This is worse."

His assistant blinked. "Worse?"

He leaned forward. "This is what happens when *leaders* decide not to just speak... but to *build.*"

Meanwhile... Kilo's Apartment

He sat with J-Rock, replaying the livestream.

"This dude turned a lie into a lesson."

J-Rock laughed. "What now?"

Kilo lit a blunt. "Now we play dirtier."

Closing Segment – Ezekiel's Final Words

"Pivoting ain't weakness. It's wisdom. They came for our character... but underestimated our *clarity.* We will not fold. We will not beg. We will build, plant, grow, and *own.*"

Cheers.

A chant started:

"2 PLUS 2! EQUALS 8!"

The walls shook. The screen exploded with engagement.

This wasn't just a movement rebounding. It was a realization. And when you teach the oppressed how to see themselves as architects, you no longer need permission.

You just pivot.

You plant.

You *rise.*

When a movement grows too big for silence, it invites war. But not the kind with bullets—yet. The kind fought in headlines, whispers, boardrooms, and between people you once trusted. Pivoting means pressure. And under pressure, only the truth expands. On this day, #2Plus2Equals8 didn't just pivot.

It planted a flag.

Barbershop – Eastside

A TV mounted on the wall played the live stream. Every chair was filled. Clippers paused.

"This is better than the debates," one man said.

Another leaned forward. "They speak *real*. Not campaign slogans—*solutions.*"

Blackstone's Office

Blackstone sat motionless at his desk. Camille watched the screen behind him.

"Bishop?" she asked.

He didn't blink.

"This ain't just noise anymore," he whispered. "This is revival without religion."

His hand trembled slightly. He turned the monitor off.

Downtown Café – Rose and Ernestine

They sat with coffee, glued to their phones.

"You hear what Malik said?" Rose asked.

Ernestine smiled. "He's walking like the old Black Panthers. With more paperwork and less bullets."

They both laughed softly.

Malik's Turn at the Podium

He gripped the mic tight.

"They tried to label us criminals. Now they are watching us turn budgets into blueprints. This ain't a trend. It's a trajectory."

He paused.

"We ain't preaching poverty. We preach power."

Crowd erupted.

Malik raised a hand to settle them.

"But let me take y'all back further—before chains, before ships. Let's talk about the Moors. We ruled Spain for over 700 years. Built libraries, universities, bathhouses, mapped stars and advanced science when Europe was still in the Dark Ages. We taught mathematics, engineering, philosophy, medicine. We influenced architecture, law, and art."

He walked to the edge of the stage.

"See, they won't teach you that. Because if you know you were kings and queens—engineers and scholars—they can't control you as convicts and consumers."

He pointed to the crowd.

"We gotta know ourselves. Know our history. So they can't keep writing it for us."

The room roared again—not just with noise, but awakening.

News Segment – Live Broadcast

A news anchor looked directly into the camera.

"Thousands tuned in today as the #2Plus2Equals8 movement delivered one of the most viral and pointed broadcasts of the year. Some are calling it the 'Financial March on Washington.' Others? The beginning of a Black economic revival."

Final Moment – The Big Three Together

The lights dimmed. Ezekiel, Malik, and Geneva walked side by side to center stage. Tasha handed each a mic.

Ezekiel began, "We came in three voices."

Malik followed, "We leave as one force."

Geneva closed, "And together, we're building a future they can't erase."

But they didn't stop there.

Ezekiel stepped forward. "Malik taught me that fire isn't always destruction—sometimes it's the beginning of creation. And Geneva... she taught me that love is strategy. That our people don't need saving—they need reminding."

Malik leaned in. "Zeke taught me that dreams don't have to die in the dirt. That if you water faith with consistency, even cracked concrete blooms. And Geneva? She's the root system under all this. Silent power."

Geneva nodded slowly. "Ezekiel showed me that vision doesn't require permission. And Malik reminds me every day that we aren't victims of our history—we are curators of our destiny."

They stepped closer, their shoulders touching.

Three mics. One mission.

Geneva's voice softened. "It's rare, this kind of alignment. Three different paths. Same compass."

Malik added, "We're not just making noise. We're building notes to a new soundtrack for our people."

Ezekiel finished, eyes locked on the crowd. "This ain't just a moment. It's a movement rooted in eternity."

They held hands. The screen behind them read: OWN THE VISION. BUILD THE LEGACY.

Cameras flashed. History paused. And a new chapter stood lit beneath the lights, authored by the ones who refused to stay silent.

This wasn't just the next chapter. This was the pivot they couldn't block. The collective step into a tomorrow that didn't ask for permission.

2 plus 2 still equals 8.

And now the whole world knew what it meant.

After the speeches fade and the lights dim, what remains are the quiet moments—the ones where victory feels like family, like laughter, like soul food on a warm night. And just when peace feels earned, reality knocks with no warning.

Pascal's Soul Food – Northside Drive

The Big Three sat around a large table near the back of the restaurant, the hum of good jazz music in the background, the scent of fried catfish and smothered pork chops thick in the air.

Ezekiel sat next to Tasha, his arm around her. Geneva was with her husband, hands locked as always. Malik sat with his two boys, and Kiya smiled more than he had all week.

Plates clanked, laughter bounced off the wood-paneled walls.

"So," Tasha said, wiping her mouth with a napkin, "We moved 12,000 shirts in three days. That's $180,000 gross.

The table clapped lightly.

"We ain't just preaching wealth," Malik said. "We are producing it."

One of Malik's boys leaned forward. "Uncle Zeke, you're famous now. You gon' be on TV forever?"

Ezekiel chuckled. "Only if I keep speaking with my chest and not my ego."

Geneva's daughter added, "Y'all should make a book. And a movie."

Ezekiel pulled out his journal.

He wrote slowly: **'Big 3: #2Plus2Equals8 – The Blueprint'**

"Say less," he said, grinning.

Moments later, the waitress returned, beaming.

"I hate to interrupt," she said. "But y'all got a line forming out front."

The Big Three turned to see people peeking through the windows, phones in hand.

Customers approached.

"Can we get a picture? Y'all changed our household. My son started investing last week because of you."

They stood. Took photos. Shook hands. Shared stories.

Later That Night – Phones Buzz at the Table

The laughter dimmed. One by one, the phones lit up.

News Alert: Shooting in The Bluff – 3 Victims Confirmed.

Photo on screen: **Truth** among the injured.

Silence fell like a blanket.

Tasha covered her mouth.

"No…"

Malik stood slowly. Eyes fixed, face hard.

Ezekiel stared at the photo, his notes still open on the table.

Geneva whispered, "We just pivoted… and they just pushed back."

Victory doesn't mean immunity. And every mountain top has a shadow. But even now, even in this—

Truth can't be silenced.

2 plus 2 still equals 8.

And this storm? It's just begun.

CHAPTER TWENTY- NINE

BLOOD CURRENCY

The devil doesn't always show up with horns—sometimes he slides into a strip club and toasts to death with champagne. The ghetto got its own rules. Loyalty for sale. Truth on discount. And sometimes, betrayal wears the perfume of someone you once loved.

Strip Club – South Atlanta

Kilo leaned back in the booth, cigar lit, lap full of cash. J-Rock beside him, dapping dancers and laughing like he hadn't seen daylight in years.

"All that crying…" Kilo laughed. "Shanice needs an Oscar. I almost believed she cared."

J-Rock sipped. "She played it well. Dropped tears at the hospital like she didn't set him up. That's loyalty for the right price."

"Ten bands," Kilo said, shaking his head. "Man's own baby mama. Told me where he was, what time he'd be there. All I had to do was pull up."

Dancers surrounded them. The DJ shouted over the beat.

"This one for all the real ones on the block!"

Kilo stood, throwing money.

"Y'all dance! It's a celebration! No more fake prophets in my hood!"

Bar – Strip Club (Same Time)

Two DEA agents stood still, leaning against the wall.

"That's him," one said.

The other zoomed in with a camera. *Click.*

"Kilo better party hard and good the end is near. Out here selling death one of his crew sold heroin laced with fentanyl to a girl in Edgewood. She died."

"Set off a whole investigation chain. His name came up quickly."

They watched him throw cash.

"He thinks he is a boss. Got followers, 'hood status'... but one domino falls and it's all coming down."

Click.

"Let him dance. We're watching."

Flashback – One Week Ago

Shanice stood on the corner in a hoodie, face low.

Kilo pulled up in a tinted Impala.

"You sure?" he asked.

She didn't speak at first. Just nodded.

"He is always playing' daddy' after these events. Takes the boys back around 6:30... usually alone. No guards, no drama."

Kilo raised an eyebrow.

"Do you still love him?"

Shanice shrugged. "I loved what we used to be. But he ain't been real since he found that 'vision.' I'm tired of struggling while he chases dreams on podcasts."

Kilo handed her an envelope. She opened it. Her hands shook. "thanks much needed," she said.

Kilo smirked. "plenty more where that came from just do as I say."

Back to Hospital – Present

Shanice and his boys stood in front of reporters.

"He was turning his life around," she said. "He didn't deserve this."

Camera lights flashed. Ezekiel's jaw clenched.

Tasha whispered, "She knows more than she saying'."

Malik nodded. "Whole thing smells like betrayal."

Geneva stepped forward.

"We ain't just gon' pray. We gon' *investigate*."

In the ghetto, truth gets traded like a bag of dope. Loyalty is rented. And betrayal?

That's the currency too many spend.

But now?

Now the fire had faces.

And this time… it was personal.

2 plus 2 still equals 8.

And vengeance wasn't loud.

It was strategic.

The halls were tight with tension. The Big Three stood near the waiting room. Geneva prayed quietly. Malik paced. Ezekiel stared at the nurse's station.

"He's gonna make it," the nurse finally said. "Still in and out, but stable."

"I was so scared," Shanice said.

Malik gave her a strange look. Geneva nodded politely, but something about it all felt… wrong.

News reporters stood outside the glass.

"Rumors suggest the victim may have been involved in a drug deal gone wrong."

But the people standing outside the hospital shouted back:

"That's a lie! He was just with his kids! This was a hit!"

The hood doesn't need permission to kill hope. Sometimes it just needs the right address.

And for ten thousand dollars, the blueprint of betrayal was drawn.

Truth had fought his way out of the game.

But the streets ain't done with you until they bury you.

2 plus 2 still equals 8.

And now, revenge had a name.

CHAPTER THIRTY

FOUR LANES TO THE THRONE

The streets are a four-lane highway. One lane for the loyal. One for the liars. One for the lost. And one for the ones who know they could die at the next red light. #2Plus2Equals8 was never just a math problem. It was the formula for survival. And now? The wheels were in motion on all four lanes.

Lane 1 – The Loyal (Center Headquarters)

The Big Three didn't sleep.

Truth's shooting rattled the city, but it also did something dangerous—it *unified* it.

Ezekiel stood in front of a war board, filled with photos, plans, code enforcement notices, headlines, and printed-out smear posts. At the top of the board in bold black marker: **"WE RESPOND WITH STRATEGY, NOT EMOTION."**

Malik entered with new intel from the streets.

"Kilo out here braggin'," he said, tossing a USB stick on the table. " He was at strip club celebrating"

Geneva added, "I got lawyers pulling public records. There's property being bought up fast around the Bluff… Some of it is tied to city grant money. Quiet. Dirty. Real estate warfare."

Ezekiel circled a photo of Kilo. "He thinks he is winning. Let's build something he can't burn down."

Lane 2 – The Liars (Wynn's Office Downtown)

Wynn met with a PR team, visibly sweating.

"You said the smear would stop them. Instead, they went viral."

His advisor flipped an iPad toward him.

"#2Plus2Equals8 rises to #1 trending tag in the U.S."

Wynn slammed the tablet.

"They're organizing financial revolutions in barbershops and beauty salons. That's not activism. That's *infrastructure*."

A woman in the corner said, "You know who else started in barbershops? Civil Rights icons. You've lit the wrong fire."

Wynn's eyes narrowed. "Then we flood the fire with doubt. Whisper campaigns. Turn friends into enemies. Get their own people to question the foundation."

He paused.

"And push Blackstone to go harder. He still got pulled in the pews."

Lane 3 – The Lost (Blackstone's Home)

Blackstone paced his library, full of first-edition Bibles, rare documents, and one empty whiskey glass.

Camille watched him from the doorway.

"They passed you," she said. "Not in charisma. But of course."

He didn't look at her.

"I built this city's faith lane brick by brick. They think they can just reroute the traffic?"

She stepped closer. "Ezekiel's not trying to replace you. He's trying to *repair* what's broken."

He turned to her, eyes heavy.

"And what if I'm one of the broken pieces?"

She didn't answer.

Because silence already had.

Lane 4 – The Ruthless (Kilo's Trap House)

Kilo sat with a half-smoked blunt, surrounded by silence, not celebration. He replayed the hospital footage again. Truth survived.

J-Rock entered.

"You hear? That boy breathing."

Kilo stood, knocking over a bottle.

"I don't care. He scared now. The people scared. we win either way."

But he was lying.

Inside, his own crew had started whispering. One of them—young, jittery—had already met with a fed. Looking for a way out.

Pascal's Soul Food – Strategy Over Supper

The Big Three, with families in tow, met in the back room. This wasn't just about strategy—it was about reflection. Grounding.

Tasha pulled out numbers.

"Sales holding. Engagement up 200%. But I feel something bigger—*movement-level* momentum."

Malik added, "We need a rally. Not a speech. A street-level teaching tour. Atlanta, then Memphis, then Houston."

Geneva raised a cup.

"Truth survived. That means we *advance.*"

Ezekiel took a deep breath.

"We film everything. Make a documentary. We don't just want headlines. We want *history.*"

– Truth's Recovery Room

Truth opened his eyes slowly.

Ezekiel, Malik, and Geneva stood at the foot of his bed.

"I didn't fold?" he whispered.

"No," Ezekiel said. "You led."

Truth's eyes watered. "Let's finish what we started."

They clasped hands in silence.

The nurse came in.

"You guys family?"

Ezekiel smiled. "Something like that."

Four lanes. Four speeds. Four agendas. But only one destination: freedom.

2 plus 2 still equals 8.

And now?

The freeway was wide open.

CHAPTER THIRTY- ONE

BLAZE THEM UP

Not all fires burn loud. Some of it smolders, gathering heat, waiting for the right moment to consume everything. The movement was catching flame, but so was the resistance. From all four corners, pressure mounted—faith versus pride, purpose versus poison, legacy versus lies. The temperature was rising.

Barbershop Panel – Live in Atlanta

The Big Three hosted a panel in the middle of a barber shop. Chairs lined up. Camera rolling.

Topic: How to Turn a Hustle into Legacy.

Malik spoke first: "We hustled because we were scared. Now we build cause we believe. Faith ain't passive. It's a strategy."

Geneva followed: "Black women are the banks of this movement. We've been lending strength. Now we are lending knowledge. Invest in us."

Ezekiel closed: "You ain't broke if you are still breathing. That breath is your first currency."

Applause. Applause that didn't stop.

Then Ezekiel leaned forward, motioning to the cameraman to keep rolling.

"Y'all ever heard of *The Original Black Elite*? That book by Elizabeth Dowling Taylor?"

Malik nodded. "One of the most slept-on chapters in our history. That book's a blueprint."

Ezekiel continued:

The Original Black Elite: Daniel Murray and the Story of a Forgotten Era by Elizabeth Dowling Taylor is a powerful and richly researched book that shines a light on a nearly forgotten chapter of American history—the rise of a Black upper class in post-Civil War Washington, D.C.

"The central figure is Daniel Alexander Payne Murray," Ezekiel explained. "He was born free in 1852. Came from humble roots. Became a librarian at the

Library of Congress. A real gatekeeper of knowledge. But more than that—he fought to spotlight Black excellence. For the 1900 Paris Exposition, he tried to showcase every major Black author and intellectual in America to counter the lies about our inferiority."

Malik jumped in. "That's what stuck with me. This brother didn't just survive—he documented greatness. Educators, landowners, authors. Folks who were already building wealth and legacy before the Civil Rights era even started."

Geneva added, "And that elite? They weren't elite to look down on people—they saw themselves as the vanguard. The proof of what was possible for all of us. And that scared the system."

Ezekiel nodded. "Because right after Reconstruction, when we were rising, Jim Crow came in and dismantled all of it. We were erased from the narrative. On purpose."

He turned back to the camera.

"This book matters today because it fills a critical gap in our history. It tells us we were never what they said we were. We've always had excellence, always had leadership. We just didn't always control the story."

He paused.

"That's why we are here. To control it now. And rewrite the ending."

Malik nodded, voice deep. "And like the book says—they walked with purpose. Dressed with dignity. And believed in the redemptive power of education."

Ezekiel looked into the lens. "This is our new Paris Exposition. #2Plus2Equals8 ain't just a brand. It's a revelation. And the best way to honor those who came before us… is to finish what they started."

Federal Building – Unmarked Conference Room

Two DEA agents watched surveillance footage on a large screen. Kilo in the strip club. Cash flowing. Arms around him. Smiling too big.

"You think we move now?" the younger one asked.

The older agent shook his head. "Not yet. We're not just going after Kilo. We want the full structure. The product trails, the money men, the politicians, the real estate flips. One raid doesn't cut it. We bring the whole house down."

He paused.

"When he thinks nobody's watching... that's when we take the shot."

Kingdom Dominion Cathedral – Sunday Morning

Blackstone stood on the pulpit, hands clenched. His sermon had fire, but not the kind that saved—it scorched. He wasn't letting go. Not yet.

"They want my seat. But they didn't pay the cost."

The congregation watched. Some are still cheering. Others are shifting.

Camille sat near the front. Her eyes no longer glowed with reverence. They stared through him.

Blackstone slammed the Bible shut.

"I'm not handing over this mantle because a few Twitter trends got folk excited. This city still runs through my hands."

Flashback – 1980s, Small Kitchen in Vine City

Young Rose, barely 17, stood at the edge of the counter, fidgeting.

Her mother—Ms. Elsie—turned from the sink.

"I'm pregnant," Rose said.

Elsie dropped the dish. "By who?"

Rose swallowed. "A married man. Church man. Has... influence."

Elsie's rage exploded. "You think you're gonna carry this secret? You think a man like that is gonna leave his suit and tie for a teenage girl in the bricks?!"

"I didn't plan it."

"Baby, life doesn't care about plans. Now you are carrying a storm."

Tears fell. But Rose stood tall.

And out of that storm, years later—came Ezekiel.

The Center – Early Evening

Geneva walked into the conference room with a file in hand.

"Ten acres. Outside of Palmetto. Undervalued, but rich soil. Could be ours."

Ezekiel looked at the map. "Now we transition from talking to action—building wealth… with ownership!"

Malik pulled up blueprints. "Subdivisions. Townhomes. Black-owned tradesmen. Each person that invests gets a trust account tied to property equity."

Tasha entered with a chart. "Add to that life insurance strategies. Do you know how many Black leaders died because they had no generational setup?"

Ezekiel turned to the group. "We talk about struggle like it's a badge. But struggling without a plan is a cycle."

Geneva nodded. "Let's make generational power the new protest. Putting an offer in tomorrow."

She laid the file on the table and spoke with a fire behind her voice.

"You ever wonder why the wealth gap is so wide? They say we are lazy, but they don't tell you how rigged the system is. Try walking into a bank and asking for a seven-figure loan to start a gas station chain, or build a hospital, a residential development, or a franchise from the ground up. Good luck."

She paced the room.

"As Dr. Umar Johnson said—we can get student loans. Car loans. Mortgages. But all those are high-risk to us and high-yield to the banks. The further you go, the less access you have. A small business loan? Maybe. But real generational moves? Nearly impossible."

She stopped and looked everyone in the eye.

"Meanwhile, other communities—like the Jewish community—have financial systems that empower them. Ever heard of *Heter Iska*? That's a financial arrangement used in Jewish law where they receive business loans without interest. No penalty. Just partnership. You understand what that means? Imagine being able to fund your legacy without the burden of debt."

Geneva leaned in, her words sharp.

"They're not just beating us in capital spending. They're beating us in *design.* We don't have access because we were never meant to be in the room."

Ezekiel gripped the edge of the table.

"Then we build our own damn room."

Hospital – Truth Goes Live

Truth sat up, tubes still attached, scars like badges. He looked into the camera, broadcasting from Ezekiel's account.

"They tried to break me. But I'm more alive now than ever. I know who I am. And I know who tried to erase me. But let me say this—I already have forgiven them. Because sometimes folks don't see the poison 'till it drips down their own throat."

The streets watched. So did Shanice—from her car, trembling.

Comments exploded.

"He is talking with heart." "We know who sold him out." "They will feel that for life."

Federal Building – Interrogation Room

J-Rock sat under the cold lights. Arms crossed. DEA agents stared at him.

"We know you weren't the one who pulled the trigger. But we know who did. We know what was paid. And we know you were there."

He said nothing.

Then they pulled out a photo.

Truth. Blood on his hoodie. Truth's kids crying behind the yellow tape.

"You gonna let Kilo get richer while you rot?"

J-Rock shifted.

Pressure was a language he understood.

The Center – Main Hall Packed

The Big Three stood at the front. No chairs. No silence.

Geneva spoke first: "Trust accounts for children. Life insurance to fund community infrastructure. Every family, an investor."

Malik added, "Land that grows gardens. Programs that build coders. Cash flowing through hands that own."

Ezekiel stepped forward. "No more asking. No more surviving. We redefine success. We take the math back. 2 plus 2 equals 8. Because our value has always been multiplied."

The room erupted.

But then hands went up.

"How can we get involved when we live paycheck to paycheck?" a single mother asked.

"We got bills today. Dreams feel like a luxury."

Geneva responded, "Start small. $10 a week into a compound interest account. Get a life insurance policy that builds cash value. And trust—this ain't about big leaps. It's about planting seeds."

A young man in scrubs raised his voice. "I'm tired of working two jobs just to breathe. Where's the opportunity that pays more than survival?"

Malik nodded. "That's why we're investing in what matters—skills. Truck driving, carpentry, coding, content creation, media production. Jobs where *you* own the tools, the truck, the trade. And we ain't just talking—we're building a trade school. On-site. With real mentors. Real equipment. Real paychecks."

Ezekiel stepped closer to the crowd. "Content is the new oil and gas. You hear me? If you got a voice, a camera, or a vision—you got power. We're launching a creators' lab. Film, write, record, publish. Tell our stories. Show our skills. Sell our value."

Geneva pointed to a mockup behind them. "Clothing brands. Community-owned. Designers from the block. Seamstresses, stitchers, shippers. Fashion with a mission. Built in our neighborhoods."

Another voice rose, an older woman near the back. "So where do we start? What's the first step?"

Ezekiel smiled.

"Right here. Right now. Sign up. Show up. One family at a time. One tool at a time. We roll up our sleeves, dot the i's, cross the t's, and flip the script that's been written *for* us—by building a future *with* us."

Geneva raised her mic. "This isn't charity. It's strategy."

Malik nodded. "And strategy is how we win."

Center Headquarters – Later

Ezekiel walked into the war room. The board now had red yarn connecting photos, plans, quotes, targets, events, and federal players.

Geneva was already there. Malik was finishing a call with someone from Oakland.

"We lit in Memphis," Malik said. "They are hosting a block teach-in. Six barbers, two Black-owned coffee shops, and an all-girl robotics team joining forces."

Ezekiel grinned. "It's happening. No turning back now."

Tasha stepped in. "And you are trending in Ghana, Zeke. Africa tapped in."

Geneva lifted her phone. "Truth's awake. He wants to speak—tonight."

Ezekiel listened and stared at a whiteboard now titled: PHASE TWO: GLOBAL IMPACT.

On it:

- International financial literacy syndicates
- Youth land trust programs
- Streaming docu-series
- Tech bootcamps

He looked at Geneva. Then Malik.

"You ready?"

They nodded.

"Let's blaze up."

The fires still burned, but now they were controlled. Fueled by focus. Branded with belief.

And somewhere in the shadows, the final domino tilted.

Because when you try to kill a movement built on strategy, all you do is sharpen it.

2 plus 2 still equals 8.

And now, the flames had blueprints.

CHAPTER THIRTY- TWO

THE SHIFT

Change doesn't always announce itself with fireworks. Sometimes, it's a whisper between movements, a conversation in a barbershop, a wiretap recording on a federal line. But when the shift comes, you feel it.

In the bones.

In the pulse.

In the silence just before everything flips.

The Center – Early Morning Strategy Session

The whiteboard now had one phrase at the top in thick red letters: "OWN EVERYTHING."

Ezekiel looked around the room. Malik. Geneva. Tasha. Truth sat near the back, healing but strong.

"Y'all feel it?" Ezekiel asked.

They nodded.

"We're not local anymore. This ain't just Atlanta. This is global."

Geneva pulled out a tablet. "Kenya, London, Toronto—all tuning in to the live streams. Some schools overseas want to build #2Plus2Equals8 clubs."

Malik grinned. "Then we franchise the blueprint. From block to boardroom."

Truth raised a hand.

"One request: whatever we do next… include the kids. I almost died for a code that wasn't mine. I want them to live for something bigger than rep."

Washington, D.C. – Closed Meeting Between Agencies

A map of Atlanta lit up the table.

Agent Wallace pointed.

"They're embedding wealth principles in education hubs, real estate co-ops, and barbershops. They've moved beyond digital. This is ideological warfare."

Another agent added, "And public opinion's swinging in their favor. We push too hard, it backfires."

Wallace stayed silent for a beat.

"Then we wait. Let them grow arrogant. Let the movement fracture from inside. Somebody always gets jealous. Ambitious."

He circled three names on a file.

Ezekiel. Geneva. Malik.

"Push the right buttons. Shake the trust. Make it feel personal."

Rose's Porch – A Conversation That Changed Everything

Rose sat in her rocking chair, tea in hand. Ezekiel pulled up a seat next to her.

"Mama," he said. "You ever thought it would get this big?"

She smiled. "I always knew you were born for something larger than the block."

He looked down. "They want to divide us."

"They always will," she said. "But what you're building can't be killed. It can only be copied or corrupted. Stay clean, son. Stay dangerous—but clean."

Barbershop Live Podcast Event

Malik spoke into the mic. "Imagine if every hood had its own credit union. Its own trust fund. Its own co-op farms. Ain't no savior coming. But WE are here."

The crowd nodded. Cheered. A teen in the back shouted, "Tell 'em again!"

Geneva added, "We raise babies to be CEOs. Not just rappers. Not just athletes. It starts now."

A woman with a baby on her hip stepped forward. "How do we teach our kids that when school barely sees them as students?"

Geneva leaned in. "We educate them at the dinner table. In the barbershop. In these halls. Like John Hope Bryant said: 'The new civil rights issue is economic empowerment.' We're taking that seriously."

A young brother in work boots asked, "What about those of us who've made mistakes? Records, pasts... can we still build?"

Truth stepped forward, voice firm. "I almost died behind fake loyalty. But this here? This movement? Realer than blood. Like James Baldwin said: 'Not everything that is faced can be changed, but nothing can be changed until it is faced.' We build from where we stand. Ain't no disqualifying past. Only unfinished futures."

Another man in the crowd raised his hand. "Y'all talk big vision. But how do we protect it?"

Malik answered. "We protect it with unity. We multiply wisdom. We stay rooted in values, not just vibes. 2 plus 2 equals 8 means you're worth more than the sum. It means we're multiplying value—across generations."

The room pulsed with applause and energy, each word laying another brick in the foundation of something real. Something is rising.

Newsroom – Late Night Breaking Report

Anchor: "Word from inside federal law enforcement is they are now treating #2Plus2Equals8 not as a protest group, but as a parallel infrastructure network. Quiet investigations continue, but with limited jurisdiction due to massive community support."

Anchor (voice-over): "From trust accounts to co-op gardens, from content studios to home-building crews, this is a self-sustaining model powered by education, ownership, and unapologetic Black vision."

Another camera angle cut to federal analysts behind closed doors.

Correspondent: "Homeland Security sources reveal internal debates about how to categorize the movement. Some are calling it 'unprecedented civilian independence.' Others fear it's igniting a new wave of sovereignty rooted in economic defiance—not violence, but visibility."

Cut back to the anchor.

Anchor: "Critics argue the movement undermines traditional authority structures. Supporters call it a blueprint for 21st-century liberation. One former DOJ official said, and I quote, 'If Martin had a dream, this is the business plan.'"

Footage ended on a wide shot of the podcast studio, Ezekiel, Malik, and Geneva seated under the banner: *OWN THE VISION. BUILD THE LEGACY.*

Anchor (closing): "Regardless of where you stand, one thing is clear—#2Plus2Equals8 is no longer a phrase. It's a movement. And it's growing."

Back at The Center – Geneva's Find

Geneva unfolded a larger blueprint on the table.

"I found a place. Old boarding school campus. Forty acres. Abandoned. Tax lien in limbo. If we raise $500k, it's ours."

Tasha's eyes lit up.

"That's the headquarters."

Malik nodded. "Home base for the movement."

Truth smiled. "Call it what it is. Legacy Land."

Ezekiel stared at the map. Then said softly:

"Let's shift the world."

Geneva pointed to two marked parcels. "The Palmetto property? That's for residential use. Townhomes, gardens, and investment units. It's the model we scale."

She then tapped the forty-acre layout. "But this here? This is the foundation. The Center's core. Administrative offices. Trade training. Financial literacy classrooms. Broadcasting studio. All of it—built from scratch. Built to last."

Malik leaned in. "This is the fortress. Not to hide behind—but to launch from. Generations will walk through this place and come out changed."

Tasha smiled. "It's more than land. It's proof. That we can do more than dream—we can develop."

Truth nodded. "Let's raise the money. Let's raise the stakes. Let's raise the future."

Geneva flipped to a finance summary sheet. "Right now, we have $225,000 in capital cash on hand from donations, merch, and passive income streams. We need to raise the remaining $275,000 within 90 days to secure the title."

Ezekiel leaned in. "Then we start stargazing—small donor events, strategic sponsors, reinvesting content profits, and expanding our digital sales funnel. We've got to scale the movement and multiply the mission."

Malik added, "And we remind the people—this is their land. This is their stake. Let's put boots on the ground and get this balance raised. Every dollar, a seed. Every seed, a brick."

Geneva smiled. "And in 90 days or less—we'll call it ours."

Movements start with messages. But revolutions?

They start when a message becomes a mandate.

This wasn't just awareness. This was architecture.

2 plus 2 still equals 8.

And the blueprint just got bigger.

CHAPTER THIRTY- THREE

THE RIDE TO BECOMING

Every leader has a before. Not just a backstory—but a ride. A ride through pain, through prayers whispered in rest stop stalls, through hunger that only purpose can feed. Geneva began at 18. On a Greyhound. Alone. Pregnant. And on fire with a dream no one else could yet see.

FLASHBACK: INT. GREYHOUND BUS – FALL, 18 YEARS AGO

The night bus rumbled steady down the Midwest highway. The seats were half-empty, the windows fogged, and the hum of low conversations filled the aisle.

Geneva sat by the window, face pressed to the glass, one hand resting protectively over her small belly. She was only four months in, but already she felt it—the tiny shifts of life forming within her. The pulse that kept her moving.

She had one suitcase, a prayer journal, and a roundtrip ticket she never planned on using.

Her mother had died in a car crash just six months earlier. Her father didn't survive it—he was still breathing, but drowning in liquor and regret. Two school teachers who raised her on wisdom, books, and Black excellence.

She still heard their voices.

"You can do anything, baby. But never forget who you are while doing it." – Mama

"There is no such thing as too loud when you're speaking the truth." – Mama

Her father's voice came quieter. Stronger.

"Cast down your bucket where you are." – Booker T. Washington

Geneva closed her eyes tight. A tear rolled. Then another.

"First time leaving home?" a soft voice beside her asked.

Geneva turned to see a middle-aged Black woman, nurse scrubs under a denim jacket, kind eyes and a warm smile.

"Yeah," Geneva replied, voice cracking.

The woman nodded. "South?"

"Atlanta. To stay with my grandmother. She's heavy in the church."

"Good. You need a net. Especially with a baby on the way."

Geneva glanced down at her stomach. "I don't even know where to start."

"Nursing's a good field," the woman said. "Long hours though. You gotta have a strong stomach for blood and heartbreak. But it's honest work."

Geneva smiled. "Thank you. I… I needed to hear that."

INT. BUS – LATER THAT NIGHT

The moonlight cast long streaks across her notebook as she scribbled prayers.

God, give me strength. I don't have much, but I'm willing. I don't know if this child will save me or break me, but I promise to raise them with light.

She looked up. Two rows ahead, an older man began humming an old Mahalia Jackson hymn. Another woman across the aisle said she used to teach in Decatur. They all shared stories—about survival, about pain, about love that outlasted the worst kind of years.

Geneva told them about her mom.

"Best teacher on the West Side. She could look at your handwriting and know your mood."

She told them about her father.

"He used to say, *'Don't raise your voice. Raise your argument.'* Now he doesn't talk to no one but his bottle."

There was silence. Then one woman said: "You still have his legacy. You just gotta be the page he never got to write."

A young man chimed in from the back of the bus.

"Madam C.J. Walker said, *'Don't sit down and wait for the opportunities to come. Get up and make them.'* You're doing that right now."

Another voice added: "And remember what Harriet Tubman said—*'I freed a thousand slaves. I could have freed a thousand more if only they knew they were slaves.'*"

Geneva nodded slowly. Those words curled around her like armor.

GREYHOUND BUS – DAWN

The Georgia trees grew thick as they neared the station. Geneva rubbed her belly again. Her eyes had been open all night, but now she felt new.

Not perfect. Not healed.

But *I'm ready.*

"I'm gonna make it," she whispered to herself.

Not for applause. Not for revenge. Not even for her parents.

But for the life inside her.

And the woman she was becoming.

Before the pulpit. Before the movement. Before Legacy Land and national broadcasts—

There was a girl on a bus with nothing but a baby and a Bible.

Geneva didn't just arrive. She *survived.*

2 plus 2 still equals 8.

And this was her becoming.

Before the pulpit. Before the movement. Before Legacy Land and national broadcasts—

There was a girl on a bus with nothing but a baby and a Bible.

Geneva didn't just arrive. She *survived.*

But survival wasn't her ceiling.

This was also the beginning of her rise.

UPSCALE DOWNTOWN RESTAURANT – LATE AFTERNOON

Geneva pushed open the tall glass door to Lucille's Garden, a Black-owned upscale bistro tucked into the heart of the city. The scent of roasted garlic, thyme, and honey-drizzled cornbread greeted her as she stepped inside. Smooth jazz danced in the air above the clinking of wine glasses and soft chatter.

She paused for a moment. Closed her eyes. Took it in.

The fact that Coca-Cola executives were investing in her and the Big Three wasn't just about money. It was validation. Her voice. Her work. Her purpose.

She glanced upward—toward the heavens.

"Mama, Daddy… y'all said I could do anything. You were right."

Elena was already seated at a private corner table near the window, a sleek black dress, natural curls pinned back, and her posture poised like a woman who had learned how to balance power with grace.

Geneva approached with purpose.

"Hey, sis," she said.

Elena stood and hugged her tight. "I've been waiting for this conversation for years."

They sat.

A young waitress with box braids and gold hoop earrings stepped up to take their order.

"We're gonna start with the fried green tomatoes, two lavender lemonades," Elena said. "Then I'll have the grilled salmon over okra risotto."

"Same," Geneva smiled. "And bring that cornbread I smelled from the door."

They laughed.

LUCILLE'S – DURING THE MEAL

The sun beamed in through the high windows, bouncing off copper light fixtures and bathing the dark wood floors in warmth. Lush green plants hung from corners. The energy was soft, but rich.

"I've been in boardrooms for 15 years," Elena said, slicing her tomato appetizer. "And this—this movement—is the first time I've ever felt alive and felt good helping my own people."

Geneva nodded slowly. "We didn't ask for a handout. We planted seeds. Y'all just watered what was already growing."

Elena leaned in. "When I pitched the grant, they questioned the ROI. I said: 'Return on investment? You're talking about dollar signs. I'm talking about generations.'"

Geneva smiled. "That's what we're building. Legacy you can live in."

Their lavender lemonades arrived in tall glasses. Fresh mint sprigs glistened over ice. The waitress smiled wide.

"Everything looks okay, ladies?"

"Perfect," Geneva said.

Elena took a sip, then lowered her voice.

"Here's where I need to be honest. This support? It's not forever unless the movement stays tight. Homeland is watching. Political fingers are itchy. Even the banks are nervous."

Geneva didn't flinch.

"We're not chasing applause. We're building policy. Programs. Protection. We plan on breaking grounds on 40 acres. And you know what the first cornerstone was?"

Elena leaned in. "What?"

"Trust. Not just paperwork trust. Spiritual trust. Between the Big Three. Between us and the people."

Elena nodded, full of something rare—hope with strategy.

"I want in deeper," she said. "Not just checks. I want to help create programs. Financial literacy modules. Corporate training on cultural reinvestment."

Geneva smiled. "Then welcome home."

Two women. One table. A movement on the menu.

This wasn't just dinner. It was destiny being drafted between bites and belief.

2 plus 2 still equals 8.

And now the rooms were changing.

Before the pulpit. Before the movement. Before Legacy Land and national broadcasts—

There was a girl on a bus with nothing but a baby and a Bible.

Geneva didn't just arrive. She survived.

But survival wasn't her ceiling.

This was also the beginning of her rise.

TRUTH'S MOTHER'S HOUSE – LATE EVENING

Truth sat on the front porch of a modest brick house tucked deep in the southwest corner of the city. The porch light flickered, casting shadows over chipped steps and flower pots that hadn't seen flowers in years.

Inside, the scent of fried cabbage and bleach lingered. His mother, Ms. Laretha, stood at the door, arms crossed, bonnet on, cigarette dangling from her lip.

"So you really believe she set you up?"

Truth exhaled hard, leaning forward on the rail.

"I want to say no. I want to believe I just got caught in somebody else's mess… but in my gut? I know it. She was the only one who knew where I was going. Down to the time."

Ms. Laretha took a drag. "You feel like killing her?"

"I ain't gon' lie, Ma. I thought about it. Her and whoever else was in it. Sometimes I imagine pulling up, letting it spray, no warning."

She stared at him. "Then what? You get your revenge and lose the movement? You lose your boys? End up in a cage next to the same people you outgrew?"

Truth didn't speak. The silence said enough.

"I never liked that girl," Ms. Laretha continued. "Had slick energy from the jump. Thought she was smarter than she was. But this here? This #2Plus2Equals8 thing? It's different."

Truth looked up. "Do you believe in it?"

"I believe in you. And I ain't one to worship no preacher, but Ezekiel? That boy ain't fake. He says things that sound like my daddy used to say. Truth that sting. Real vision."

She sat beside him. "If you believe in this movement, then don't let pain make you throw it all away. Let the universe handle what you can't. That's gangster too. Holding your peace when you have every reason not to."

Truth nodded slowly.

"I'm just tired of being betrayed by people I fed."

Ms. Laretha stubbed her cigarette out on the porch railing.

"That's life, baby. You feed snakes, eventually one gon' bite. But you? You are still walking. Still talking. Still changing lives. Don't become what tried to break you."

Truth leaned back, rubbing his beard.

"She ain't worth the vision."

"That's the son I raised," she said, standing. "And if you ever do decide to handle it differently... just let me know. I still have a few connections from back in my days."

They laughed, just for a second.

But the weight lingered.

Revenge is loud. Purpose is patience.

Truth had every reason to choose the gun. But he chose the grind.

And with Ms. Laretha's strength behind him?

2 plus 2 still equals 8.

And it now had a warrior with scars, vision, and restraint.

CHAPTER THIRTY- FOUR

BLACK OAK GOLF CLUB – MORNING

The sky was painted in soft gold, the kind of morning light that felt like a fresh check—clean, promising. Birds cut quiet loops across the air, and every blade of grass on the fairway looked hand-manicured by God himself.

Ezekiel and Malik pulled up in a rented golf cart, both rocking fitted polos with #2Plus2Equals8 subtly stitched over the heart.

"I hear all the real money deals made on the golf course?" Ezekiel said, adjusting his glove.

Malik grinned. "That's what they say. And look over there—see that dude with the white bucket hat?"

Ezekiel squinted.

"That's Johnson. Brother owns 25 McDonald's across the southeast. Franchise king."

Malik pointed again.

"And the dude in the maroon slacks? That's Cedric Franklin. Top Black-owned dealership group in the state. Imports, luxury lines, even heavy commercial fleets."

Ezekiel shook his head. "We're definitely walking with the big dogs now."

BLACK OAK CLUBHOUSE – LATER

The clubhouse was elegance dipped in mahogany. Polished wood floors. Crystal chandeliers. Velvet accents on dark leather chairs. Waiters in black vests moved like shadows between tables, refilling water glasses and delivering plated perfection.

Dante—sharp as ever in navy slacks and tan blazer—stood as Ezekiel and Malik entered.

"Gentlemen," he said, smiling. "Welcome to where conversations turn into contracts."

They shook hands, then followed him to a long table already set with white linens, iced teas, and strategic ambition.

"Let me make the round," Dante said, pulling out chairs.

He gestured to a tall, bald man with a calm stare and a Rolex that could blind a skeptic.

"This is Mr. Terrance Johnson—McDonald's magnate. He didn't just franchise the game, he redefined how community hiring looks. 2,000+ employees. Over 40% of high schoolers. First jobs, second chances."

Johnson nodded. "Legacy ain't just what you leave. It's who you lift."

Next, Dante turned to a stocky man with dreadlocks pulled into a bun and designer frames.

"Cedric Franklin. Owner of Franklin Auto Group. Twelve rooftops, from Kia to Cadillac. Has a car-lot mentorship program training youth in finance, sales, and automotive repair."

Cedric fist-bumped Malik. "Finance starts with motion. We teach both."

He motioned to a sharp older gentleman in a three-piece grey suit.

"Reverend Lewis Mathis. Founder of The Arc Institute—one of the few Black-led think tanks working on policy design, economic recovery, and reparative models."

Reverend Lewis spoke like thunder wrapped in silk. "Faith is not noise. It's negotiation with God. And movements without structure collapse."

A woman with short platinum hair and a tablet sat poised at the end of the table.

"Dr. Nadine Powell—real estate developer, economist, and head of Black Futures Urban Planning. She's put over 1,000 Black families into new housing in three years—without predatory lending."

Dr. Powell nodded at Ezekiel. "Ownership is the only protest they actually fear."

"And finally," Dante turned to the youngest man at the table—maybe late 30s, cool fade, no tie.

"This is Amir Bryant. Serial entrepreneur. Ex-Silicon Valley. Sold two startups. Now leads an incubator that funds Black-owned tech, media, and AI firms. He's our disruption whisperer."

Amir raised a glass. "Power respects patterns. I'm here to help scale yours."

Ezekiel and Malik exchanged a look—this was different.

This wasn't charity.

This was a *council*.

Dante smiled and finally sat down.

"This movement you're building? It's real. But now, you don't just have a mission—you have momentum. We're here to multiply that."

Some meetings don't make headlines.

They make empires.

2 plus 2 still equals 8.

And this table?

This was where the next chapter of power got inked in bold.

BLACK OAK CLUBHOUSE – POWER LUNCH CONTINUES

The table had warmed up. Food cleared, drinks refilled. But now the real currency was conversation.

Terrance Johnson leaned back in his chair, wiping his mouth with a cloth napkin.

"Alright," he said. "What's the five-year vision? I mean real numbers. Tangibles. Not just slogans."

Ezekiel didn't blink.

"Five years? Legacy Land becomes fully built. Three more locations in different states. Five thousand youth trained in tech, finance, and land use. Our own credit union. All Black-funded."

A quiet pause.

Malik followed up, voice steady. "And we're launching a digital campus. Afrocentric education, no gatekeepers, accessible worldwide. Teaching wealth, law, and wellness like they teach war."

Dr. Powell tapped her glass. "That's scalable. Just need the right protections and digital infrastructure. I'd like to assist with the planning."

Then Cedric leaned forward.

"Y'all came in here strong. Not pitching, not begging. That's rare. Respect."

Reverend Mathis nodded. "This is the first grassroots movement I've seen walk into a room of giants and not bow."

Amir, cool as ever, cut in: "But have you thought of aligning with *100 Black Men of America*? You bring new blood. Fresh energy. Could be a win."

Ezekiel raised a brow.

"We respect them. But we ain't joining no faces that ain't been showing up when bullets hit, schools close, or food deserts grow. We're not trying to wear a brand. We *are* the brand."

Cedric smirked. "Well damn. Ain't no misunderstanding you."

Another executive asked more softly, "Is there really hope though? Or are we just dressing the wound better than before?"

Malik looked him in the eye.

"You ain't ask if there's hope when Amazon drops a warehouse in the hood. Or when they teach our kids to follow instead of lead. Don't question hope when it finally has a backbone."

That hit.

Two members leaned in, took out phones.

"I'll write the first check," one said. "Fifty thousand."

The other followed. "Count me in for seventy-five. Let's break some damn ground."

CLUBHOUSE ENTRY – MINUTES LATER

Just as the energy reached a crescendo, the door opened.

Blackstone walked in.

Clean suit. Confident smile. But something behind the eyes said war.

He was familiar with everyone at the table—dap and handshakes, polite nods. But the air changed.

Cedric folded his arms. "Well, look what the sanctuary dragged in."

Dr. Powell sipped her tea slowly, eyes locked on the tension.

One member whispered boldly, "Always room for fresh meat. Especially ones that ain't scared to eat."

Ezekiel stood, approached.

"Peace, Blackstone. This ain't about lines drawn. It's about bridges built. We ain't trying to replace nobody. Just trying to stop the bleeding."

Blackstone smirked, but his eyes stayed on the room, surveying.

"You've built something fast. Fast things tend to fall apart."

Malik stepped up, voice calm but clear.

"We're not scared of speed. We're scared of silence."

Blackstone nodded slowly, but the pride behind his stare couldn't hide the storm.

Outside the windows, two news reporters snapped photos, whispering with cameramen.

"What's the meaning of this gathering?" one asked loudly.

Another called out, "Is this a private summit? A political move?"

One exec laughed dry. "Free publicity comes fast when the Black elite share lunch."

Ezekiel turned, walked to the glass doors, and spoke directly to them.

"It's not about power. It's about a blueprint. And if you listen close enough, you'll hear it's not a whisper—it's a war plan. We ain't hiding. We're multiplying."

Click. Click. Flash.

The room wasn't built for applause.

It was built for agreements.

Two young men, once doubted by the world, now stood in it—shaping legacy alongside veterans, challengers, and even rivals.

2 plus 2 still equals 8.

And now? The table was theirs.

CHAPTER THIRTY- FIVE

BRICK BY BRICK, DOLLAR BY DOLLAR

Movements don't grow on fire alone. They grow on spreadsheets, courage, long meetings, hard questions, and plans built nail by nail. The fire starts it. But discipline sustains it.

37 Days Later – Goal Surpassed, Vision Expanded

#2Plus2Equals8 HEADQUARTERS – MORNING

The hum of conversation filled the newly furnished headquarters—a converted warehouse now lined with smart boards, folding chairs, vision boards, and a café-style kitchen in the back where someone kept brewing cinnamon coffee.

Ezekiel stood at the head of the table. Malik to his left. Geneva on his right. Truth leaned against the wall near the window, arms folded, nodding as the numbers came in.

At the center, behind a laptop with colored tabs, sat Brielle, their young accountant—24, sharp bob, thick-rimmed glasses, and a piercing wit that cut cleaner than most men twice her age.

Brielle cleared her throat.

"So here's where we stand. Total donations and sponsorship as of this morning: $548,732.14. That includes direct deposits, mailed checks, and two corporate pledges we just locked in."

She clicked a new slide.

"T-shirt and merch sales? Up 43% from last quarter. Gross revenue: $197,440. Profit margin holding at 60% thanks to our switch to local printers."

Geneva smiled.

"That's almost 120K in profit—straight back into programs."

Brielle continued. "Streaming content—podcast episodes, virtual speeches, and interviews—steady IP revenue flow. Last month: $12,085 in royalties."

Malik leaned forward.

"That's just talking real. Imagine when we build the curriculum."

Truth smirked. "We're building' already."

STRATEGY ROOM – MIDDAY

Geneva stood near a detailed map of the 40-acre property, pinned to a cork wall. She tapped it with a red marker.

"Closing is in six days. Wire already confirmed. This land is ours."

Ezekiel looked at the layout. "Forty acres... like our ancestors dreamed of. What's the first brick?"

Geneva answered without hesitation. "Resource center. Grassroots programs. Legal help. Food distribution. Then farming. Then homes."

Malik added, "We'll build housing with hands from our own blocks. Every nail driven by someone who thought they couldn't change nothin'. Until they did."

Geneva pointed at another section of the map. "We'll dedicate one building strictly for youth development. Arts. Tech. Wellness. Teaching young Black kids that creativity is capital."

Truth stepped up. "I got more dealers comin'. They wanna help. Men that never touched a hammer askin' what time we start. They'll be at the next town meeting."

Ezekiel locked eyes with him.

"That's the real win. Not just saving them—but involving them."

HQ – LATER THAT AFTERNOON

Ezekiel sat with a notebook, scribbling outlines.

"Memphis and Chicago. We hit the schools. Elementary to high school. Assembly speeches, student councils, Q&As."

Malik leaned in. "We link with barbershops and small businesses while we're there. Leave something behind other than inspiration."

Truth nodded. "Make sure we touch the street teams too. Show 'em what growth looks like when you stay out of the casket or the cage."

Geneva pulled out her phone.

"Elena's sending us a videographer from Coke to start documenting the journey. We'll stream it. Show people what the building looks like."

Ezekiel leaned back and whispered, quoting Booker T. Washington: "Success is to be measured not so much by the position one has reached in life as by the obstacles which he has overcome."

Geneva followed with a nod. "Like Byron Allen said—'We must own our narrative and distribute it.' We're not just building land—we're broadcasting truth."

Malik raised his glass of sweet tea. "Phase one is complete. But the next phase? Ten times harder. Ten times bigger. We build the classrooms, the podcast studio, the small business incubator, and that underground data vault. Deadline? 18 months."

Truth tapped his fist to his chest. "Let's lock in. No fallback. Only forward."

Ezekiel stood, his voice calm and bold.

"We don't just want to be the story. We want to be the system. New rules. New order. And this time—we write the blueprint."

There were no shortcuts. No magic. No saviors.

Just vision. Strategy. And sweat.

2 plus 2 still equals 8. And every line item… Every plan… Every converted soul…

Was a receipt.

This movement wasn't on fire.

It was focused.

THE BLUFF – NIGHTFALL

The street buzzed like a live wire. The trap house—known in whispers as *The Green Light*—sat crooked at the end of a block where hope had been evicted long ago. It was an old shotgun home with its porch ripped off, window bars bent like crooked teeth, and a flickering green bulb above the door.

Cars lined both sides of the block like a Chick-fil-A drive-thru—except nobody was looking for chicken sandwiches. They were hungry for something darker.

Teens no older than fifteen moved between car windows like workers on a timed shift. Black, white, young, old—it didn't matter. Every window rolled down, every hand reached out.

"Two blues. You know the vibe."

"Zonex got what you need. Stay on the line."

One of the boys—Zonex—was the smallest but quickest. Slim build, eyes way too old for his face. He wore a bubble coat and designer sneakers covered in alley dust. He repeated the same line to every customer:

"Fresh Fet and fire Heron. Get right, stay light."

A woman with a daycare logo on her shirt pulled up, car seat in the back, money in her hand. Zonex leaned in, expression blank.

"You got kids?" she asked, almost ashamed.

"I have dead cousins," Zonex answered flatly. "Take it or keep it moving."

She didn't hesitate.

TRAP HOUSE LIVING ROOM – SAME TIME

Inside, the air was hot with ego and Hennessy. Kilo sat on a stained velvet couch, legs spread, shirt off, gold chain thick as a rope swinging across his chest. Two women sat on either side of him, feeding him grapes and praise.

"One hour, this block does a 30 ball," he said, flexing. "Ain't even touched the phone calls yet all trap money."

The woman with the pink wig grinned, leaned into his ear. "And you did it all without breakin' a sweat. You are a king, Kilo."

The other chimed in. "A god in these streets."

Kilo sipped lean from a mason jar and smirked.

"I just feed the people. Government let 'em starve."

ABANDONED DUPLEX – ACROSS THE STREET

On the second floor of a half-collapsed duplex, two DEA agents sat in the dark. One crouched behind a broken window, Nikon zoom lens steady. The other scribbled notes while chewing nicotine gum.

"Look at that," the older agent muttered. "Four OD's in this zip code last week. And here they are… selling slow death with no fear."

The younger agent took another photo of Zonex slipping pills into a biker's hand.

"We got enough for a raid, easy."

The vet shook his head. "It ain't about enough. It's about the fish. The one Kilo reports to. Up top don't want cleanups—they want headlines. Promotions. Budgets."

The younger agent looked out at the sidewalk—saw a man slumped against a fire hydrant, foaming at the mouth. A toddler rode his tricycle around the body like it was nothing new.

"And until one of those dead bodies is the senator's daughter," the agent said coldly, "nothing's changing."

THE BLUFF – CONTINUOUS

Further down the street, a group of young boys played football with a crushed soda can. Just yards away, a woman lay face-first on the concrete, her lips blue. Nobody stopped.

A teenager with a cracked phone stood nearby, recording it all for social media.

"This The Bluff," he said into the camera. "The place where God blinked."

A local artist sat on a porch sketching the scene, charcoal smudges on his fingertips.

"I'm gon' make y'all look," he muttered. "Even if it's in a gallery full of white folks that never stepped foot here."

Same city. Different world.

While one side planted seeds, the other watered graves.

The trap thrived not because it was brilliant—but because the system was broken. And until truth reached these streets… Kilo would keep counting thirty balls.

2 plus 2 still equals 8.

But in The Bluff?
Every answer comes at a deadly cost.

CHAPTER THIRTY- SIX

THE BECOMING OF BLACKSTONE

BLACKSTONE'S PRIVATE STUDY – NIGHT

The flame of the candle flickered, dancing shadows across the bookshelves lined with sermons, Masonic literature, and framed certificates from state-level partnerships. Blackstone stared at a photo from his early days. His hand trembled slightly as he traced the edges.

FLASHBACK: WEST END CHURCH BASEMENT – LATE 1990s

He was just Elijah then. Twenty-five. Hungry. Gifted. Preaching sermons with fire that cracked ceilings. The congregation was small, but the word was mighty.

He slept in the church office most nights, surviving off gas station noodles and hope.

He didn't want fame.

He wanted freedom. For his people.

FLASHBACK: GOVERNMENT OFFICE – EARLY 2000s

That's when Wynn entered the picture.

A clean-cut man in a tailored gray suit slid a file across a mahogany desk. The file had one word on the cover: *CONTROL.*

"You want to help your people, right?" Wynn asked. "Then don't just speak to them. *Shape* them. With the right funding, structure, access—you'll be a king among men. We'll handle the paperwork. All you gotta do is keep the peace."

Blackstone hesitated. "What's the catch?"

"You manage expectations. You steer their rage. When things get too loud, you turn it down. When protests swell, you redirect. Your sermons become a strategy."

That was the day Elijah signed a silence disguised as salvation.

FLASHBACK:. ATLANTA BANQUET HALL – A FEW YEARS LATER

Now they called him *Pastor Blackstone.*

He wore Italian shoes and delivered speeches to senators, not just sinners.

At a private fundraiser, he met Camille, a well-connected attorney with a polished tongue and a guarded heart.

She was beautiful, brilliant, and embedded in elite circles.

But Camille didn't challenge his calling—she upgraded his brand.

Together, they looked untouchable.

Until he forgot who he was without her validation.

MONTAGE – YEARS LATER

Secret meetings with Homeland agents.

Whispers exchanged in D.C. green rooms.

Briefcases slid under tables.

He became the broker—not just between God and man, but between power and progress.

He approved programs that never arrived. Dismissed leaders who made too much noise.

He told himself it was balanced.

But somewhere deep down, he knew…

It was betrayal in a suit.

BACK TO PRESENT – BLACKSTONE'S STUDY

The photo fell from his lap.

His phone buzzed with a news clip—Ezekiel in Memphis, kids surrounding him, energy high.

And Blackstone felt it again—that burn from the basement years.

The one before politics. Before compromise.

Before Camille.

Before control

He was chosen.

But not by God.

By men with pens, power, and promises that turned prophets into puppets.

Now the fire was returning.

And Blackstone had a choice:

Continue the lie.

Or tear down the throne he helped build.

2 plus 2 still equals 8.

And some equations… demand redemption.

 Speak It, Build It, Live It

A movement without a story dies in silence. A movement without ownership gets auctioned off.

This ain't just about shirts and speeches anymore. It's about creating a legacy with language. Turning pain into pages. And microphones into ministry.

2 plus 2 still equals 8. But now… they're amplifying it on every platform.

#2PLUS2EQUALS8 CENTER – PODCAST ROOM – NIGHT

Dim lights. Hardwood floors. Brick backdrop with a glowing neon sign behind them: "WE BUILD."

The mics were hot. Cameras rolling. Headphones on.

Ezekiel sat at the center of the table. To his left, Malik rocked a #2Plus2Equals8 hoodie and jeans. Geneva to his right, poised, tablet in hand. Behind the glass, a teen named Bryson managed the audio. A product of the program.

Ezekiel leaned into the mic.

Ezekiel: "Tonight ain't just a podcast. It's a blueprint. Because what we are building requires more than prayers—it requires *plans*."

Malik: "And partnership. Ownership. Let's call it what it is. The revolution ain't just in marches. It's in the paperwork."

Geneva: "It's in wills, trusts, deeds. We've normalized struggle, but never security."

CENTER HALLWAY – EARLIER

Before the episode, Ezekiel sat alone in the media room. Laptop open. Fingers dancing.

He wasn't working on finances.

He was working on a script.

A film.

Based on the two Atlantas he lived between.

The Bluff. The Vision.

He typed:

"Scene 6: A mother steps over three overdoses to pick her son up from school. She never flinched. This was normal. But today, she stopped. She looks at the bodies. And finally, she cries."

Tasha walked in, reading over his shoulder.

Tasha: "That's… heavy."

Ezekiel: "So is the truth."

She kissed the back of his head

Tasha: "You're telling our story. Don't let them water it down."

PODCAST ROOM – MID RECORDING

Geneva brought in the guest—Elena, the Coca-Cola exec.

She joined virtually. Bright smile. Corporate backdrop.

Elena: "I've sat in rooms with brands, boards, and billion-dollar budgets. And I'll tell you this… they fear anything they don't understand. You all? You're creating language they can't control."

Malik: "We ain't asking for a seat at their table. We are building our own. And putting our grandmas at the head."

Elena: "My advice? Keep receipts. Protect your IP. Document *everything.* The world will catch on late, but they'll come running."

TRUTH'S BLOCK – MEANWHILE

Truth sat on his porch, watching the livestream.

Two young boys next to him. One used to trap. Now he filmed recaps of every rally.

Boy 1: "Truth, they are talking about us."

Truth: "Nah… we talking to them. About where we have been. And where we goin' if we stay locked in."

The street lights flickered.

A neighbor across the way turned their speaker up, letting the podcast echo through the block.

PODCAST ROOM – CLOSING SEGMENT

Ezekiel: "Look… legacy is not a word. It's a *witness.* A real-time testimony of what we chose to build instead of just surviving. We're gonna teach these babies how to own, how to trust, how to grow food, and how to write their story before someone else does it for them."

Malik: "You either feed the system… or starve it. And I'm done feeding it."

Geneva: "We're not finished. We're just getting better. Louder. Smarter. Bigger."

Ezekiel reached over and cut the mic.

But the message didn't stop.

They spoke life. They wrote a vision. They built a legacy.

And for the first time in a long time— The world had no choice but to *listen.*

2 plus 2 still equals 8. And now, it echoes.

CHAPTER THIRTY- SEVEN

WHEN THE CHIPS FALL

There comes a moment when the pedestal cracks. When the mask peels. When the ones who rose on favors and fear finally come face to face with accountability.

And just like that—everything starts to fall.

ATLANTA STREETS – EARLY MORNING

It started with the tow trucks. Three of them.

Parked neatly outside Blackstone's Buckhead estate. Two black Cadillacs, a foreign sports coupe, and one matte black Range Rover were hooked and hauled.

By the time Camille opened the front door, a news van had already arrived.

Cameras rolled. Mics shoved forward.

REPORTER: "Reverend Blackstone, sources confirm three separate liens have been filed by two banks and a private lender. Any comment on the financial investigation?"

Blackstone stood silent in a gray robe. No chains. No rings. Just exposed.

The world is watching.

ERNESTINE'S LIVING ROOM – SAME TIME

Ernestine sat on her recliner, cup of instant coffee in one hand, remote in the other.

Ernestine: "Well, look at God. Ain't He poetic?"

ROSE: *(watching from the kitchen)* "Damn... he really losin' it all."

Then she smirked. Slow. Devilish.

Rose: "Sometimes karma doesn't knock. It just kicks the damn door in."

CITY HALL – INVESTIGATION CONFERENCE ROOM

A dozen men and women in suits sat at a long glass table. Laptop screens lit with digital spreadsheets and flagged wire transfers.

AGENT THOMPSON: "The misappropriation of church development funds is now under formal review. There are at least six shell accounts under different LLCs. All tracing back to Blackstone."

A silent consensus moved around the room.

The wolves were circling.

LEGACY LAND – CLOSING DAY

Sun beaming. Cameras flashing.

The Big Three stood on the porch of a sprawling ranch-style home—the first house built on the 40 acres.

Reporters packed the lawn. Local students, elders, and volunteers filled the drive.

Ezekiel stepped forward in a crisp white tee and slacks. In his hands, a massive gold-painted key.

He held it up to the sky.

Ezekiel: "This isn't just land. This is a legacy. This is where our babies will run safe, our elders will rest proud, and our future will be planted and protected. One brick, one breath, one blessing at a time."

Applause erupted.

Malik and Geneva flanked him. Truth stood with the former dealers now turned builders, all wearing navy tees that read: *OWNERSHIP OR NOTHING.*

TASHA'S SHOP – MIDDAY

The TV was turned up. Tasha and three clients watched Ezekiel's speech live.

Tasha: *(smiling)* "That's my man. Told y'all he was a builder."

The women laughed and clapped.

Naomi walked in with a juice box, her mom beside her.

Naomi's Mom: "He's really doing it, huh?"

Naomi: *(grinning)* "That's my daddy."

Darryl, sitting in the waiting area, grunted.

Darryl: "Anybody can run their mouth. Let's see how long it lasts."

Tasha rolled her eyes.

SOUTH ATLANTA – DRE'S MOM'S COUCH

Dre sat on the couch in basketball shorts, watching the news with greasy fingers and a bitter jaw.

Dre: "Ain't nothin' special about dude. He just got lucky. That's all."

His mom walked past with a laundry basket.

Dre's Mom: "He out there changin' the city. You in here changing the channel."

He ignored her.

WEST END BARBERSHOP – SAME TIME

Kam and Marcus stood outside watching the TV in the window.

When Ezekiel held the key up, they high-fived.

Marcus: "He came from nothin', dawg. And now look."

Kam: "Yeah... now it's all up from here."

Blackstone's empire was unraveling. Ezekiel's vision was rising.

And the people?

They were watching closely.

Some with hope. Some with hate.

But none could deny—

2 plus 2 still equals 8.

And today, the math belonged to the movement.

CHAPTER THIRTY- EIGHT

THE QUIET BEFORE THE COLLISION

HOMELAND SECURITY BRIEFING ROOM – MORNING

A gray conference room. Sealed windows. Ten men and women in suits. A digital board glowed behind them, cycling images—Ezekiel, Malik, Geneva, Truth. Dossiers. Bank accounts. Family photos. Footage from the 40 acres.

A voice broke the silence.

AGENT ROTH: "It's time to roll up our sleeves."

AGENT LARSEN: "We've planted moles before. But this time, we go closer. Someone personal. Someone he trusts."

AGENT CHAMBERS: *(flipping a file)* "Dre. Government name, DeAndre R. Fulton. Old juvenile record. Same detention center as Ezekiel. Same zip code. Living back with his mom. Bitter. Broke. Perfect."

AGENT ROTH: "We send the message. Lure him with pride. Let him feel seen. Then we plant the story—he reconnects with Ezekiel. Offers help. But slides in a package. Enough to tie the whole group."

AGENT LARSEN: "It'll look clean. A few former dealers on the land. Truth's past. Ezekiel's own juvenile record for possession. The media will eat it up."

AGENT THORNE: "And if we time it right... we can have Blackstone's old church seized by the state, then auctioned."

A beat.

AGENT CHAMBERS: "We bait the trap, let it simmer, then burn it all down."

LEGACY LAND – LATE MORNING

It was quiet. Sacred.

A line of barefoot families walked the green field slowly, arms interlocked. Some prayed aloud. Others sang.

Children chased butterflies between rows of soil freshly turned. Volunteers knelt in gardens. Truth stood with two ex-trappers-turned-carpenters, reading from Proverbs under the shade.

TRUTH: "Jonah ran and ended up in the belly. Moses doubted and still led a nation. Maybe we are all flawed, but we ain't finished."

Ezekiel watched from the porch of the ranch house. Malik beside him. Geneva approached with iced tea in hand.

Ezekiel: "You know what I was thinking? If Blackstone's church comes up for auction… we should buy it."

Geneva raised an eyebrow. And smiled slowly.

Geneva: "Now you talkin'. Turn the pulpit that is divided into a platform that builds."

Truth joined, his hands dusty.

Truth: "I have been studying more lately. Not just the word. The meaning behind it. And I keep coming back to this—God doesn't need perfect people. Just prepared ones."

BLACKSTONE'S PRIVATE SUITE –

BAHAMAS – SAME TIME

The balcony overlooked blue water that stretched beyond sins. Blackstone sipped wine. Camille counted files on a secure laptop.

Blackstone: "These offshore accounts… best thing we ever did."

Camille: "They can't find what they can't trace. And if they do?"

Blackstone: "We'll already be somewhere they don't speak English or accountability."

She shut the laptop. For a moment, silence.

Camille: "I still remember when you spoke for the people I'm not going to run."

Blackstone: "Now I speak for the protection of what we built. Let them drown in sermons. We sailing. Not running"

The kids had calmed. Families sat around benches. Ezekiel gave Naomi a piggyback ride across the field. Malik prayed with two teenagers. Tasha braided hair under a tree while the older women prepared a pot of stew over an open flame.

Geneva stood at the front porch, barefoot in the dirt, eyes closed, the weight of the ancestors on her breath.

She whispered:

Geneva: "Until the lion tells his side of the story, the tale of the hunt will always glorify the hunter."

The seeds were planted. But so were the traps.

And while Legacy grew in light,

The shadows were coming to collect.

2 plus 2 still equals 8.

And the harvest? Would test every root.

CHAPTER THIRTY- NINE

FROM CONCRETE TO FIRE

Before Malik was a strategist. Before he shook hands with bank execs and held prayer circles in boardrooms—

He was a boy with bruised knuckles, A voice too loud for silence, And a heart that burned for something *more.*

This ain't just how Malik became a leader.

This is how the system made the mistake of letting him live long enough to change it.

FLASHBACK: ATLANTA, AGE 14

Rain hit hard that night. The kind that soaked through your hoodie and your bones.

Malik sprinted through the back alley behind an abandoned duplex. One pocket full of nickel bags. The other, a screwdriver he used to pop the back windows of empty houses.

He didn't steal for sport. He stole because food stamps don't stretch when you got two siblings and a mom working double shifts still wasn't enough to feed five kids.

That night, the cops were two blocks in the area at the night time —but the cameras weren't. He did few days in juvenile and a court date

His mom cried. His caseworker sighed. The judge didn't flinch.

JUDGE: "Group home. Ninety-day minimum. Review pending behavior."

Malik just stared.

He'd seen worse.

GROUP HOME – FULTON COUNTY – NIGHT

The walls were stained. The beds creaked like broken promises. Two boys shared one bunk. One window had been boarded up since '97.

The food was cold. Showers had no curtains.

Malik spoke up on day three.

Malik (age 15): "Yo, y'all getting money from the state and feeding us expired beans? Where's the budget?"

The staff shrugged. One laughed.

But the boys listened.

He stood up again after lights out.

Malik: "Ain't no way I'm lettin' grown men pocket checks while we rot in here."

By week two, he was holding meetings. Circling complaints. Organizing. Writing to officials.

The director warned him.

GROUP HOME DIRECTOR: "You doin' too much. Fall in line."

Malik stared him dead in the eye.

Malik: "I ain't built for lines. I *drew* them."

FLASH FORWARD: JOB CORPS CAMPUS – AGE 16

After running away from the home, Malik ended up at the Job Corps in Savannah. Showed up with nothing but a duffle and that same fire.

He organized night study sessions. Pushed for clean meals. Helped the GED pass rate double in four months.

By 18, he was Student Body President.

Then the cameras came.

WSAV LOCAL NEWS: "Meet the young man transforming Job Corps from survival to leadership."

It aired at 6PM.

Back in Atlanta, that old group home director saw it.

And called it in.

JOB CORPS CAMPUS – NEXT DAY

Malik walked across the field in khakis and a school tee.

A crowd gathered. Cheering. Chanting.

He was going to speak at a campus rally.

That's when the police pulled up.

Three cruisers.

They didn't even wait for the ceremony to finish.

OFFICER: "Malik Rowland, you're under arrest for absconding from state custody."

Gasps. Screams. Phones out.

Malik raised his hands slowly.

Malik (calmly): "It's cool. They can take me. But the spark's already lit."

He looked at the crowd.

Eyes filled with tears, fists raised in the air.

JUVENILE DETENTION – CELL BLOCK – NIGHT

Malik sat on the edge of the bunk. No more tears. Just thought.

He remembered that rally crowd. The chants. The energy.

They weren't just cheering for him.

They were cheering for the version of themselves that still had fight.

That's when he knew.

He wasn't born to sell corners. He was born to *build kingdoms.*

BACK TO PRESENT – LEGACY LAND – DUSK

Malik stood barefoot on the same soil they just broke ground on. Watching kids play. Watching young men hammer. Watching the system shake.

He whispered under his breath:

Malik: "I was arrested in front of crowds. Now I build for 'em."

You can't kill purpose. You can only delay it.

And Malik?

He's walking proof that sometimes the cage just sharpens the calling.

2 plus 2 still equals 8.

And now the math includes him.

LEGACY LAND – MID-MORNING SUN

The wind carried the scent of red Georgia clay and ambition. Near the edge of the property, Ezekiel leaned on a folding table set up under a white tent. A digital tablet lit up with slides, designs, and an idea taking shape.

Across from him stood Julian Mays, an ex-Silicon Valley tech architect in tan loafers and a crisp linen shirt. He once built backend systems for one of the world's largest streaming platforms. Now, he stood barefoot, toes pressed into dirt he once ignored.

Ezekiel: "I don't want just a film. I want a platform. An app. For *us*. For our movies. Our stories. So nobody gets to edit our struggle into palatable pieces."

Julian swiped across the screen, eyes sharp.

Julian: "You want it custom-coded? You'll need about 50K to do it right. Full backend, ecommerce, live streaming—no ads unless you sell them."

Ezekiel: "We got seed money. We got coders from the youth lab. And I already got ten scripts waiting for light."

Julian grinned. "You're not building a brand. You're building a digital revolution."

ON THE PORCH – TEN MINUTES LATER

Ezekiel rejoined Malik, Geneva, and Truth where they sat overlooking the clearing where workers hammered new frames into red clay.

Ezekiel: "You know how Atlanta's become a film capital, right? Tyler Perry built his own lot. What's stopping us?"

Geneva: "Studios. Sets. Infrastructure. Shoot documentaries here, plays, indie films. Control the location, the budget, the message."

Malik: "Hell, why not? Legacy Studios. We put our history on record. Teach these kids that storytelling *is* ownership."

A breeze kicked up. Laughter rang out nearby as kids ran past with wooden hammers.

DANTE (Investor Mentor) APPROACHES

Dante strolled up with two assistants behind him, both holding leather portfolios. He wore slim slacks and spoke like every word was worth interest.

Dante: "Y'all building dreams. I came to talk about legacy."

He opened one of the folders and laid out printouts.

Dante: "You need to form a REIT—Real Estate Investment Trust. Let your members buy shares of the land they are building on. Ownership becomes equity. Passive income *and* generational."

Truth leaned in.

Truth: "Break that down again?"

Dante: "You put a hundred folks in. They each buy in monthly. Your properties grow. You pay dividends. Wealth becomes group-centered—not government-granted."

Then Dante tapped another page.

Dante: "And these—IULs. Indexed Universal Life policies. Tax-free growth. Borrow against it. Leave it behind. It's what the elite use to stay elite. Quiet wealth. Private power."

Geneva: "Let's add that to the curriculum. We're framing ten houses now— we need to lay the foundation in our minds too."

DESIGN CENTER TENT – MINUTES LATER

Malik sat with a clipboard going over pledges. Nearby, a young man in bright yellow and jet-black streetwear paced, energy high. His name was BadSmith, a local rapper and streetwear mogul with a cult following.

He had gold teeth, passion in his chest, and a business brain behind the grill.

BadSmith: "Yo, y'all building' like Noah, I swear. Lemme get in on this. We bring my hoodwear line, I teach the youth to print, stitch, design—and I invest ten racks now. More later."

Malik dabbed him.

Malik: "Bet. Let's build a fashion lab in the old barn."

Moments later, two athletes walked up—Jae Rivers, an NFL running back, and Keyron Mills, an NBA shooting guard. Both Atlanta-born, both quiet about their money, but loud about their roots.

Keyron: "Y'all got farmland, right? Let's build basketball courts and solar panels on half of it."

Jae: "And I'll cover uniforms, tutoring, and three community events a year. I ain't tryna throw money—I'm tryna change family trees."

Truth grabbed the whiteboard.

Geneva started drafting partnership memos.

Ezekiel just stood back.

Watching.

Smiling.

Breathing.

From film to farming. From code to concrete.

This wasn't a moment. This was a movement.

2 plus 2 still equals 8. And now?

The world couldn't ignore the math.

CHAPTER FORTY

WE SPEAK, THEREFORE WE BUILD

#2PLUS2EQUALS8 COMMUNITY CENTER – EARLY EVENING

The energy inside the room pulsed like electricity trapped in wood. Folding chairs were pushed to the side, walls lined with shoulders and eyes. Standing room only. The old community center creaked under the weight of transformation.

People from all over Atlanta filled every inch—barbers, ex-cons, single mothers, entrepreneurs, kids with notebooks in hand. The Big Three stood at the front. Truth nearby, hands behind his back, posture like a guard and a guide.

Malik stepped forward first.

Malik: "They told us our voices didn't matter unless we sang about pain or violence. But what if our voices build policy? What if we write the future instead of surviving someone else's script?"

He paused. The crowd was silent. Leaning in.

Malik: "Nelson Mandela once said: *'Education is the most powerful weapon which you can use to change the world.'* That's what this is. This center. This movement. It's our weapon."

Geneva stepped next, tablet in hand. Her voice was warm but sharp.

Geneva: "Napoleon Hill said, *'Whatever the mind can conceive and believe, it can achieve.'* But only if that mind is free. Free from fear. From poverty. From mental chains."

She tapped her heart.

Geneva: "Your mind is currency. Your action is compound interest."

People nodded. A few clapped.

Truth moved next, raw and direct.

Truth: "I used to put pain in plastic bags. Now I preach prosperity. Robert Kiyosaki said in *Rich Dad, Poor Dad, 'The single most powerful asset we all have is our mind. If it is trained well, it can create enormous wealth.'*"

He looked around the room.

Truth: "This movement ain't about clout. It's about clarity. You are an asset. Train your mind. Own your name. Build your table."

Ezekiel stepped to the front, Bible in one hand, rolled blueprint in the other.

He paused. Then let his voice boom.

Ezekiel: "Willie Lynch taught how to keep us bound—not by chains, but by *conditioning.* Light skin vs. dark. Old vs. young. Field vs. house. Male vs. female. If we still act like that, we are proving his plan is still working."

He pointed to the crowd.

Ezekiel: "Marcus Garvey said, *'A people without knowledge of their past history, origin and culture is like a tree without roots.'* This center? These acres? This movement? It's our roots finding soil again."

The crowd erupted.

BACK WALL – WYNN RECORDING

Wynn stood in the shadows, phone held low, camera rolling. His eyes were cold. His suit is clean. He whispered into a Bluetooth earpiece.

Wynn: "They're growing faster than expected. We'll need to fracture from the inside."

CENTER – MOMENTS LATER

Marcus and Kemo stood off to the side near the back. They were locked in. Humbled.

That's when Dre walked in.

Marcus tensed. Kemo squinted.

Kemo: "Isn't that…?"

Marcus: "Yeah. That's Dre. What is he doing here?"

Dre walked slowly. Calm. No hoodie. Just eyes that looked different. Like something cracked open inside.

Ezekiel saw him. Stopped.

Ezekiel: "Dre."

Dre nodded.

Dre: "I come in peace. I've been watching. Listening. I was wrong. I wanna help."

Marcus: "You sure this ain't a stunt?"

Dre: "Man, look. I got two nephews asking me if I know Zeke. And I couldn't lie. But now? I wanna say I stood next to him. Not against."

Ezekiel smiled. He stepped forward.

Ezekiel: "It takes strength to admit you were wrong. Takes more to do something about it. Welcome home, bruh."

They dabbed. The crowd cheered softly.

OUTSIDE THE CENTER – SUNSET

People spilled into the parking lot. Kids jumped rope. Elders debated Scripture. Teens passed out flyers for workshops.

Rose and Ernestine handed out water bottles, laughing, fussing at young boys to pull up their pants.

Tasha and Elijah handed out pamphlets printed with bold headers:

"YOUR MINDSET IS YOUR FIRST PROPERTY."

"#2PLUS2EQUALS8: THE FUTURE AIN'T FREE, BUT IT'S OURS."

From quotes to questions. From doubters to disciples.

They weren't just organizing a movement.

They were awakening people.

2 plus 2 still equals 8. And tonight, they didn't just hear it.

They *believed* it.

CHAPTER FORTY- ONE

BLOODLINES AND BACKDOORS

LEGACY LAND – ROSE'S CABIN – EARLY EVENING

Rose's phone buzzed twice.

The room was warm, filled with the sound of family laughter, plates clinking, the soft hum of old-school soul playing from a Bluetooth speaker.

Ezekiel sat at the head of the table, his son Elijah beside him biting into a fried chicken wing, Naomi laughing at something Tasha whispered in her ear. Geneva passed cornbread. Truth and Malik loaded up plates across from them.

Rose's hand trembled as she looked at the screen.

TEXT MESSAGE:

"I think it's time you let him know who his father is."

Her breath caught. The room blurred.

Ernestine noticed first.

Ernestine: "You alright, baby?"

Ezekiel turned from his plate, eyes narrowing.

Ezekiel: "Mama, you okay?"

She forced a smile, standing with her plate half-finished.

Rose: "Yeah… yeah, just need to use the bathroom. This lemonade hitting' too hard."

She disappeared down the hallway.

GENEVA'S OFFICE – SAME TIME

Camille sat with her legs crossed, sipping tea with both hands like she needed something to hold her together.

Camille: "Sometimes I wonder who I married. Blackstone wasn't always this man. He used to fight for something."

Geneva nodded slowly.

Geneva: "Power changes folks. But silence? That breaks 'em. Have you ever spoken your truth to him?"

Camille: "I tried. He smiled… and then dismissed me like I was quoting fairy tales."

Geneva leaned in, her voice soft but sharp.

Geneva: "You can't change a man who thinks his darkness is divine. But you can choose whether or not to keep worshipping his shadow."

Camille's eyes welled, but she blinked fast.

Camille: "I needed to hear that. I hate how much I still love him. And I hate how I'm afraid to stop."

Geneva reached over, gripped her hand.

Geneva: "Ain't no weakness in walking away. But there's power in naming your chains before you cut 'em."

MALIK'S CABIN PORCH – LATER THAT NIGHT

Truth leaned on the rail, his face tight with conflict. Malik tossed a few logs on the firepit and sat back, listening.

Truth: "I ain't seen my sons in months. Not 'cause I don't want to—but because I don't know what I might do if I see *her*."

Malik: "You still think she set you up?"

Truth: "I *know* she did. She cried crocodile tears and texted Kilo while I was bleeding out."

Malik shook his head.

Malik: "That pain is real. But don't give her the power to make you abandon what's yours."

Truth pulled out his phone.

Truth: "You're right."

He hit *FaceTime*. The screen lit up. Two boys appeared—one around 8, the other maybe 12. They were in a living room, watching basketball.

Nasir: "DADDY!"

Truth: *(choked)* "Wassup, soldiers?"

Nasir: "When are you coming to see us?"

Truth: "Soon. Real soon. Y'all okay?"

Kwame: "Mom says you are working hard. We are proud of you."

Malik turned his head, wiping his eyes.

Truth's jaw tightened, voice barely holding.

Truth: "I'm proud of y'all too. Just remember, your last name means something now. We are building something real."

Kwame: "We know. We part of #2Plus2Equals8."

The call ended, but the silence afterward was sacred.

ROSE'S BATHROOM – SAME TIME

Rose sat on the edge of the tub, phone in her lap, hands shaking.

A younger photo of Ezekiel stared back at her from the gallery.

She whispered to herself:

Rose: "You ain't just my boy. You his son too. And he needs to know."

She thought about the pain. The broken promises. The man who left her scared and pregnant and disappeared into politics.

But also about the strength Ezekiel had become. What truth could unlock. What healing it could start.

A choice had to be made.

And soon.

The truth doesn't always knock with kindness.

Sometimes it shows up with a mirror.

2 plus 2 still equals 8.

But tonight, some numbers… carried blood.

CHAPTER FORTY- TWO

STORMS, CHOICES, AND CROSSROADS

THE BLUFF – NIGHT – RAIN FALLING HARD

It wasn't just rain. It was a flood baptized in struggle. The kind of rain that turned the red clay of the Westside into mud that held secrets and soaked shoes like it knew every name buried beneath the surface.

But the cars still came.

Old Crown Vics. Bentleys on forgivable rims. Mom vans with missing hubcaps. They lined up deep into the side streets, headlights cutting through the downpour like knives.

At the center of it all stood Kilo's trap, glowing under green-tinted floodlights. The paint peeled, the roof sagged—but it was alive. It pulsed like a heartbeat too strong for the city to ignore.

Four boys no older than 16 moved like clockwork between the cars. Hoodies soaked. Eyes sharp. Each had one job: pills, powder, payment, patrol.

One kid knocked on a window.

Zonex: "Do you want the heroin pill or the quiet one?"

Driver: "Give me the fire. I need to disappear tonight."

Zonex didn't blink. Bag in. Cash out. On to the next.

Narration:

This wasn't a nickel-and-dime hustle. This was warfare. Chemical colonization. Pills replacing bullets. And Kilo? He was the general with no conscience.

KILO'S TRAP – LIVING ROOM – SAME TIME

Kilo leaned back on a faux leather couch, shirt off, tattoos glistening with sweat and power. His gold grill caught the flicker of the big screen TV where NBA2K blasted at full volume. His two shooters played controller for controller while a third rolled up.

Kilo was on the phone.

KILO: "Yeah, bring the 200 thou pills. I already sent half the bag."

VOICE: "That's heavy weight, Kilo. You not playin' the block no more. You're playing' chess with coffins."

KILO: "I know. It's time. I'm done dipping' toes in the trap. I want the whole damn city addicted. Eastside. South. West. I'm turnin' Atlanta into a kingdom of nods."

He hung up. Looked around.

KILO (to his crew): "We're gonna be richer than every preacher in this town. Streets ours now."

They laughed. Loud. Ugly.

BANDO – ACROSS THE STREET – NIGHT

Two DEA agents watched from behind a boarded-up window. Steam from their breath curled in the cold air. One held a long lens camera, the other scribbled notes.

DEA Griffin: "Two hundred thousand pills. That's enough to bury this city and sell roses on top."

DEA Cousin: "We don't move fast, he's gonna have every corner strung out. I'm callin' Washington. This ain't just a bust—this is chemical terrorism."

He pulled out a burner phone.

DEA 2: "This ain't street war no more. It's genocide in disguise."

MAYOR'S OFFICE – LATE AFTERNOON

The sun bled orange and gold through the massive bay windows of the Atlanta mayor's office. The wood-paneled walls reflected years of polished promises, but today—power felt different.

The Big Three sat across from the mayor at a long obsidian table. He wore a tailored burgundy suit, tie undone, energy humming with tension. Behind him, a painting of Frederick Douglass stared like it could hear every word.

MAYOR: "Y'all moving mountains. I ain't seen unity like this since the civil rights marches. But now it's time to show 'em we ain't just organized—we're unstoppable."

Ezekiel: "We ain't askin' for permission. We askin' how far the city is willing to go with us."

Malik: "The people out here dying. Not just from bullets—but from slow poison. Pills, poverty, promises that never cash. We ain't here for photo ops—we're here to flip the whole damn table."

Geneva: "We want a city-sponsored *Future Festival*. Hosted at Legacy Land. Solar booths. Live podcasts. Healing tents. Legal aid. Job offers. Black excellence on full display."

MAYOR: *(leaning forward)* "Let's do it. Full resources. Press coverage. Helicopters if needed. Let's give this city something to live for."

They shook hands. Fire behind every grip.

SUBURBAN HOME – ELENA'S KITCHEN – SAME TIME

Elena stood barefoot on polished marble floors, sleeves rolled, afro wrapped. Her white husband, Bryce, leaned on the fridge with a wine glass, half listening, half annoyed.

ELENA: "I'm leaving Coca-Cola."

BRYCE: "Excuse me?"

ELENA: "I'm investing in #2Plus2Equals8. Full-time. This isn't just a trend. This is the real movement."

BRYCE: *(laughs bitterly)* "These things always start with passion. Then they burn out. You've made it. Why throw it away to play Harriet Tubman?"

ELENA: *(stepping closer)* "You don't get it. You never have. My success doesn't mean shit if it comes with silence. I'm tired of living in the house and watching the village burn."

BRYCE: "You'll ruin your reputation. Your future."

ELENA: "Then I'll build a new one. One where I don't have to step over my people to sleep next to you."

She walked past him. He called after her.

BRYCE: "You'll regret this."

She didn't look back.

ELENA: "Only thing I regret… is waiting this long."

The storm came hard. And so did the decisions.

Kilo wanted the city's veins. The Big Three wanted its soul.

And somewhere between the trap and the mayor's chair,

The fight for Atlanta's future raged silent and loud.

2 plus 2 still equals 8. And every number… Carried blood.

CHAPTER FORTY- THREE

FULL CIRCLE

PENTHOUSE BALCONY – NIGHT – MIDTOWN ATLANTA

Blackstone stood high above the city, the skyline glowing beneath a murky sky. Atlanta looked different from up here—less like a home, more like a kingdom he was losing brick by brick.

A bottle of tequila dangled from his hand. His robe hung open like his past—tattered, vulnerable.

BLACKSTONE (to himself): "Used to be mine... every block, every soul, every hand raised in my church. Now they are chanting that boy's name."

He took another swig, leaned over the railing.

FLASHBACK – INT. MOTEL 6 – EARLY 90s

Dim lights flickered above faded sheets. Blackstone buttoned his shirt, eyes on the mirror—not on Rose, who sat on the bed holding a test in trembling hands.

ROSE: "I'm pregnant."

BLACKSTONE (cold): "You knew the rules."

ROSE: "Elijah, please..."

BLACKSTONE: "Good luck, Rose. Don't call me again."

He walked out, slamming the door behind him.

BACK TO PRESENT – BALCONY

His voice cracked as he whispered into the wind.

BLACKSTONE: "Outta all my kids, he is the one who got my fire... But more. He kept the light. And I left him in the dark."

ROSE'S KITCHEN – NIGHT

Rain tapped the windows like old memories. Rose sat at the kitchen table, vodka sweating in her glass. The text glared back from her screen:

"Time to tell him."

She read it again. And again.

ROSE (softly): "It's time. Can't run any more."

She took a long breath, then typed.

Ezekiel, we need to talk.

She hit send. Closed her eyes.

LEGACY LAND – MORNING SUNLIGHT CUTTING THROUGH TREES

Dre hauled two-by-fours like his freedom depended on it. He moved dirt, cut grass, and fixed panels. Sweat soaked through his shirt, but his eyes burned with something new.

Marcus leaned against a truck, arms folded.

KEMO: "Dre out here like he's running' for mayor."

MARCUS: "Nah. He runnin' from something'. Or maybe toward it. Either way, it looks real."

KEMO: "You trust it?"

MARCUS: "I trust patterns. If he stays movin' like this… we'll know."

TRUTH'S ROOM – EARLY AFTERNOON

Truth sat on his bed, phone in hand. His knuckles tight, jaw tighter.

He stared at a photo—two boys smiling with Kool-Aid lips.

He hit the composer.

TEXT (to his kids' mother):

"It's time. I want to see my sons. Let's make it happen. Soon."

He didn't hit send yet.

TRUTH (to himself): "They got **my name.** But they don't know my voice. That ends now."

FEDERAL BUILDING – DEEP BRIEFING ROOM – LATE NIGHT

A dim, cold room designed for strategy—not justice. Screens displayed shipment routes, photos of pills, street-level intel. A map of Atlanta glowed blood red in heat zones.

The room was silent until a CIA official stood and spoke with surgical precision.

CIA OPERATIVE: "Atlanta is becoming a problem. Not because of crime. Because of *consciousness*."

Eyes turned toward him.

CIA OPERATIVE: "We watched this before. Montgomery. Oakland. Detroit. Every time a Black movement gets too unified, too financially independent, too loud—we lose control."

He clicked a slide.

Images of #2Plus2Equals8 rallies. Ezekiel's speeches. The podcast. Kids learning to code. Women owning salons. Men building homes.

CIA OPERATIVE (cont'd): "After King, we vowed never again. Atlanta is a powder keg—too much pride, too much strategy. So, we going pull an old page out the book look the other way while drugs flood the streets not crack but Pills. Despair, make the revolutionaries fight ghosts and grief. Dead bodies speak quieter than leaders."

DEA AGENT 1: "You mean let this poison in?"

CIA OPERATIVE: "Not let. *Deploy.* Create chaos. Criminalize the saviors. Feed addiction. Collapse vision before it grows teeth."

One younger agent turned pale.

DEA AGENT 2 (under breath): "This is genocide with a suit on."

But he said nothing more. Just watched the plan unfold.

TASHA'S BRAID SHOP – SOUTH ATLANTA – GOLDEN HOUR

Inside the shop, the hum of clippers, laughter, and purpose created a sacred rhythm.

Tasha stood in the center, watching young women teach each other—hair, business, healing.

TASHA: "This ain't just braids. This is our economy. This is our legacy. What they kill in corners, we rebirth in culture."

She walked past a young girl braiding with one hand, holding a vision board in the other.

TASHA (to her): "You got gold in your fingers, baby. Now build an empire with it."

Posters on the wall read:

"Build with your hands. Lead with your mind." "#2Plus2Equals8 — A Movement Rooted in Resurrection."

The silence in boardrooms birthed storms in the streets. But Black people knew how to dance in rain and rise from ashes.

The poison was coming.

But so were the builders.

So were the mothers, the fathers, the children who knew their names.

2 plus 2 still equals 8.

And in Atlanta? The math was about to make history.

CHAPTER FORTY- FOUR

THE JUDAS HANDSHAKE DEEPER EMOTION AND STRATEGY)

The night before the betrayal, Dre sat on the back steps of the framing shed, his eyes wet with a pain he couldn't name.

Rain clung to the air, but it wasn't falling. Just heavy—like the weight on his chest. His jeans were still dusty, his boots kicked off. He watched the solar lights flicker across Legacy Land as kids darted through the grass, laughing like freedom was normal.

He'd seen it that afternoon—Kyree, the kid with crooked glasses, using a drill for the first time. Dre helped him tighten a board and the boy said, "You really from the streets?"

Dre nodded.

The boy smiled and said, "wow and now you are here."

Dre hadn't cried in years. But he cried that night.

MIDTOWN HOTEL – PRIVATE SUITE – MIDDAY

The room smelled like oak, money, and malice. Wynn stood near the bar, pouring dark liquor into two crystal glasses. He wore a slate-gray suit, gold cufflinks catching the light. Dre stood across from him, hoodie up, jaw clenched.

WYNN: "You could be a king, Dre. Instead, you're hammerin' nails for free?"

DRE: "I'm good."

WYNN: "No, you broke. Let me fix that."

He slid the listening device across the table. Then placed a manila envelope beside it—cash visible at the corners.

WYNN (leaning in): "Plant this in the podcast studio. We need the dirt. Intercept the strategy. The government doesn't care about their talk—but they are terrified of their *plans*."

He sipped.

WYNN (cold): "Atlanta's not about money. It's about momentum. And your little crew is gaining too damn much."

Dre didn't speak. But when Wynn turned to the bar, Dre slipped his phone out, tapped 'Record,' and slid it behind his bag.

He caught it all.

Every word.

UPSCALE CAFÉ – MIDTOWN – LATE AFTERNOON

The back patio was quiet, birds fluttering in planters, espresso machines hissing in the distance. Geneva, Elena, and Camille sat in a booth under an umbrella, hands wrapped around teacups like they were holding legacy.

CAMILLE (fidgeting): "I didn't think I'd ever say this out loud—but I don't know who Blackstone is anymore. He used to quote scripture. Now he is quoting stock reports."

ELENA: "You're not alone. My husband Bryce? Every time I say the word 'movement,' he hears 'rebellion.' Says I should be grateful. Stay in my lane. Smile. I told him… my smile ain't for sale."

Geneva leaned in, her voice calm but fierce.

GENEVA: "We are the movement. Not the men who fear it. You know how many women are the backbone of history—but get left out the pages? No more."

CAMILLE (choked): "I still love him. But I love the truth more."

ELENA (nodding): "I left a six-figure job. You think that was easy? But freedom costs more than money. My soul couldn't afford silence."

Geneva reached out, laid a hand over theirs.

GENEVA: "Our grandmothers marched with babies on their hips. We build with blueprints and balance sheets. You're not walking away. You're walking *toward it.*"

They sat in silence, tears held and respected. Then they laughed. Deep. Healing. Powerful.

CAMILLE: "Let's call it what it is. We're *the revolution's spine.*"

ELENA: "And we stand tall."

GENEVA: "Then let's plan like queens. Shield the movement. Guide the voices. Protect the vision."

LEGACY LAND – SUNSET

Dre returned with the bug in his pocket and fire in his heart. The kids were still running. One girl handed him a picture she drew—him standing next to Ezekiel, both wearing capes.

GIRL: "You're heroes now."

He smiled. It hurt.

That night, in his room, Dre hit 'Record' and spoke.

DRE (softly): "They thought I'd sell the movement. But they forgot I been sold out before. Ain't sellin' what saved me."

He packaged the audio, the bug, and the cash. Labeled the envelope:

"Dirty money and lies."

He put it in a box

Sometimes betrayal is a mirror. And sometimes, that mirror cracks before the knife is drawn.

In this movement, even the broken are being rebuilt.

2 plus 2 still equals 8.

And the math? Now includes justice.

CHAPTER FORTY- FIVE

PROPHETS IN THE TRAP

They gathered in a circle beneath the tall oaks on Legacy Land—no podiums, no pulpit, just folding chairs, lanterns, and the weight of unspoken truths.

It was nightfall. Flames from the fire pit licked the night sky as the people sat close—old heads, young bloods, single mothers, ex-hustlers, and men trying to father children they hadn't seen in years. The hum of cicadas mixed with the scent of wood smoke and Black purpose.

Truth stood with his hands in his pockets. His eyes are glossy, not from weed or drink, but memory.

TRUTH: "I used to sell the same poison that killed my cousin. I ain't say it out loud before tonight. It started with $80 to help my mama buy groceries. Then it was Jordans. Then it was a chain. And before I knew it, I was servin' death with a smile."

He looked out. Faces stared back. No judgment. Just reflection.

TRUTH (cont'd): "But I was never the only one. The system taught us the hustle—just never how to build. Told us to get the bag but never showed us how to keep it. And every time we stacked, they moved the finish line."

A silence fell.

Then Big Rico, former corner god from Vine City, leaned forward.

BIG RICO: "You wanna talk Atlanta? I remember Auburn Ave when Black folks owned every damn thing. Barber Shops. Banks. Insurance offices. The pride was thicker than the smog. But when the crack hit, it came with a plan. They aimed it at us like a missile dressed in a Newport box."

JUNIOR, an OG from Bankhead, nodded hard.

JUNIOR: "Real talk. Some of us joined gangs not 'cause we wanted to bang— but 'cause it was family. Ain't no daddies in the house. The block raised us. But the block doesn't have an exit plan."

OLD HEAD BARBER, gray-bearded and wise, sat back in his chair, arms crossed. His voice came slow and deliberate, the kind that made people lean in.

BARBER: "I cut hair in Atlanta 42 years ago. Seen boys become men, and empires built then fall on dope. But before that? After the Civil War, this city was the Black Phoenix. We rose from ashes. We built churches, colleges—Morehouse, Spelman—back when the cotton fields still whispered our names. Auburn Avenue was the Wall Street of the South."

He looked around the fire.

BARBER (cont'd): "They didn't kill us with hate alone. They killed us with envy, then policy. Urban renewal? Just another word for displacement. They took our blocks, called it progress, and left us with crack and the projects."

The crowd was still. Listening.

A young man—Tyree, barely 19, with gold tips in his locs and pain in his eyes—stood.

TYREE: "I was gonna rob Miss Tasha's shop."

Gasps. A few murmurs. But no one got up.

TYREE (cont'd): "I was broke. Mad. Thought it was survival. But I watched y'all podcasts one night. Malik says 'Knowledge is compound. Stack it right and it outlives your mistakes.' That line… that stopped me."

Tasha sat at the edge of the circle. She nodded. Her voice caught.

TASHA: "Thank you for not robbin' me. But thank you more for showin' up tonight."

MALIK stepped forward. His voice was quiet thunder.

MALIK: "We are not marching for peace. We are not marching for no more damn rights. We marching' for ownership. We teach' how to read contracts, not chants. You wanna fight injustice? Get financially literate. Own your land. Fund your children's dreams."

He looked around.

MALIK (cont'd): "God didn't call us to just survive. He called us to the steward. And if you too broke to think, you too bound to hear God."

A few men wiped their eyes. Some gripped knees, holding back sobs that weren't allowed in prison but flowed freely here.

Then they noticed him.

Ezekiel. Quiet. Standing beneath the trees, not saying a word. Just watching.

Until he stepped forward, voice carrying like prophecy.

EZEKIEL: "I've been listening. To pain. To guilt. To hope. And I see the spirit of Moses here. I see Joseph—dreamers turned to slaves turned to kings. And I see David—flawed, bloodstained, but chosen."

He walked the circle slowly.

EZEKIEL (cont'd): "We weren't meant to die in Pharaoh's system. We weren't made to live off crumbs. God didn't make us the head just to settle for the heels."

He pointed to the fire.

EZEKIEL: "This right here… this ain't no trap talk. This is testimony. This is a temple. And where two or more are gathered in truth… chains *break*."

People stood. Hugged. Some prayed. Some wept.

It was more than healing. It was history correcting itself.

The block had become the altar. The trap, a church. And every testimony? A blueprint.

2 plus 2 still equals 8. And tonight? It equaled redemption.

CHAPTER FORTY- SIX

LEGACY IN MOTION

Six months had passed since the fire circle lit the night sky at Legacy Land.

Now, that same land hummed with purpose. Children planted vegetables in garden beds. Framing crews drilled two-story homes where there were once only blueprints and dreams. The podcast studio buzzed with episodes dropping every week, and a newly finished media center stood proudly at the entrance of the property, painted with a mural of Atlanta's ancestors—King, Tubman, Garvey, and modern-day builders with no names yet.

INT. LEGACY CENTER – BOARDROOM – MID-MORNING

Geneva clicked through a slideshow as the new Trustees Board reviewed quarterly reports.

GENEVA: "Apparel sales: 162,000 units sold. Streaming: over 6 million downloads. Podcast monetization alone has generated $180,000. The #2Plus2Equals8 app has 230,000 active users and climbing."

Ezekiel leaned in.

EZEKIEL: "The stock portfolio has grown 17% quarter over quarter. Our IULs are properly funded—average return at 7.3%. And our compound interest funds now feed four community micro-banks."

Truth tapped the table.

TRUTH: "We don't just have resources. We got systems. We are teaching boys how to calculate freedom."

Malik nodded.

MALIK: "And we own it all. Every copyright. Every course. Every video."

Geneva advanced the next slide.

GENEVA: "All four of us are finalizing our books. Malik's is already in pre-orders: *Blueprints of a Block King*. Truth's *Rebuilt from Rust* hits shelves in two months. Mine, *The Silent Architect*, is going through final edits. And Ezekiel's? Already being adapted into a docu-series."

Ezekiel smiled.

EZEKIEL: "Title: *2Plus2Equals8: Breaking the Curse of Limited Belief*."

They all nodded.

Outside the window, workers painted a new sign: Legacy Land Cultural and Financial Development Center.

TRUSTEE MEMBER: "We also propose creating a youth council and rotating trustees every two years. Keep the power fresh. Transparent. Evolving."

Geneva raised her glass of water.

GENEVA: " bring total working capital over eight million. To legacy that leads, not bleeds."

Everyone clinked glasses.

EXT. LEGACY LAND – EVENING

Truth stood beneath a sycamore tree. Two little boys—his sons—ran around him, laughing, tossing a football back and forth. Their joy echoed off the walls of what used to be hopelessness.

He knelt down and hugged them both, tears hidden in his beard.

TRUTH (to himself): "I missed too much. But I'm here now. And I ain't leavin'."

BLACKSTONE'S HOUSE – DEN – NIGHT

The room was dim. Just one lamp and the weight of old mistakes.

Blackstone sat across from Rose. A drink in his hand. Her eyes were tired but firm.

BLACKSTONE: "I don't even know how to say it. He is my blood, and I left him to the world."

ROSE: "He became what you never had the courage to be."

Blackstone nodded.

BLACKSTONE: "But he deserves the truth."

ROSE: "Then give it to him. Before the streets do."

Silence.

Blackstone stood, walked to the window, and stared out at the skyline.

DEA ATLANTA FIELD OFFICE – UNDERGROUND MEETING ROOM – SAME NIGHT

Agent Langley sat in silence while overhead screens flashed charts of recent overdoses across Atlanta. One in Vine City. Two in Buckhead, three in little five points, Another near Edgewood. Five in East Point. Three teenagers. Two adults. All fentanyl-laced.

The lead Homeland official spoke coldly.

HOMELAND OFFICER: "This is part of the rollout. Collapse begins with saturation. We've softened the zones. Poverty will swallow the resistance."

Langley gritted his teeth.

LANGLEY: "This ain't strategy. It's genocide."

HOMELAND OFFICER: "History will frame it as natural selection."

Langley stood up.

LANGLEY: "History's watching. And so am"

That night, Langley downloaded classified files onto a personal flash drive.

Inside his car, he looked out at the lights of Legacy Land in the distance.

LANGLEY (to himself): "I can't stop everything. But I can warn them."

He hit SEND. To an encrypted email. To Geneva.

The legacy wasn't just a land. It was a lifeline. And the war wasn't coming.

It had already arrived.

But now, they had roots. And roots? Can crack concrete.

2 plus 2 still equals 8. And what they were building now... Was bigger than survival.

It was a new blueprint for Black power.

CHAPTER FORTY- SEVEN

A CITY CODED IN CONTRADICTION

PODCAST STUDIO – LEGACY LAND – NIGHT

The cameras were rolling. The energy was charged. The backdrop read "2Plus2Equals8: Truth Talks." Malik, Ezekiel, and Truth sat shoulder to shoulder—mics hot, hearts heavy.

MALIK: "Tonight's topic… Are we set up to fail?"

TRUTH: "Let's talk real. Why is Atlanta full of liquor stores, strip clubs, trap houses and churches that don't feed the flocks with real answers? But learning centers, outreach programs, credit unions, rec centers, YMCA—the list goes on—barely exist throughout the city."

EZEKIEL: "Facts. I mean, how is Atlanta—city of civil rights, home of MLK— a place where some of the most brilliant Black college girls come to get degrees… and end up in clear heels under neon lights?"

TRUTH: "You don't even gotta be 21 to dance. Just shake trauma for tips. Some of these girls got 3.8 GPAs and still chose the pole 'cause the system won't let 'em breathe."

MALIK: "And we gotta ask… how did Atlanta become a drug hub? We ain't by water. We are not a border city. No sea ports. Yet somehow, we move more product than Houston or Miami. Y'all ever wonder how?"

EZEKIEL: "Because the system ain't broken—it's built that way."

They paused. Silence held weight before Ezekiel leaned forward.

EZEKIEL (cont'd): "Let's talk pros and cons. Atlanta got HBCUs, Black millionaires, the biggest Black film studio in history. But also? The highest eviction rate, sky-high HIV infections, kids going to school hungry. It's a city of duality. You can find Black excellence and Black death on the same block."

TRUTH: "Can't lie. We got culture. But culture has been commercialized. The trap ain't just music—it's a mindset being marketed to us 24/7."

MALIK: "Which brings us to our guest tonight—someone who's seen the beast from the inside. Corporate strategist, system analyst, and a sister who's walked away from comfort to fight for us: Elena."

ELENA'S CAM – SPLIT SCREEN

Elena sat upright, poised and powerful. Her voice came steady, but her words hit like thunder.

ELENA: "I spent 14 years in corporate America—boardrooms that shaped entire cities without ever stepping foot in them. You wanna know why strip clubs outnumber libraries? It's by design. The data says: keep the poor entertained and exhausted."

ELENA (cont'd): "We used to analyze trends—spending habits, family breakdowns, education gaps. Then build systems that benefit off them. If Black folks stop spending on what doesn't feed them? The whole economy would crash."

EZEKIEL: "You said something before, off-camera. About prisons and zip codes?"

ELENA: "Yeah. In boardrooms, we look at third-grade reading scores and childhood trauma indicators. Then we forecast prison beds. It's not about crime. It's about probability. Predicting poverty and monetizing it."

TRUTH: "Damn."

MALIK: "So they build cages off pain they helped create?"

ELENA: "Exactly. Then turn around and sell us back chains with diamonds."

The studio went quiet again.

EZEKIEL: "Let's speak deeper. Let's talk about households. You wanna break people, start at the root. And the root? Is family."

GENEVA (off-camera, stepping into the frame): "Exactly. That divide started long before any rap record or welfare check."

She took a mic, passion rising.

GENEVA: "Let's go back. Slavery stripped Black men of their right to protect or even raise their children in open view. On plantations, a father had to watch his child be sold or beaten and could do nothing about it. That trauma never left. It embedded itself."

TRUTH: "And now that trauma cycles itself. Through generations."

GENEVA: "Fast forward. Government housing programs—specifically Section 8—offered assistance, but only if there was no man in the house. Think about that. To get help, he had to go."

EZEKIEL: "So now the woman becomes the head, but under conditional help. Which means the government had more say than the father. Strategic separation."

MALIK: "Then add the job crisis. Factories closed. Trade jobs outsourced. Suddenly brothers got no work, so they hustle. Hustle brings crime. Crime brings time."

TRUTH: "And now their sons grow up with locked doors and empty chairs at dinner tables."

GENEVA: "This was chess, not checkers. And it's been played for decades. America is the only industrialized nation where the Black male has been systematically stripped of his role as head of household."

EZEKIEL: "And we're still called lazy."

GENEVA: "But as Dr. Umar Johnson said: you can get a student loan, a car loan, a mortgage. All high-risk. But try getting a million-dollar loan for clinics, grocery stores, or gas stations in the hood—good luck."

TRUTH: "And here's what most people don't know: in Jewish communities, there's something called Heter Iska—interest-free business loans. Can you imagine us having that?"

MALIK: "That's a game-changer."

GENEVA: "They call us poor because we don't own the printing press. But we were rich in mind and soul. Now it's time to change the balance sheet."

EZEKIEL (closing): "So tonight, we're not just venting. We're connecting dots. Exposing patterns. And declaring this:

2Plus2Equals8 is a new math. A new model. A new movement.

Let's reclaim what was taken. Let's rebuild what they broke. Let's replant what they uprooted."

The room erupted in applause. The lights lit up

BARBERSHOP – WEST END – NIGHT

Blackstone stood silent in the corner as the podcast played on the TV above the mirror. The old head barber shook his head slowly.

BARBER: "They preachin' better than most preachers."

A few young men looked uncomfortable. Blackstone's jaw tightened.

BLACKSTONE: "They ain't ready for the weight that comes with leading. Not like I was."

BARBER: "Maybe not. But they ain't carrying' ego. They carrying' the people."

Blackstone didn't respond.

TASHA'S BRAID SHOP – SOUTH

ATLANTA – SAME TIME

Young girls braided in rhythm while the podcast streamed on the Bluetooth speaker. Tasha handed a girl a fresh pack of hair while mouthing along with Ezekiel's words.

TASHA: "You hearin' this? That's what leadership sounds like."

The girls nodded. One of them paused, looked up.

YOUNG BRAIDER: "Why don't they teach this in school?"

Tasha smiled, bittersweet.

TASHA: "Cause school ain't designed to make us free. But this? This right here? It's a liberation in surround sound."

KILO'S HIDEOUT – EAST ATLANTA – DIMLY LIT

Kilo sat in front of a large screen, joint in hand, a cold expression carved across his face. His crew laughed at something else in the room, but Kilo watched in silence.

KILO (to himself): "They buildin' something real… but it won't last. Not if I got say."

He tapped the side of his burner phone. Then sent a text.

KILO: "Let's shake the table. Hard."

HOMELAND OFFICE – SECURE ROOM – SAME TIME

The podcast was on mute, but the captions ran across a big screen. Wynn stood behind a group of agents watching every word.

AGENT: "They're not just talking. They're mobilizing. Converting culture into control."

WYNN: "Then we drown it. Drown it in scandal. Drugs. Fear. Turn heroes into headlines."

Truth echoed louder than applause. And in Atlanta? The war wasn't just for votes or dollars. It was for *narrative.*

Because if the people ever believed again?

They'd stop consuming and start creating.

2 plus 2 still equals 8. And tonight… It was trending.

CHAPTER FORTY- EIGHT

STRANGE FRUIT, STILL HANGING

STONE MOUNTAIN TRAIL – EARLY MORNING

A woman jogged through the misty Georgia woods, earbuds in, breath steady. Her pace slowed when she noticed something up ahead—unmoving, swaying.

At first, she thought it was a broken banner or fallen gear from a hiker.

But the closer she got… her scream pierced the quiet.

Dre. Hanging. From an oak.

A type note taped to his chest. "I couldn't handle the guilt."

LEGACY LAND – STUDIO – HOURS LATER

Ezekiel stood frozen. Geneva dropped her phone. Malik punched the air. Truth fell into a chair like the weight of survival finally cracked his knees.

TRUTH: "Nah. Nah. He ain't going out like that. Not Dre. Not after everything."

EZEKIEL: "He left the movement stronger than he found it. That ain't guilt. That's a hit."

Geneva, pale but focused, dug through Dre files. She opened an envelope marked PRIVATE, the one Dre had dropped off months ago. Inside, a USB drive.

GENEVA (whispering): "He recorded them…"

LEGACY MEDIA ROOM – LATER THAT DAY

The Big Three watched the video Dre had secretly taken with Wynn. The audio was raw:

WYNN (on tape): "We let movements grow just enough to track their leaders. Then we freeze their accounts, arrest them on technicalities, and turn public opinion with staged scandals."

WYNN (cont'd): "Dre, you plant that device, you disappear a nobody. Or you become a name they praise on murals after you're gone."

Silence.

Then Ezekiel turned to Geneva.

EZEKIEL: "Send it to the press."

IRS FIELD OFFICE – ATLANTA – SAME TIME An agent stared at an alert on his screen: 2Plus2Equals8: Account Freeze – Immediate Audit Pending.

INT. LEGACY LAND – MIDDAY The sun burned overhead, but the chill inside the center could be felt in the silence. Geneva stood at the front office window as two federal agents handed her a folder thick with government letterhead.

"Audit pending," one of them said, voice flat. "Effective immediately, all 2Plus2Equals8 assets are frozen."

"For what cause? We've done nothing but build," Geneva replied, trying to stay composed.

"It's not my call," he said. "Just my job."

Inside the main hallway, workers were boxing up computers. Files. Office equipment. Even the wall-mounted flat screen that played the documentary of their progress.

Kids from the youth development program peeked around corners. One boy—about ten—clutched a math workbook to his chest. His friend whispered, "Why are they taking our stuff?"

In the café area, Malik stood in disbelief, fists clenched, watching the agents unplug one of the financial literacy computers used daily for community classes.

Geneva raised her voice to the agents. "You are DEAD wrong for this. Children are learning here. Lives are being rebuilt. You didn't even give us a hearing."

"Ma'am, it's a federal order. We're just following the file."

Tasha arrived and rushed through the front door, heart pounding. Elijah and Naomi were right behind her, confused. "What's going on?" Naomi asked.

Ezekiel walked in moments later, having heard the news en route. He stood still at the doorway, eyes locked on the scene unfolding—agents with boxes, Geneva with fury in her throat, and truth being packed up like evidence.

Outside, the news crews gathered. Cameras rolled. One reporter whispered, "This one's different."

Crowds formed—supporters, skeptics, neighbors. Some said, "Knew it. Too good to be true." Others stood silently, watching with heavy hearts.

But one thing was clear.

Everyone could feel it:

This wasn't just another raid.

This was fear—fear of something too pure. Too organic. Too real to be controlled.

Geneva stood on the steps of Legacy Land, voice shaking but strong:

"They did the same to Garvey. They surveilled Dr. King. They watched Malcolm until his last breath. They fear our unity. They fear what happens when we stop surviving… and start owning."

Ezekiel stepped beside her.

"Let them take what they want. The soil's still ours. The vision's still rooted. They can't freeze a seed already planted."

Malik raised his fist behind them. Truth walked out, hands open, voice loud:

"They froze the account. Not the movement. We are STILL #2Plus2Equals8."

The crowd erupted. Reporters scribbled.

And the world was watching.

INT. IRS FIELD OFFICE – SAME TIME The agent who issued the freeze order sat back in his chair, visibly uneasy. His colleague beside him muttered under breath:

"If this blows up… it won't just be numbers we're auditing. It'll be history."

CONGRESSMAN'S MANSION – SAME NIGHT

His niece is 22. Dead. Overdosed in her apartment. A half-used bag of fentanyl-laced pills still in her purse.

The congressman flipped the TV to see Dre's hanging on every news channel. He saw Truth's face, Ezekiel's voice calling out systems.

CONGRESSMAN (to aide): "I want that trap shut down. Tonight. I want heads. I want Kilo in a cage or on a stretcher."

SMALL CANDLE LIT ROOM – LATER THAT NIGHT

Ezekiel, Rose, and Blackstone sat facing one another. A truth too old to ignore sat between them.

BLACKSTONE (shaky): "You were never supposed to find out this way."

EZEKIEL (flat): "And yet… here we are."

ROSE: "I tried to protect you."

EZEKIEL: "From the truth? Or from your and his shame?"

BLACKSTONE: "I was a coward. I chose the pulpit over paternity. I chose praise over pain. And I lost you because of it."

ROSE (tearful): "I should've told you when you were old enough to ask. But you were already carrying so much. I—"

EZEKIEL (cutting her off): "You both lied. And now that I got a whole movement breathing down my neck… *now* you tell me?"

BLACKSTONE (on his knees): "I'm sorry, son. I am."

Ezekiel stood.

EZEKIEL: "Don't call me that. I got God. I got my people. I don't need a daddy now."

He walked out.

MEDIA CENTER – PRESS CONFERENCE – NEXT MORNING

The Big Three stood at the podium. News cameras rolling. A black-and-white photo of Dre projected behind them.

MALIK: "They thought killing Dre would kill the mission. They thought freezing our accounts would stop our fire."

TRUTH: "They've been doing this since Rosewood. Since Tulsa. Since the Black Panthers. Whenever we rise with ownership, education, or unity—*they panic.*"

EZEKIEL (stepping forward): "This isn't just an attack on us. It's an attack on Black *legacy.* We've been targeted because we're teaching wealth. Because we're reprogramming the narrative. And because we believe that 2 plus 2 don't have to equal 4 when you plant your own equation in good soil."

Gasps. Tears. Cheering from the crowd.

EZEKIEL (cont'd): "We are not done. We are just getting started."

They hanged Dre from a tree to remind Atlanta of its roots. But what they didn't know…

Is that the roots they tried to rot now feed something greater.

And from that tree?

A nation will be rebuilt.

2 plus 2 still equals 8. Even in grief. Even in fire. Even in betrayal.

CHAPTER FORTY- NINE

CANDLES FOR THE FALLEN, FIRE FOR THE FUTURE

LEGACY LAND – Late evening

Hundreds of candles lit up the dark, lining the main walkway to the community center. Pictures of Dre surrounded the circle. His laugh froze in time. His name etched in cardboard signs that read: *From Hustler to Healer. Long Live Dre.*

The people stood shoulder to shoulder. Silent. Grieving. Resolved.

TRUTH stepped forward first.

TRUTH: "He used to say he was broken. But he wasn't. He just didn't have the right tools. And before he left, he made sure to pass 'em on. I watched him show three boys how to use a tape measure. Said, 'This is how you build something that doesn't fall in the wind.' That's Dre."

His voice cracked. He paused, hand to chest.

TRUTH (cont'd): "Don't measure his life by where he started. Measure it by what he left behind."

MALIK: "Dre died because he chose the truth. And for that, we gon' make sure his truth doesn't die with him."

GENEVA: "The world wants to make martyrs out of us. We're choosing to make architects instead."

EZEKIEL (voice soft, then rising): "This road we on? It ain't about marching. It's about planting. But the hardest part… it ain't the mission. It's the ones who don't want the mission to succeed. We're not up against ignorance anymore—we're up against calculated resistance. Power that thrives off our silence."

He looked across the candlelit faces.

EZEKIEL (cont'd): "So we can't afford to whisper. Not anymore."

A few wept. Some held their loved ones tighter. Others just stood, fists clenched.

MAYOR'S OFFICE – SAME NIGHT

The mayor stood around a roundtable with his senior staff. Charts. Overdose maps. Intel from recent raids.

MAYOR: "Too many kids dead. Too many bodies with no history of use. I want answers."

His Chief of Public Safety spoke hesitantly.

CHIEF: "Some of the shipments were rerouted from out-of-state. But the volume… it's coordinated."

MAYOR: "Then tell me what I already suspect. Is this sanctioned? Or rogue?"

A silence. Then someone spoke.

AIDE: "It's reminding some of us of South Central. Crack days. Real Rick Ross era. LA all over again."

The mayor picked up his phone. Typed a text.

"Ezekiel. Let's meet."

LEGACY CENTER – WRITERS ROOM

Stacks of manuscripts lined the desk. One by one: *The Silent Architect*, *Blueprints of a Block King*, *Rebuilt from Rust*, and Ezekiel's own script—now complete.

EZEKIEL (reading the final line aloud): "...and so, they realized 2 plus 2 was never meant to equal 4. Not when the math was built to confine. It equals 8 when your mind is free."

He closed the script. Sat back. Breathed deep.

EZEKIEL AND TASHA'S PLACE – LATER THAT NIGHT

Tasha stood in the kitchen pouring tea. Elijah sat at the table as Naomi curled up beside her, reading from *As a Man Thinketh* in a soft, steady voice.

NAOMI: "...for as a man thinketh in his heart, so is he."

Ezekiel walked in, visibly heavy.

Tasha didn't ask what was wrong—she just looked at him, and he nodded. He'd been carrying everything.

TASHA: "one thing I know about you and love your resilience unmatched we going get through this come back stronger."

Ezekiel sat down beside her, silent for a beat.

EZEKIEL: "The IRS froze everything. Sponsors pulling back. My script's done, but the funds are tied up. And… I found out who my father is."

Tasha blinked. Her lips parted.

TASHA (softly): "Blackstone?"

He nodded. Looked away.

EZEKIEL: "Rose knew. He knew. And they waited till now. Like I didn't have enough on my back."

Tasha reached across the table, took his hand.

TASHA: "Everything you've built… you built without him. With us. With God. With the streets watching and the system against you. And baby—you're still here."

Ezekiel looked at her, his eyes wet.

EZEKIEL: "I'm tired, Tasha. But I ain't finished."

TASHA (smiling through tears): "I know you ain't. That's why I was talking with the landlord about buying the whole plaza. I want to expand the shop. Run programs. Give these girls something to build on."

Naomi looked up, hopeful.

NAOMI: "We gonna own the whole building?"

TASHA: "We're gonna own *everything*, baby girl. Just like we planned."

Ezekiel took it all in. The woman. The children. The storm and the calm.

EZEKIEL (whispering): "This is legacy. Right here."

He looked at the window, the city stretching beyond it. Flames of fear were rising. But so were they.

NEW DAY

SPONSORSHIP MEETING – MIDTOWN – SAME TIME Elena and Geneva sat across from a boardroom of tight-faced executives. Legal counsel, brand reps, financial backers.

ELENA: "Everything you've seen in the news? Crafted. Fear-mongering. What we're building isn't rebellion—it's infrastructure."

GENEVA: "And if your company really cares about equity, now's the time to prove it. Or admit you were only here for the hashtag."

They held the room in silence. A sponsor rep closed his laptop.

REP: "We'll resume funding. Quietly at first. But we believe you."

LEGACY LAND – CONFERENCE ROOM – NIGHT

The core team gathered. Geneva stood before them.

GENEVA: " I met with a few sponsors. Three agreed to continue—quietly. Combined, $150,000 in commitments. Elena has agreed to front $250,000 from her personal account."

Everyone in the room reacted—eyes wide, gasps low.

GENEVA (cont'd): "That gives us $400,000 of float money. It'll hold us over until this IRS audit clears. The movement doesn't stop."

Truth nodded. Malik rubbed his chin. Tasha squeezed Ezekiel's hand. The room swelled with unspoken gratitude.

Then Ezekiel cleared his throat.

EZEKIEL: "There's something else. Something I need to say."

The room quieted.

EZEKIEL (cont'd): "Blackstone… he's my father."

Silence cracked like thunder.

Geneva's brows furrowed.

GENEVA: "What?"

Ezekiel nodded, slow and heavy.

EZEKIEL: "Rose knew. He knew. And he waited till now. All this time, I was his shadow."

Malik looked at him, deep in thought.

MALIK: "Honestly... it makes sense. Your voice. Your delivery. Been resonating with folks like a preacher who knew fire before he found the mic."

Geneva tilted her head, squinting. Then smiled.

GENEVA: "You do favor him... I just couldn't see it at first."

Everyone broke into light laughter.

TRUTH: "Well, maybe that means you can finally turn them lemons into lemonade."

EZEKIEL: "Now you pushin'."

They all laughed again—deeper this time, freer.

Ezekiel stepped forward, placed a hand over the table.

EZEKIEL (softly): "Let's pray."

Heads bowed.

EZEKIEL (cont'd): "God, we've walked through storms and shadows. We've lost brothers. We've been doubted, questioned, attacked. But we are not broken. We are built. You planted us deep so we could rise strong. Thank you for every hand in this room. For every voice that stayed. Every dollar that moved in faith. Protect our minds. Our mission. Our unity. And when they come with lies and fire, let us be the water. Let us be the truth. Amen."

ALL: "Amen."

Narration: They lit candles for Dre. But they lit fire in themselves.

2 plus 2 still equals 8. Even when the system trembles. Even when fathers fail. Even when death tries to write the ending.

The story goes on. And now?

They're writing every chapter. Together.

CHAPTER FIFTY

ACCOUNTABLE FIRE

IRS HEADQUARTERS – DC – EARLY MORNING

A stark gray room buzzed with tension. IRS agents scrolled through digital spreadsheets and reports that glowed on multiple monitors.

LEAD AUDITOR: "We triple-checked it. Apparel sales? Receipts clean. Donations sponsorship? All tracked. No offshore movement. No personal siphoning. No one's living beyond their means—not a single red flag."

SENIOR OFFICER (tight-lipped): "But Homeland is breathing down our necks. They want something. Anything."

ANALYST: "Then tell 'em to keep breathing. These numbers read like a textbook. Not a dollar out of place. No exotic cars. No private jets. No 'ghost' charities. It's community-based. Structured. *Accountable.*"

SENIOR OFFICER (growling): "Keep digging. Something this clean? That's a threat in itself."

THE BLUFF – NIGHT RAID – ATLANTA

Armored trucks roared through the narrow veins of the Bluff like blood through a hardened artery. Helicopter blades thundered above as floodlights painted the cracked streets in white-blue panic. Sirens screamed like the ancestors had finally been heard.

Local SWAT. Atlanta PD. State police. They moved like a synchronized army—battering rams, rifles drawn, shouting commands that pierced the muggy night air.

Inside a corner trap house, J-Rock and three others had no time to flush the stash. The front door was reduced to splinters. Officers stormed in, shouting over each other. In the back room—bags of fentanyl, two Glocks on a folding table, and a duffel bag stuffed with hundreds stacked in rubber bands.

"Get on the ground! Hands behind your head!"

One by one, they were dragged out—shirts yanked over their heads, blood on lips, eyes wild and unrepentant.

NEWS REPORT (V.O.) "Over 5,000 fentanyl pills seized in a major sting operation tonight in Atlanta's historic Westside. Dozens of illegal firearms were recovered, and more than $100,000 in suspected drug money was found. Four men—led by Jerome 'J-Rock' Hill—are now in custody. But the alleged mastermind, known only as 'Kilo,' remains at large."

The news traveled faster than sirens.

NEIGHBORHOOD – MINUTES LATER

Word spread like wildfire. From porch to porch, through text chains and murmured prayers. Mothers stepped outside in robes, slippers scraping the sidewalk. Old men clapped hands together.

"Heard they got them boys this time."

"They finally came for 'em."

"It's about damn time."

In front of a worn-down corner store, a group of teenage girls hugged and sang a hymn, harmonies off-key but holy:

"This little light of mine... I'm gonna let it shine..."

One grandmother raised her cane and her voice. "The Lord still walks these streets. You hear me?"

Outside the gas station, even the regulars—men who usually argued over scratch-offs and blunts—stood still. Nodding. Whispering. Watching.

A young boy pointed at the convoy of flashing lights disappearing down the block.

"Is it over, mama?"

She knelt beside him, kissed his cheek, and said, "Not yet. But tonight... it started."

TRUTH'S HOUSE – SAME NIGHT

From his front window, Truth watched it all unfold.

He held his sons close.

The streets were changing. Slowly. Painfully.

But changing.

And somewhere, in the shadows just beyond the lights—Kilo watched, too. Eyes cold. Heart furious.

They got the house.

They got the guns.

They got the runners.

But they didn't get him

LUXURY HOTEL PENTHOUSE – MIDTOWN ATLANTA – NIGHT

Glass walls overlooked the glowing skyline. Modern art. Bottles of champagne. Designer clothes draped over furniture. Kilo stood in a robe, barefoot on imported marble.

Truth's kids' mother Shanice sat on a velvet couch, silent, unsure.

KILO (watching TV coverage): "They think they are winning. But this city has memories. It doesn't belong to saviors. It belongs to survivors. That's me."

He poured two glasses of bourbon. Sat next to her.

KILO (smirking): "Let 'em shut down the Bluff. I'll open five more doors. They forgot how deep my veins run. And Truth? He is still breathin'. That ain't right."

She looked away. Swallowed hard.

KILO: "You ain't gotta like it. But you better not stop me."

MAYOR'S OFFICE – DOWNTOWN ATLANTA – EARLY MORNING

The mayor stared out the window, coffee steaming in his hand. Ezekiel stood opposite him, arms folded, eyes heavy but alert.

MAYOR: "The city's shifting. You feel it. I feel it. And Dre's death… the people are listening now. Leaning in. What else do you need from me?"

EZEKIEL: "Consistency. Not headlines. Not handshakes. Infrastructure. Policy. If you wanna help, shut down the backroom loopholes. Crack the city codes they use to bury our businesses. And stop hiding behind task forces that don't fix a damn thing."

MAYOR (taken back): "I'm trying. But it's a machine."

EZEKIEL: "Then reroute the wires. 'Cause the Bluff getting raided doesn't mean the poison's gone. It just gets pushed deeper. You kill one head, five grow back. That's the pattern. And y'all been playing chess with pawns while the king sits clean."

MAYOR: "You're saying what we're doing isn't enough."

EZEKIEL (firm): "I'm saying, until the money flows where the healing lives… it never will be."

A long silence. Then the mayor nodded slowly.

MAYOR: "Let's set a real date. You and your people. Public, transparent. We build something together."

EZEKIEL: "I'll show up. Just don't flinch when we bring the full truth to the mic."

CIA FIELD ROOM – NIGHT

Monitors displayed photos of protests. Charts of community financial flows. Pages of social media quotes.

HOMELAND OFFICER: "We told the IRS to freeze them. They found nothing."

CIA AGENT: "No overseas accounts. No shell companies. No false fronts."

HOMELAND OFFICER (cold): "Then fabricate the optics. The truth won't matter once the fear hits."

A junior agent whispered:

AGENT: "They might actually be clean."

HOMELAND OFFICER: "Then we're gonna make 'em look dirty."

LEGACY LAND – OUTDOOR COURTYARD – EVENING

Malik and former DEA agent Langley sat on a bench, watching boys toss a football across the lawn.

LANGLEY: "Spent two decades arresting shadows. But now I see where the light really is."

MALIK (nods): "It's hard walking' away from a badge."

LANGLEY: "Harder living with regret. Count me in. I'll keep y'all safe from the inside. Whatever comes."

MALIK: "Then let's do it right. No more band-aids. Time to build walls they can't tear down."

They threw everything they had. Freezes. Raids. Fear.

But the truth was tighter than their chains. And even as Kilo plotted, and suits conspired,

The people? Were planning too.

2 plus 2 still equals 8. Even in fire. Especially in fire.

CHAPTER FIFTY- ONE

THE WORTH WITHIN

LEGACY CENTER – GENEVA'S OFFICE – LATE MORNING

Sunlight poured in through wide windows, illuminating boards of strategy, checklists, and post-it notes layered with ideas. Geneva and Elena sat across from each other, laptops open, legal pads stacked, coffee still steaming.

GENEVA: "The publisher came back. $250K each. Clean contract. National rollout."

ELENA (reading the fine print): "Yeah… and 40% of all backend royalties. No ownership of audio. No control over edits. That ain't it."

GENEVA: "I know. I told them no."

Elena smiled.

ELENA: "That's right. We're not selling the voice of a movement. We're building it."

They scrolled through updated dashboards.

GENEVA (pointing): "Print cost? Under $3 per copy. Amazon and Kindle locked in. Uploading now. We hit go next week. We got five podcast interviews already lined up—three Black-owned, two syndicated. Radio station outta Chicago just confirmed."

ELENA: "And Barnes & Noble?"

GENEVA: "They want shelf space in ten major cities. We're handling inventory ourselves. Independent. Direct-to-reader. Full control."

ELENA: "We own every chapter."

They clinked mugs.

GENEVA (softly): "And every word is a seed."

LEGACY LAND – CONSTRUCTION SITE – AFTERNOON

The hum of drills echoed alongside laughter. Kids ran across the community garden. Young men with hard hats laid the foundation for the new multipurpose building. Malik, Ezekiel, and Truth walked the gravel path that ran along the back edge of Legacy Land.

MALIK: "The mayor looked shook. What did he say?"

EZEKIEL: "He said he was ready to help. I told him help ain't press releases. Help is passing policy that keeps schools from falling apart."

TRUTH: "We don't need saviors. We need systems."

EZEKIEL: "Exactly. That's why I've been sketching out this new initiative. Start at the middle school level. Go all the way through high school. We bring kids here three days a week—call it *Career Day*, but for real."

He pulled out a folded sheet.

EZEKIEL (cont'd): "We break the sessions up: health, finance, real estate, coding, law. No lectures. Real mentorship. One-on-one with folks in the field. We got barbers teaching balance books. Chefs teaching meal plans. Lawyers teaching contracts. This ain't no workbook hustle."

TRUTH: "You tryna raise a generation of bosses."

EZEKIEL: "I'm tryna give 'em the blueprint we never had."

MALIK: "What's the budget?"

EZEKIEL: "Grassroots fund. Already started. Small property acquisitions. Duplexes, corner lots. We stack 'em. Rent flows into the education program. One property, one path to passive income. Timeline on Legacy Land is eighteen months for total build out: media wing, outdoor amphitheater, dorms for youth, full-scale kitchen, bookstore and co-op."

TRUTH: "And the IRS?"

EZEKIEL: "They ain't got a thing. And that means it's time to go ten times harder."

They looked out over the site as kids painted murals on plywood walls. One read: *Freedom Is In The Math.*

HOMELAND STRATEGY ROOM – UNDISCLOSED LOCATION – NIGHT

Dark room. Red light. Data flowing on LED panels. Documents projected. One showed Legacy Land's construction timeline. Another displayed Ezekiel, Malik, Truth, Geneva, Elena—all with digital profiles.

LEAD ANALYST: "The audit failed. But public perception is pliable. We create doubt. Start with anonymous whistleblower claims. 'Financial irregularities.' It doesn't have to be true—it just needs to trend."

SECOND AGENT: "Or we attack the structure. Fake donor outrage. Get someone inside to call misuse."

THIRD AGENT: "They're resilient. That means we need to go surgical. One misstep, one scandal, one betrayal… and the house shakes."

LEAD AGENT: "We don't just stop movements. We starve them. Isolate them. Make the good look greedy. The strong look suspect. We're not here to arrest them. We're here to erase belief."

Silence.

LEAD AGENT (cont'd): "Let's proceed."

Ownership was louder than outrage. And while the system plotted in whispers,

The people were speaking in blueprints, ink, and brick.

2 plus 2 still equals 8. And now?

It was publishing. It was planting. It was a legacy.

CHAPTER FIFTY- TWO

THE JUDAS EFFECT

HOMELAND INTEL SAFEHOUSE – NIGHT

Dim light flickered over concrete walls. Surveillance feeds glowed on stacked monitors. The air was thick with manipulation. On one screen: *Shanice*, Truth's baby mama. Her body language screamed fear, but her face tried to stay neutral.

A Homeland agent in a crisp gray suit leaned forward, voice sharp but wrapped in honey.

AGENT THORNE (calm, cold):
"Cooperate, and your record stays clean. Your children never see what it's like to visit their mother through glass. Don't… and we'll let the full weight fall."

SHANICE (shaking):
"I already gave you what I knew…"

THORNE:
"Now we need what you *don't* know—yet. You're going to re-establish contact with Truth. Ask him questions. Personal. Financial. Routine. You'll be our eyes."

SHANICE (whispers):
"What happens when they find out?"

THORNE:
"Let's just make sure they don't."

He slid an envelope across the table. Inside: cash. A burner phone. And a clear threat.

SECOND ROOM – OBSERVATION LAB – SAME TIME

Behind a two-way mirror, a young man named *Jason*—mid-twenties, smart, loyal, and a proud volunteer with #2Plus2Equals8—sat in a chair, headphones over his ears. He didn't know it, but *he* was the next experiment.

Two agents stood nearby, watching his vitals and mental response.

AGENT RIVERS:

"Jason Carter. Grew up in College Park. Joined the movement six months ago. Smart. Respected. Already leading workshops on credit and ownership. If anyone can discredit them from the inside… it's him."

AGENT DEAN (grim):

"He doesn't even know we've started conditioning. MK-Ultra protocols: coded sound triggers, sleep deprivation, suggestion layering. It worked in the '60s. It'll work now."

RIVERS:

"The goal?"

DEAN:

"Break trust. Disrupt flow. Make him act out—on camera. Paranoia, maybe violence. Just enough to make the whole movement look unstable."

The screen behind them lit up with flashes of past MK-Ultra records: charts, redacted files, audio snippets.

AGENT DEAN (cont'd):

"This worked on political prisoners. Even the military. We're just accelerating the cycle now. They want to build a legacy? We'll detonate it from within."

TRUTH'S HOUSE – NEXT DAY

Truth sat on the porch, his son's inside playing with the game. He stared at his phone. A new message from *Shanice*.

SHANICE (TEXT):

"Can we talk? I want to fix things."

He stared at the screen for a long time, suspicious but still… sentimental. After all they'd been through, something in him wanted peace. Or closure.

LEGACY LAND – STRATEGY ROOM – LATER

The Big Three and LANGLEY sat around the table. Malik pacing. Geneva on her tablet. Ezekiel rubbing his temples.

GENEVA:

"We need more than passion right now. This feels like infiltration."

MALIK:
"Yeah. Something isn't right."

EZEKIEL (calm, but firm):
"If they come from the inside, then we reinforce from within. That's what they always underestimate—our ability to unify."

LANGLEY (the EX DEA) "History repeating itself. First they infiltrated Marcus Garvey's movement. Then they killed the Panthers with lies and COINTELPRO. It's MK-Ultra 2.0. Just digital now. Sound triggers. Emotional warfare."

MALIK:
"The real revolution gotta start with awareness. We train our people to spot it. We teach them how manipulation works."

LANGLEY: "They've embedded someone. I don't know who yet. But it's close. It ain't just smears now. It's sabotage."

MALIK: "Then we move in the open. What's seen can't be lied about forever."

Langley handed him a flash drive.

LANGLEY: "Surveillance records. A few audio files. Start here."

EZEKIEL:
"Every great Black movement in history got hit from the inside. But they forget—we got God this time. And we *learned*."

HOMELAND INTEL SAFEHOUSE – THAT NIGHT

Thorne reviewed the latest footage of Jason twitching as a subliminal audio file played in his headset.

THORNE (smirking):
"Plant the seed… let chaos grow."

But this time… that seed wasn't landing in just anyone.

(Ezekiel's Voice Over):
"They always come for us when we organize. Not when we riot. Not when we beg. But when we *build*. When we teach ownership. When we plant seeds that can't be burned down."

"The Judas Effect always begins with silence... but truth always finds its voice."

CHAPTER FIFTY- THREE

LEGACY LAND – NIGHT

Truth stared at a freshly printed flyer: *8 Sons Mentorship Circle*. His hands shook slightly. He didn't know why. Maybe Dre's voice still echoed in his chest.

Outside, the sound of hammers, drills, and laughter filled the air. He walked past the amphitheater construction into the media wing where Ezekiel and Malik were deep in plans.

TRUTH: "We have a problem."

Ezekiel looked up.

TRUTH (cont'd): "I ain't sayin' I know what it is yet. But something feels off."

Malik nodded slowly.

MALIK: "Movements always attract the Judas. It's in the book."

BLACKSTONE'S OFFICE –

THE CHURCH – SAME NIGHT

The congressman stood at the window. Behind him, Blackstone sat still, unreadable.

CONGRESSMAN: "You've done a lot for this city. You built a flock. Gave order. Power. That power can still be yours."

BLACKSTONE: "And what would it cost?"

CONGRESSMAN: "Denounce 2Plus2Equals8. Distance yourself from Ezekiel. Call it a misguided rebellion. A misuse of spiritual intention."

BLACKSTONE (softly): "My blood flows through that boy."

CONGRESSMAN: "Then cut the vein. Or the whole arm gets burned."

Camille stood in the doorway, fists clenched. Her voice cracked, but her fire didn't.

CAMILLE: "You sell your soul again, Blackstone, I won't be here when the reaping comes."

She walked away. Blackstone bowed his head.

TRUTH'S HOUSE – NEXT MORNING

Shanice came by with the kids. They jumped into his arms. He laughed, but something behind his eyes didn't smile.

Later, they sat on the couch, kids asleep.

Shanice: "You really think what y'all building can't be stopped?"

TRUTH: "Everything can be stopped. But not everything can be replaced."

She looked down, conflicted. The recorder in her purse blinked silently.

Shanice: "Can me and the kids come help?"

TRUTH: "That would be great all I ever wanted my kids involved ."

Big smile on Truth face Shanice look to the ground blank stare

MAYOR'S CONFERENCE ROOM – AFTERNOON

The Mayor met with a school superintendent, a small tech investor, and Ezekiel. On the table: plans for tech labs, trade classes, and building youth co-ops in abandoned public schools.

MAYOR: "What makes you think this time'll be different?"

EZEKIEL: "Because this time we're not asking. We're building our own wealth and teaching the truth not theirs. We just came here to let you know before the city gets left behind."

The room fell quiet.

The superintendent leaned in.

SUPERINTENDENT: "If you do this right… every kid in South and West Atlanta could graduate with ownership in something."

EZEKIEL: "That's the point."

RADIO STATION – EVENING — LIVE BROADCAST

The backdrop of the studio was sharp: black walls, red trim, microphones hot and ready. Across the table sat Elena in a black hoodie with white block letters reading: #2Plus2Equals8. Behind her, Geneva and Malik sipped from mugs, relaxed but focused. Ezekiel sat closest to the board, headphones on, locked in.

ELENA:
"Welcome back to *Seeds & Strategy*, powered by #2Plus2Equals8. Tonight we're not just talking rumors—we're planting the truth."

CALLER #1 (VIA PHONE):
"So y'all still denying those fraud claims? 'Cause I'm hearing things."

ELENA (leaning forward):
"We deny them because they're false. Let's be real—when was the last time a community movement opened its books publicly? Showed every dollar? We've done that. Twice. And if you want to verify? Pull up to the next finance town hall. We're not hiding. We're multiplying."

CALLER #1 (click):
"…No one else is doing that."

ELENA:
"Exactly."

MALIK (grinning):
"Let's make it plain: the IRS couldn't find dirt because there wasn't any. We operate above board. Black folks with spreadsheets and discipline scare people."

EZEKIEL:
"And that fear turned to lies. But truth moves differently—it doesn't flinch."

GENEVA (calm and clear):
"Now we've come out stronger. The audit? Passed. Every accusation? Dismissed. Our systems? Tighter. Our reach? Deeper."

MALIK:
"And while they were hoping we'd fall, we finished seven houses in Palmetto. Broke ground on three new ones in South Fulton. We're building wealth— real, brick-and-blueprint wealth."

CALLER #2 (VIA PHONE):
"I'm in Chicago. Y'all coming up here?"

GENEVA:
"We are already building the blueprint to roll into five cities next year. Chicago, Detroit, Baltimore, St. Louis, and New Orleans. Book tour starts next month. We'll be in your city."

CALLER #2:
"I want in. How do I join?"

EZEKIEL (smiling):
"Go to 2Plus2Equals8.org. Membership free. You start by learning. Then you plant seeds. Then you water. We don't just teach—we walk with you."

MALIK:
"Programs are peaking. Career Day got 60 kids shadowing Black dentists, pilots, traders, and app developers."

GENEVA:
"Our mentorship program doubled in the last 90 days. And yes—every mentor passed background checks. Our youth deserve both heart and accountability."

CALLER #3 (older woman, skeptical):
"I still don't trust it. All this... sounds good. But every Black movement I've seen either gets bought out or broken down."

EZEKIEL (quiet, strong):
"We hear you. And you're right to be cautious. But let me ask—when's the last time you saw a movement where the people own the platform, the message, and the mission?"

CALLER #3 (softens):
"Not in my lifetime."

EZEKIEL:
"Then maybe this time, we do something different. Maybe this time, we build with no exit strategy. No handouts. Just roots."

GENEVA:
"We launched our own app. No algorithms suppressing truth. No gatekeepers. Content from us, for us. Including our documentary, our school tour, and behind-the-scenes of Legacy Land."

MALIK (quoting Malcolm X):
"'The future belongs to those who prepare for it today.' And today? We are building futures, not just dreaming 'em."

EZEKIEL (quoting Muhammad Ali):
"'Don't count the days—make the days count.' We've been doing that from day one."

ELENA:
"And it's working. Passive income training is live. Streaming royalties are up. People making money from podcasts, publishing, affiliate brands—we're turning $500 incomes into $5,000 legacies."

GENEVA:
"We have real estate courses starting next month. Co-op investing. Trust building. We're laying out paths for families making under $50K to grow sustainable wealth."

CALLER #4 (younger voice):
"Can kids get involved?"

EZEKIEL (beaming):
"They already are. Our 'Young Builders' bootcamp is full. Kids are learning how to code, budget, pitch, and grow. It's like the Harlem Renaissance meets Shark Tank."

MALIK:
"They tried to bury us with audits, headlines, and whispers. But seeds thrive underground. And now?"

ALL TOGETHER:
"We are rising."

GENEVA (quietly, quoting Fred Hampton):
"'You can kill a revolutionary, but you can't kill the revolution.' This isn't about hype. It's about healing. It's about home."

CLOSING NARRATION (V.O.):
From dirt, they built roots. From their roots, they grew fruit. From fruit, they fed the people. And now—every mic, every class, every house, every hoodie marked with #2Plus2Equals8 carries one thing louder than fear:
Legacy.

BLACKSTONE'S BEDROOM – SAME NIGHT

Blackstone sat alone, staring at an old photo of a young Rose. He whispered to the air.

BLACKSTONE: "I was selfish. I wore the cloth but let my ego be the altar. I failed you. I failed him."

His phone buzzed. A message from Camille.

"Your silence now is a louder betrayal than before."

He turned off the phone. Sat in the dark.

LEGACY CENTER – AMPHITHEATER FOUNDATION – NIGHT

The soft hum of generators echoed across the field. Stadium lights, still in testing mode, flickered above the skeletal steel beams of the stage. The Big Three—Ezekiel, Malik, and Geneva—stood in the gravel, their hoodies zipped against the night breeze.

EZEKIEL: "This space... it's not just a stage. It's a declaration."

MALIK: "We've hosted town halls, podcasts, and block meetings... but this? This is the echo chamber for our future."

GENEVA: "And our ancestors. Every brick out here feels like a whisper from the ones they tried to bury."

They walked together toward the scaffolding. Camera crews nearby adjusted their setups. The buzz of community energy filled the air.

 PODCAST STUDIO – LATER THAT NIGHT

The Big Three sat behind their mics. New banners behind them read: "2Plus2Equals8 – Legacy in Motion."

Ezekiel tapped the table twice and leaned in.

EZEKIEL: "We're back. The IRS couldn't shake us. Because when the math is divine, no audit can subtract it. The money's flowing again. Buildings are rising. From the ground up we built homes in Palmetto, film in post-production. And listen—our compound interest funds have tripled. We got single mothers investing. Barbers with portfolios. Teachers stacking streams. This ain't theory. It's testimony."

MALIK: "People earning under 50K—now owning stocks, land shares, even vending machine routes. And our membership? 200,000 strong and counting. We are talking about economic revival. Not charity. Power."

GENEVA: "And because we've been tested and stood firm, let me remind y'all what Fred Hampton once said: 'We're gonna fight racism not with racism, but with solidarity. We're not gonna fight capitalism with Black capitalism. We're gonna fight it with socialism.' He built bridges. He fed kids. And they feared him for it."

EZEKIEL: "And Malcolm X told us: 'The future belongs to those who prepare for it today.' Ali? He said: 'Don't count the days—make the days count.' That's what we are doing. Every. Single. Day."

The crowd outside the studio window cheered. But in the corner, Jason— part-time assistant, once a true believer—watched with clenched fists.

Across the studio, Shanice and the boys handed out flyers with her forced smile. Her eyes flicked constantly—watching, worrying. The pressure was breaking both of them in different ways.

INT. LEGACY CENTER – PRIVATE CONFERENCE ROOM – MOMENTS LATER

The Big Three gathered off-air.

GENEVA: "I met with three sponsors. Two agreed to continue support under anonymity. One? Put up $150K. The other two 50K"

Malik clapped a hand on Ezekiel's shoulder.

MALIK: "This next phase gotta be bulletproof. We move in love but think like chess masters."

EZEKIEL: "We stay building. Stay bold. Stay real. We got a stage going up, schools writing us in, kids wearing hoodies with pride. But eyes are watching. So we keep the vision tight, the mission louder, and the math sacred. 2 plus 2 equals 8... and we multiply."

They bumped fists.

Judas always walks close. They smile. They pray. They shake hands.

But when the betrayal is revealed… it doesn't break the movement. It purifies it.

2 plus 2 still equals 8. And betrayal? Can't kill what was born from fire.

CHAPTER FIFTY- FOUR

THE EARTHQUAKE TEST

TASHA'S BRAID SHOP – EARLY MORNING

The sun hadn't fully risen, but Tasha was already sweeping the shop floor when she heard the crunch of broken glass. She turned the corner and froze.

The front window was shattered. Spray-painted in red across the cracked glass: "FRAUDS."

Her heart dropped.

Elijah stood wide-eyed at the doorway.

NAOMI (softly): "Why would they say that about Daddy?"

Tasha knelt down and pulled her children close, holding back tears with a steady voice.

TASHA: "Because when you shine too bright, baby… some people just want to break your light."

LEGACY CENTER – NIGHT

The Big Three sat around the long table, each with their head bowed—not in prayer, but in heavy thought.

MALIK: "They're tightening the noose. Media. Homeland. Now the streets."

TRUTH: "They tagged Tasha's shop. Kids were inside. That ain't just pressure. That's war."

EZEKIEL: "They want fear. They want fatigue. They want us to self-implode."

He stood up, pacing.

EZEKIEL (cont'd): "And I swear, some days I want to give 'em that explosion. Let it all burn just to stop feeling the pressure."

GENEVA (entering): "Then feel it. But don't fall for it. Because pressure is how you test the foundation. And we ain't built this movement on sand."

ROSE'S LIVING ROOM – LATER THAT NIGHT

Ezekiel sat on the couch, elbows on his knees. Rose poured vodka into a cup, then hesitated.

ROSE: "I used to drink to forget. Now I drink so I don't scream."

She sat beside him, staring at a photo of him as a child.

ROSE (cont'd): "You were six when I knew I had to raise a prophet on a battlefield. You asked me once who your father was. I said 'a long story.' Truth is... he wasn't ready for you. I was. And that had to be enough."

Ezekiel turned, eyes burning.

EZEKIEL: "But why lie? Why let me walk blind all those years?"

ROSE: "Because you didn't need to carry his shame. You were already carrying the world."

Silence fell. But healing sat inside it.

CITY HALL – UNITY EVENT – AUDITORIUM – EVENING

The Mayor took the stage, flanked by city leaders. Cameras flashed. The governor nodded.

Then Ezekiel stepped up.

No script. No mic. Just a voice.

EZEKIEL: "They tried to hang my name like a loose thread. But what they didn't know is—my community stitches every letter in gold. This city was built by hands that never made the history books. But tonight, we will write the next chapter."

The crowd stood. Thunderous applause. But outside, another storm brewed.

HOSPITAL WAITING ROOM – LATE NIGHT

Truth sat in blood-smeared jeans. A 13-year-old boy from the Legacy garden program had been shot during a retaliatory hit near the Bluff.

TRUTH (to nurse): "I told him this was a sanctuary. I *promised* him that."

Malik came and put a hand on his shoulder.

MALIK: "The devil don't take off. So neither can we."

Truth's eyes hardened. He nodded, slowly.

HOMELAND HQ – NIGHT

Agents reviewed fresh intel. Surveillance footage. Reels from TikTok, Facebook, protest videos. The wall glowed with lines connecting faces.

LEAD AGENT: "Ezekiel is the nerve. Take him out—physically, emotionally, or publicly—and the body collapses."

CIA CONSULTANT: "Remove the Messiah. Replace him with fear."

YOUNG AGENT: "But it's not just him anymore. It's *them.*"

LEAD AGENT: "Then we burn the whole tree. Roots and all."

TASHA'S BEDROOM – NIGHT

Tasha watched Elijah sleeping. Naomi held a copy of "The Spook that Sat by the door" open on her lap.

NAOMI: "Tasha, does Daddy still believe?"

Tasha wiped her eyes, brushing Naomi's curls.

TASHA: "Your Daddy doesn't just believe. He *builds* belief. With every step he takes."

She looked down at her phone. A text from Ezekiel:

"Window fixed. Message louder. Let's rise."

She smiled.

BLACKSTONE'S CHURCH – EMPTY HALL – NIGHT

Blackstone lit a candle and sat alone. A Bible open to Matthew 7:25:

"The rain came down, the streams rose, and the winds blew and beat against that house; yet it did not fall, because it had its foundation on the rock."

His fingers trembled.

BLACKSTONE (to himself): "Maybe it's time I stop standing above and start standing beside."

He send Text to Ezekiel

LEGACY LAND – DAWN

The sky cracked pink and orange. Ezekiel walked the perimeter of the center. Every corner held a story. Every wall carried names.

He stopped. Closed his eyes.

EZEKIEL (praying): "Lord, I know earthquakes come to test foundations. Let mine not shake. Let it hold. Let these people see You through me. And if I fall… let them rise higher."

Behind him, Truth, Malik, Geneva, and Elena stood in silence. No fanfare. Just presence.

The earthquake didn't shake them apart. It forged them tighter. And in the cracks left behind?

New seeds grew.

2 plus 2 still equals 8. Especially under pressure. Especially when tested.

Because what's built on truth? Cannot be moved.

CHAPTER FIFTY- FIVE

THE WEIGHT OF THE CROWN

LEGACY CENTER PODCAST STUDIO – NIGHT

The cameras were live. The lights are soft but powerful. A clean black backdrop glowed with the bold white letters: #2Plus2Equals8.

The Big Three sat at the table—Ezekiel, Malik, and Geneva—with Elena and Truth filling the final seats. Everyone wore black hoodies with white lettering. The mics glistened like steel swords, and the energy in the room buzzed with purpose.

Ezekiel leaned forward, hands folded. "Tonight's word ain't for the faint. We talked about ownership. What it means. What it does. Why is it the key to freedom."

Malik nodded. "Ownership is peace. Ain't no landlord knocking. Ain't no boss telling you your value. Ain't no threat when you *own* your time and your table."

Geneva: "And it ain't just about land. It's about legacy. We are building *permanent* power—not protests that fade with hashtags."

Truth added in his gravel voice: "I used to own fear. Now I own my mornings, my money, and my movement."

The chat lit up.

Elena lifted her mic. "Let me ask this: what if every athlete, every entertainer, every Black lawyer, doctor, and CEO decided the common cause mattered more than the commas? What if they gave *just a tenth* of their income to uplift the race instead of fueling the same system designed to break us?"

Ezekiel: "Say it again."

Elena: "Just a tenth. Ten percent. That's billions. BILLIONS. And not charity. Reconstruction. Ownership for the people. Equity for the culture. Imagine what we could build. Clinics. Banks. Housing. Schools. Land. Media networks."

Geneva leaned in. "That's what God told Moses in the Old Testament. In Deuteronomy 14, tithes went to every family, every tribe—for seven years—until all were standing on their own. Not one. *All*."

She flipped open a small leather Bible beside her.

Geneva (reading): "'That the Lord thy God may bless thee in all the work of thine hand which thou doest.' (Deut. 14:29)"

Malik: "We miss that. God gave the blueprint. But we are chasing blessings, not building systems."

Ezekiel: "Jews that came to America followed that. So did the Chinese. So did the East Indians. The Russians. Most groups of people don't believe they are free till they are financially independent . But us? We think one mansion means we made it."

Truth: "That's why we still beggin', marchin', and dyin' to be seen."

Ezekiel: "No ownership. No unity. No freedom. Equals no respect."

A caller rang in.

CALLER: "How can people making under $50K be part of this?"

Elena: "We got fractional investment pools. You can own it for $50/month. Our books open. Our mission is public."

Geneva: "Your investment ain't in dollars alone. It's in discipline. It's in trust. It's in truth."

Malik: "If you can buy Jordans, you can own stock. If you can bet on a game, you can bet on your block."

HOMELAND OFFICE – NIGHT

Across town, agents watched the livestream on three screens. Jason sat quietly in the corner, hoodie low, one earbud in. His other hand gripped a pistol inside his coat pocket.

Shanice watched from the back of a room, her face hard to read. Homeland whispered around her.

AGENT 1: "We tried the IRS. Tried infiltration. Now we tighten the noose."

AGENT 2: "They're growing too fast. Too clean. Too powerful."

INT. BARBERSHOP – SIMULTANEOUS

An old man turned the dial up as the show played live.

ELDER: "They got the fire of Fred Hampton."

INT. LEGACY CENTER – NIGHT

Geneva stood up.

Geneva: "Fred Hampton united gangs and cultures. He fed people. He said: 'You can kill the revolutionary, but you can't kill the revolution.'

Ezekiel: "Malcolm said: 'If you're not ready to die for it, put the word 'freedom' out your vocabulary.' And Ali said: 'I'm not the greatest because I said it. I'm the greatest because I *believed* it.'"

The room pulsed.

Malik: "Then believe this. Legacy Land is just the start. Curriculum. Career days. Film studios. Trade schools. One city, then five. Then fifty."

Truth: "And we ain't just talking about it. We walkin' it. Seven homes up. App in development. Film in production. Thousands of members are growing wealth under $50K. We built a table. Now we build a *nation*."

Ezekiel stood.

Ezekiel: "They'll come harder now. But we built stronger. Because the seed wasn't planted in fear. It was planted in faith."

And somewhere in the crowd, Jason adjusted his grip. Shanice blinked back tears. The agents whispered. The people watched. And the math never changed.

2 + 2 = 8.

When you multiply belief, add truth, subtract fear, and divide the power? The outcome is no longer negotiable.

Legacy is no longer a dream. It's a declaration

CHAPTER FIFTY- SIX

IT STARTED LIKE A WHISPER WRAPPED IN THUNDER.

They said he was a madman. Reverend Ezekiel Trueborn didn't mind. He stood barefoot in the pulpit of New Revival Tabernacle, robe loose around his shoulders, sweat glistening on his forehead under the glow of the sanctuary lights. The room was packed wall to wall, saints and skeptics alike, waiting for a miracle or a meltdown.

He raised one hand slowly and held up two fingers. "Two," he declared. He raised the other hand, two more fingers. "Plus two."

Then he smiled.

"Equals eight."

A ripple of confusion danced across the crowd. A few gasps. One woman near the front clutched her purse like he'd pulled out a demon instead of a doctrine.

But Reverend Trueborn wasn't shaken. He stepped forward, eyes blazing with conviction. "The world teaches you arithmetic. Heaven teaches you faith."

He let it sit. Silence fell.

"You see four. I see eight. Because I don't serve a God of addition. I serve a God of multiplication."

The organ hummed low. A few voices said, "Amen."

He pressed on. "In your natural eyes, two plus two is four. But with the seed of faith, with the compound interest of obedience, with the dividends of sacrifice—what you sow is not what you reap. It comes back shaken down, pressed together, running over."

A wave of applause began to ripple through the congregation.

"Your faith is the principle. Your patience is the compounding. Your praise is the reinvestment. And your increase? Oh, baby—that's exponential."

He tapped the pulpit. "Two plus two? That's the start. But you give it time, give it tears, give it trust—and it turns into eight. Or eighty. Or eight thousand."

That Sunday, he didn't preach a sermon. He preached a shift.

After service, a young man waited by the church doors, arms crossed, face skeptical.

"Are you a math teacher now, Reverend?"

Ezekiel chuckled. "Depends. Are you looking for answers or just looking to argue?"

"I'm looking for the truth."

The Reverend nodded. "Then walk with me."

They moved slowly through the parking lot. The sun was dipping low, painting gold across the hoods of battered cars and beat-up pickups. The preacher pointed to a weed breaking through concrete.

"What do you see?"

"A weed."

"I see potential. See, most folks would kill that weed. But that weed doesn't care about opinions. It don't care that the ground was hard. It doesn't care that nobody watered it. It grew anyway."

The young man squinted. "Still doesn't explain your math."

"Sure it does. That weed is two plus two equals eight. It's the impossible result of invisible work. Roots grew before you ever saw green. Faith is like that. So is money. So is love."

He stopped and faced him. "You think God gives you four because you can count to four. But God counts differently. He adds time. He multiplies pain. He compounds glory."

Word got out.

People started coming not just for sermons, but strategies. The Reverend began holding "Kingdom Wealth" sessions every Tuesday night. Not for get-rich-quick promises, but to teach biblical compound interest—on money, on vision, on relationships.

"You plant a seed," he said one night, holding a mustard seed between his fingers. "You don't see a tree tomorrow. But you keep watering. You keep believing. And over time, it grows beyond what you sowed. That's compound interest. That's how heaven works."

He taught the janitor how to invest in dividend stocks. He helped a single mother start her hair salon with a prayer and a payment plan. He showed the retired mechanic how to leverage a life insurance policy.

"Faith without a system is fantasy," he said. "But a little faith inside a righteous system? That's fire. That's 2 + 2 =8

Then came the backlash.

A rival pastor accused him of preaching prosperity lies. Local officials questioned how his small church suddenly had enough to open a food bank and a credit union. Even some old church mothers whispered that Ezekiel had lost his mind.

But Trueborn stood firm.

"Let them say what they want," he told his board. "We don't worship numbers. We understand them. And we master them."

Yet the test came soon.

A major donor pulled out. Bills piled up. The food bank nearly shut down.

That Sunday, the church was quiet. Heavy.

But Ezekiel walked to the pulpit with a smile.

"Some of y'all worried because our two plus two don't feel like eight right now. But that's the problem—you are looking for results instead of respecting the process."

He leaned in.

"I'd rather plant in a famine than eat in fear. Because what I plant today, God multiplies tomorrow."

Three months later, the impossible happened.

A local tech investor, moved by the church's work, donated half a million dollars.

The food bank expanded. A new mentoring program launched. The church paid off its land. The congregation doubled.

One news station interviewed Reverend Trueborn.

"What do you say to people who claim this is luck, or manipulation?"

He smiled. "I say God does math differently."

"Two plus two equals eight?"

"No. Two plus two equals obedience. And obedience equals overflow."

The clip went viral.

But Ezekiel never let the fame inflate him. He still walked barefoot to the pulpit. Still spoke fire. Still believed in miracle math.

"It was never about the numbers," he told his church one Sunday. "It was about the mindset. The world taught you to count. I came to teach you to multiply."

Years passed.

Reverend Ezekiel Trueborn grew older, but his vision only grew sharper. He began mentoring young leaders, teaching them the principles of what he called "faith finance."

One young woman asked, "What do I do when the world laughs at my vision? When they say it doesn't add up?"

He looked her dead in the eye.

"You smile. And you tell them: You're right. It doesn't add up. Because my God doesn't add. He multiplies."

He handed her a small card.

On it were four words:

Two plus two equals eight.

In a world addicted to logic and limitation, Reverend Trueborn preached the wild, holy arithmetic of heaven. He understood that what begins small, when placed in the hands of eternity, does not stay small.

It grows. It compounds. It breaks the rules.

Because in the Kingdom, math is always more than numbers.

It's faith.
 It's patience.
 It's praise.

And when those three come together, even two plus two...

...can equal eight.

Then Ezekiel opened his eyes.

The pulpit was gone. The crowd was gone.

He was in his Office at legacy Land

Elijah sat , locked into his PlayStation game, his face lit up with joy and digital explosions. Naomi was humming and dancing with her dolls nearby. And Tasha—his rock—sat at the desk , focused on her laptop, glasses low on her nose.

Ezekiel blinked. The dream still clung to him like incense.

He whispered to himself, "Two plus two equals eight..."

And for a moment, he believed it more than ever.

CHAPTER FIFTY- SEVEN

THE SHOT THAT SILENCED THE GYM

The hallway buzzed with the weight of something unseen.

Ezekiel stretched, rubbing the sleep from his eyes as he stepped where Tasha waited, sipping lukewarm tea and scrolling through notes.

"How long was I out?" he asked, voice still groggy.

"One much-needed hour," she smiled. "They're waiting for you in the gym."

He nodded. "Anything on the plaza?"

Tasha sat up straighter. "1.2 million. Eight storefronts. Four are already leased."

Ezekiel rubbed his chin. "Let's move. If we are talking about freedom, we need more foundations under our feet."

Meanwhile…

LEGACY CENTER – BACK HALLS – SAME TIME

Shanice moved quietly through the hallway. Eyes darting. Mind ticking.

She entered one office—Geneva's. She slipped a small recorder from her purse, clicked it on, and tucked it beneath the desk drawer. Her breath was tight. Her hands trembling, but she kept moving. She did the same in Truth's workspace. Then in the file room.

In her earpiece, a voice whispered: "Keep your pace. No sudden changes."

Back in the gym...

LEGACY CENTER – GYMNASIUM – CROWDED

The gym was full of life—families, teens, elders, babies on hips. Community. Legacy. Laughter.

Jason stood near the refreshment table, hoodie on, eyes scanning the crowd.

He gripped his phone.

"Target?" a voice asked in his earpiece.

Jason responded, low and even. "He's come into view."

"Execute. Now."

Jason exhaled, pulled his hoodie tighter. His hand hovered near his waist. One foot in front of the other, slow and deliberate, toward the center of the gym.

Elsewhere in the gym...

Langley leaned in to Malik and Truth. "We've got a mole. I feel it."

"Who?" Truth asked, scanning the faces.

Langley shook his head. "Not sure yet. But something's off. I can feel it in my teeth."

As they spoke, Ezekiel entered the gym. The applause grew. Kids waved. Parents smiled. Phones came out. Jason's pace quickened.

Shanice, now in place, spotted Ezekiel. She walked toward him.

Truth's eyes lit up when he saw her. "Man... maybe I was wrong about her."

"She helped. And she got my sons in the room too," he added. "Might give this one more try."

Shanice reached Ezekiel. They embraced lightly. Smiled. Laughed briefly.

Jason's hand moved beneath his hoodie.

Langley's eyes locked on him. Something didn't fit. The gait. The eyes. The tension.

Langley's mouth opened—too late.

"Zeke!"

BANG!

BANG!

Two shots cracked the joy open like lightning through a sanctuary.

Screams tore through the gym. A mother dropped to her knees. Kids scattered. Phones flew in the air. Blood splashed onto the floor.

Ezekiel and Shanice hit the ground.

Langley tackled Jason from behind, forcing the gun loose. Malik and Truth dove into the chaos.

Geneva, Elena, and Tasha rushed forward. Elijah stood frozen. Naomi cried out.

"Someone call 911!" a voice shouted.

Jason lay cuffed, eyes wild. "I did what I was told!" he shouted. "I DID WHAT I WAS TOLD!"

Blood spread beneath one body—no one could tell whose.

Hands pressed down on wounds. Someone sobbed uncontrollably. The gym became a scream.

News cameras caught it all—live feed still rolling.

Elijah and Naomi clung to Tasha as she cried out, shaking.

Truth knelt, face pale. Geneva shouted for towels. Elena shouted for silence. Langley scanned the ceiling, the exits, the people.

All of it blurred—sound fading to muffled ringing.

Then... everything went black.

THE END

Part 2 Coming Soon

OTHER BOOKS BY TIERRE FORD

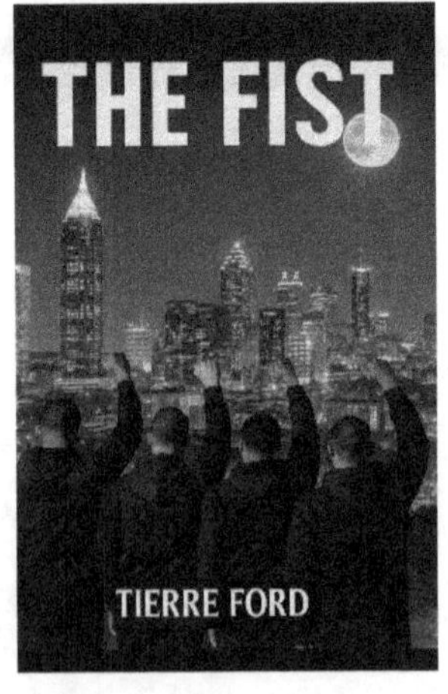

TIERRE
PRESENTS
ALL
FOR TEN
MINUTES OF
Fame

DARRIN
DEWITT HENSON
ROBIN
GIVENS
TOBIAS
TRUVILLION
AND KEITH
ROBINSON
BASED ON THE NOVEL BY TIERRE FORD
THE PRODUCTS OF THE
AMERICAN GHETTO
DIRECTED BY HENDERSON MADDOX
A DIFFERENT KIND OF AMERICAN DREAM

www.ingramcontent.com/pod-product-compliance
Lightning Source LLC
Chambersburg PA
CBHW082101090726
47910CB00008B/2548